Ryken Augmented

BOOK 2:

The Amica Kingdom Saga

by

Jonie Lax

Printed in the USA

Copyright © 2019 Jonie Lax

ISBN-13: 9-7-8057846911-9

Special Thanks to:

Katherine McNab

Joshua Garrett

Laith Hamdan

Episode 1:

Ryken Life

On the border of the Laevus Nation, a few days travel from the capital of Centrum City, Callisto bakes in the sun. He wipes the sweat from his brow, willing his mind to stay vigilantly focused on his task: the horizon.

His view is obstructed by towers of rock spouting up from the red earth. A flock of birds captures the recruit's attention momentarily, but then it's back to the matter at hand. Hours creep steadily past, minute by sizzling minute. Callisto's forehead begins to ache from the strain of his extended scrunched expression due to the sunlight.

Finally, there is movement. "Between one and two o'clock," Callisto murmurs to himself once his sixth ryken sense of spirit energy detection confirms the sight. Callisto sets out at a walk, parallel to the horizon. He starts to jog after a dozen or so steps. Just as he breaks into a full-tilt sprint, the criminal spots him, much too late. The man breaks off at an angle, but there is no escape. For every one stride of the man, Callisto matches it with three of his own. Before long, the two are within arm's length, at least as far as Callisto is concerned.

"Lethal Binding!"

Callisto reaches out for the perpetrator, extending his arms. The man drops to the ground in a last-ditch evasive maneuver, but to no avail. Callisto scoops him up, wrapping his elongated fingers around several times. Gritting his teeth from the effort, Callisto constricts his fingers and presses his palms inward. The man's futile squirming is hardly noticed, but the same cannot be said for his screaming. Before long, he passes out from the pain and Callisto's arms retract back to his sides. Then he lifts his head to his team approaching from afar.

* * *

Out the door, down the stairs, and around the corner Gaudyme runs, his mind racing even faster. *I've perfected my route. There's no way I can lose!*

"Admiratio! No running in the halls!" a teacher yells after him. Gaudyme ignores him, shooting down the hallway.

"I made it! I–" Gaudyme stops his celebration when he sees Samané already receiving his tray from the lunch lady.

His friend feigns surprise. "Oh hey, Gaudyme. I didn't expect you here so soon. That's a new record for you, buddy."

"There's no way!" Gaudyme says, flailing his arms. "My strategy was perfect!"

"Maybe you'll get me tomorrow," Samané' says, winking.

"Didn't you say that your classroom was farther away than his?" the lunch lady asks Samané.

"Way to rub it in, Grandma!" Gaudyme interrupts.

"I told you not to call me that! Now you're going to get extra mystery meat today!" She scoops a huge chunk of some greasy substance and slams it onto his plate. Gaudyme accepts it and walks with Samané toward the tables.

Samané shakes his head. "When is she going to realize that giving you extra food is not a punishment, regardless of what it is?"

"You see how much she gave me?" he exclaims. "Lunch is going to be good today!"

Gaudyme stops at an empty table as Samané continues on. Once Gaudyme notices, he picks his plate up and trots to catch up to him. "I keep forgetting we don't sit there anymore," he says, forcing a laugh.

"You know you don't have to come with me," Samané says.

"Come on, don't start with that again. Really, it's no big deal."

They reach a smaller room with a dozen worn-down chairs around two wobbly tables. Samané sits down and Gaudyme sits beside him. "I don't know why you and Lo feel like you have to eat with me," Samané says. "The humans' lunchroom is much better. I know you guys hate it in here."

"Wherever there's food, I'm happy," Gaudyme says. "Plus, you'd do the same for us, so shut it."

"But you two are the only 'humans' that eat in the ryken lunchroom. It doesn't look good to the rest of the school."

Lo walks up to the table, slamming her bag lunch down. "Are you going on about this again?"

Samané breathes an unenthusiastic greeting. "Hi Lo."

"Gaudyme and I already told you we don't care what other people think of us. We're your friends and that's all that matters."

Samané waves his hand. "Yeah, yeah, no need to get all noble on me."

"Whatever." Lo's head snaps to Gaudyme. "And if you touch that again you'll regret it!" Gaudyme swiftly pulls his hands back from Lo's lunch bag. She plops down in her rickety chair. "What a bunch of idiots you two are."

"Oh, that actually reminds me!" Gaudyme somehow finds space to stuff the last bite of mystery meat in his mouth, then rummages through his book bag.

Lo gapes. "He ate all of his lunch already?"

Samané's eyes are wide. "That might be his second broken record of the day."

Gaudyme swallows hard and slams a piece of paper on the table. "Read 'em and weep!" he exclaims, sitting back proudly.

"Whoa, an eighty-two on Mr. Gicco's mid-term?" Lo asks. "That's not bad, especially for you!"

"Hey! What's that supposed to mean?"

"Well, you're dumb."

"Oh... Hey!"

Samané nods at Gaudyme's test. "This is really good."

Gaudyme beams. "Well?"

"What?"

"What'd you get? I know you've been out for almost two months, so I promise not to rub it in too much that I beat you."

Samané picks up his book bag. "Well yeah, I could've definitely done better if I hadn't missed so much school."

Lo swallows a small bite of her sandwich. "No excuses, Samané. If Gaudyme beats you I don't–" she stops mid-sentence seeing Samané's grade resting on the table.

"A ninety-one?" Gaudyme shouts. "But how?"

"Well, what can I say?" Samané laughs.

"But what was all that crap about doing better if you didn't miss school?"

Samané shrugs. "I probably could've gotten a ninety-seven or something."

Lo kicks the loose leg out from underneath his chair. The decrepit seat completely falls apart. Samané smacks his face on the table as he falls to the floor atop the pieces of his chair. Lying on his back in a daze, he can hear Lo's laughter from above.

* * *

The long, twisting hallways of the Arena are still somewhat of a maze to Callisto. He can always get where he needs to be, eventually— the roundabout journeys are all a part of the process, or so he's been told. The Arena was designed like this purposefully as an additional line of resistance against attack, as if that was needed. Anywhere else but here could use the extra defense. Who could even approach this building in stealth? Who would be so arrogant to try and infiltrate it? Who would be dumb enough to attempt the challenge? The Arena is home to the world's most powerful ryken and a place where Callisto is now welcome. *It all still feels so surreal.*

Callisto enters the room where his team's debriefing is scheduled, but instead finds half of the ryken squad waiting on him. He approaches hesitantly. The cheerful faces put his nerves at ease about some form of catastrophe, but he's still anxious nonetheless.

"So is it true?" someone calls out.

"Is what true?" Callisto asks.

"Come on, don't play stupid," another recruit shouts.

"Is it true that you took down Lapitate all by yourself?"

Callisto scratches his head. "Uh, well, not really. Warren and Abimael had already worn him down. Tell them, guys."

"We did tell them," Warren says. "We told them how you kicked Lapitate's butt!"

"Yeah, Callisto," Abimael agrees. "There's no need to be so modest."

A recruit steps up in anticipation. "So tell us, how'd it feel to catch that creep?"

"Uh..." The crowd begins to close in around Callisto. It's at that moment that someone starts to make his way through. Callisto straightens his posture once he sees who it is. "Sir!"

The plain-appearing General Nicon Pompeii steps to Callisto. "Still with the formalities I see, Callisto—I mean, am I right?"

"Yes sir!"

Nicon sighs. "Relax, I'm not even your general. No need to be so uptight, am I right?"

Callisto relaxes his posture somewhat. "Okay, sure."

Nicon smiles. "I was just coming by to congratulate you on your last mission. Am I right? Good work."

"Thank you, sir."

"I had just received orders to provide your unit with backup once we realized the severity of the situation here at the base. Although shortly after, I was surprised to hear Lapitate was taken down, then Jove told me that you finished him by yourself. Am I right? I'm impressed to say the least."

Callisto stiffens his posture once more under the general's praise. "Thank you again, sir."

"I told you to call me Nicon." He leans in. "I'm not as uptight as the other generals, am I right?"

"Sorry sir, but I must disobey," Callisto finds himself saying. "I cannot call you by only your first name; it's disrespectful."

Nicon tilts his head. "So it's not disrespectful to disobey a direct order, but it is disrespectful to call me by my name?" Callisto freezes. Nicon bursts into laughter. "I'm just messing with you; I mean, am I right?"

In the back of the crowd a disgruntled recruit storms away. He leaves the chamber without a backward glance and almost makes it back to his room before he is stopped in the hall.

"Prix."

Prix turns immediately and bows. "General Jove."

Prix stands at attention, his lean, muscular build evident through his uniform. With his short black hair and a permanent hard look in his brown eyes, Prix doesn't have the most inviting appearance in the ryken squad. General Jove is more unwelcoming still, despite his smaller stature. "What's bothering you?" Jove asks. "I could see it from all the way down the hall."

Prix turns his head trying to hide his disgust. "I'm sure you already know, General."

"What I'm having trouble understanding is why. With Callisto's power we have grown to be the strongest division in the ryken squad."

"We were already on the road to becoming the strongest division." Prix says. "Our rise had nothing to do with him."

"You must see that your point of view is a bit biased," Jove says.

"Sir, if you would excuse me, I have somewhere I need to be," Prix manages through gritted teeth.

Jove sighs, then walks away. "As do I, Prix. I'll be seeing you then."

* * *

Tick-tock. Tick-tock. Tick-tock.

The same boring chair, at the same boring desk, with the same boring supervisor, in the same boring classroom. It's not much different than regular school, but somehow Samané finds it much more mundane. *Good old detention.* He sighs.

Normally this is nap-time for Samané, but a switch in schedule landed him in a study hall his last period of the day and asleep not long after. So instead his mind wanders.

The first week back to school had been rougher than Samané expected. It was the typical unfair ryken-human interactions he'd seen all his life, but now he was the target. After returning from Ground Zero, word spread like a disease about his active ryken blood. Not good. As a result the school had suspended him indefinitely and a legal inquiry had been opened to settle the matter, the pressing issue being Samané's participation in the martial arts program when it was strictly forbidden for ryken to partake in any sport. At the conclusion of weeks of court, with a good lawyer and Coach Srick's testimony, Samané was allowed to return to school on the grounds that it couldn't be proven that he ever used his ryken powers. And to the best of his own knowledge, he hadn't. Samané competed for the love of the fight, not because he had an unfair advantage.

Was it foolish to think no one would ever find out? At any rate, now it's just detention every day for the rest of the year and some community service, but that's better than being expelled.

He can admit, however, how interesting it has been being treated like the other hundred ryken at Centrum City High School. In a sense, it always felt like he was betraying them by pretending to be human, but now he's no different. Sitting in the back of the class, eating in a separate lunchroom, being disrespected by the humans—all the usual ryken oppression antics.

Still, Samané would suffer through things much worse with a smile if it meant that Gaudyme and Lo would not be found out. If his work at Ground Zero had uncovered their secret as well, he's not sure he could have forgiven himself.

"Hey Ryken-Boy!" the supervisor calls over. "Get up! Detention's over!"

* * *

In the general ranked training room of the Arena, Jove and Nicon spar against one another. An intense round completed, the two separate to catch their breath. "Good work as always, Jove. Am I right?" Nicon says.

"You're doing pretty well yourself," Jove says.

Today is a continuation of the two's everyday training session, and it proceeds the same as always with Nicon fighting brilliantly, but just a hair behind Jove—even less than that; a speck of difference in skill. If Jove so much as blinks at the wrong moment, Nicon will emerge victorious.

Initiating the next bout, Nicon engages Jove with a blow aimed for the gut. Jove blocks, retaliating with a punch, then a leg sweep. Nicon finds himself flat on his back. Jove tries a follow-up strike, but Nicon evades by tilting his head and counters, kicking Jove in the chest. Nicon jumps back to his feet. The two separate again, taking another second to compose themselves.

Jove wipes the sweat from his brow. "I heard you spoke with Callisto the other day."

Nicon takes a deep breath. "Sure did. I congratulated him on a job well done. Am I right?"

"If I didn't know any better I'd think you were trying to steal him from me," Jove says.

"I just don't get why you and Clamous get all the good recruits, while Gwen and I always get stiffed—I mean, am I right?"

"How would your recruits feel if they heard you speaking of them that way?"

"I tell them all the time!" Nicon exclaims. "They think I don't mean it, but I mean every word. Am I right?"

Jove's tone remains even. "Well, we'll see how Callisto compares to Prix with our next mission."

"Ah, so that's the plan? I was wondering why you were going with so much firepower for a simple rescue mission. Am I right?"

Jove cracks his neck one way, then the other. "Okay, that's enough of a break, Nicon. This is the last round so let's turn it up a notch."

"I was just thinking the same thing." Nicon says, pulling out a boomerang.

* * *

A few clouds overhead swirl around in the sky. The spring sun peeks through, providing the recovering trees and plants with much-needed nutrients. Lo and Samané raise their hands to wave goodbye to Gaudyme as they part ways going home. "You know you don't have to walk me home, Samané."

"You say that every day and every day I say I don't mind."

Lo's brow furrows. "What if I mind?"

"When have I ever cared about how you feel?"

"Watch it," Lo says, shaking her fist.

Samané chuckles. "It's my job to look after you—Callisto's orders."

"Oh, speaking of Callisto, I'm going to visit him this weekend. We talked on the phone yesterday and he said he'd be off duty and that I could."

Samané smiles. "Good stuff."

Silence. Not awkward, just silent. A breeze pushes itself past the two.

"I doubt if he's still mad, Samané."

"And what happens when you find out that he still is?" Samané asks.

"I'll talk to him," she replies after a second. "Look, this is the first time in three months I've had an opportunity to see him face to face. Since he's had a chance to cool down we can have a calm, logical conversation."

"Don't spoil your visit arguing over me. Callisto and I will settle things when the time is right."

Lo folds her arms across her chest. "I'll do what I want."

Samané shakes his head. "I swear, stubbornness must run in the Socius blood."

Lo smiles. "Of course it does."

After seeing Lo off Samané continues home, enjoying the weather, his favorite time of year slowly approaching. He enters into his house. "Hey Mo–"

In the living room, Kato sits on one couch and Shine on the other. The two were sitting in silence since before Samané entered, which is why he almost didn't notice them.

"What in the world are you doing here?" Samané asks.

Kato raises a brow. "Is that anyway to talk to a guest, kid?"

Samané moves on to Shine. "Mom, why is Kato here? I thought you said you didn't know him?"

Shine starts to laugh. "I only did that to mess with him."

Kato puts a hand to his forehead, a small smile on his lips. "No doubt I deserve it."

Samané steps into the room. "So wait, you two do know each other? Come to think of it, Kato, I still don't know how you knew Dad."

"He was actually Thralle's general back in the ryken squad," Shine offers.

"Your father was a slick one though," Kato says. "He was only sixteen when he joined but lied and said that he was eighteen."

Samané smiles. "How'd he pull that off?"

"He only had to trick Kato, which isn't really that hard," Shine teases.

"Shine, your words are like daggers," Kato says dramatically.

"Then Thralle became a general in only one year, which is the record for that status," Shine says.

"And the kid and I were friends ever since," Kato finishes. A somber mood sets over the living room, all taking a moment to long for the company of their best friend, husband and father. Kato changes the subject to get rid of the nostalgia. "Anyway kid, I'm here because Oki has the results back from the research she was conducting."

"What's the verdict?" Samané asks.

"She wanted me to fetch you so she could tell you herself. Plus, I have something I need to talk to you about anyway."

* * *

On the streets of Centrum City, Samané and Kato head to Doccue Hospital, a world renowned institution for ryken care. "We're almost there now. Can you tell me what you wanted to tell me?" Samané demands impatiently.

"Okay, okay, I'll tell you, kid," Kato relents. "I wanted to talk to you about starting a combat team of your own."

"A combat team?" Samané echoes.

"Yeah, something like a ryken squad," Kato says.

"Why would I want to do that?"

"I think it could be beneficial to Centrum City if something like that were created by a smart, reasonable ryken. Someone to protect this city from real harm."

Samané pauses, then asks, "But isn't that what the ryken squad is supposed to do?"

"Yes," Kato says, "but you know as well as I do that the job can be, and needs to be, done better."

"Of course, but there must be a more effective method of protecting the city than taking matters into our own hands."

Kato smiles. "What better solution is there in any case than taking responsibility of something yourself and putting matters into your own two hands?" When Samané doesn't respond Kato continues, "At least think about it."

With that Kato and Samané arrive at Doccue Hospital. They enter the bustling establishment, trying to keep pace with the swarming patients, doctors, and other staff zipping around them. Eventually, the two find their way to the back of the building and wait at a desk.

After they talk to the secretary, Oki comes out in a white doctor's coat rather quickly. She greets them with a warm smile. "I've been waiting for you two. Follow me."

Kato and Samané follow Oki into her office. Samané reads the title on the door as he enters. "Administrator?" he balks. "You own Doccue hospital?"

Oki laughs. "I don't own it, I just run it."

Kato slaps the back of his hand against Samané's shoulder. "I told you, when it comes to ryken care nobody does it better than my Oki!"

"Wow, I'm impressed," Samané manages, incredulous.

"Thank you," Oki says, "but let's get down to the matter at hand." The three take a seat around Oki's desk. "I've asked you to come here so I could tell you about the condition you asked me about a few weeks ago, but before I do I need you to explain it to me one more time."

Samané nods. "Sure. Back at Ground Zero when Metis and I were fighting, his spirit energy signature completely changed. It was almost impossible to identify it as his anymore."

"Would you say its composition felt denser?" Oki asks.

"Yeah, that's exactly it! It was denser and felt more pure. Purer than any other energy I've felt before."

Oki rests her chin on her hand thoughtfully. "I see...this all makes perfect sense. Tell me one last thing. Moments before this, was Metis put into a life or death situation?"

Samané leans in. "Yes, I had just hit him with my Corkscrew Kick. Any other person would've blacked out at that point. I'm still having a hard time believing that Metis took the full brunt and didn't."

"That's because he did black out," Oki says.

"What?"

She stands. "Metis might have something known as concitaline."

Episode 2:

The Novice Pack

"Concitaline?" Samané asks.

Kato and Samané sit in front of Oki Lusha's desk, confusion plastered over their faces. Oki stands opposite them, providing answers. "It's a hormone previously seen only in the first generation of ryken."

"How the heck is Metis the only ryken in three hundred years to have it?" Kato asks.

"I don't know," Oki says. "All I know is from Samané's account of what happened during that fight, and my research, Metis definitely has it."

"I'm lost," Samané says. "What is concitaline?"

Oki starts to pace behind her desk as if giving a lecture. "Concitaline is a hormone very similar to adrenaline. When humans and ryken are put in what we call *fight or flight* situations hormones are released in our bodies: adrenaline, norepinephrine and cortisol. But for a special kind of ryken there is another hormone released called concitaline. Essentially, what concitaline does is condense all the spirit energy in a ryken's body. From the energy reserves to the daily-used spirit energy, all of it is condensed into an accessible form for immediate use. By doing this, a ryken's spirit energy could increase to as much as double the original level."

Realization settles upon Samané. "That would explain why I was so easily beaten after I landed that kick."

Oki continues. "There are risks and side-effects to such a reaction though. While in the Concitaline State, the body shuts down overly taxing cognitive processing in the brain. In other words, when a ryken enters this state it is next to impossible for him or her to control their actions. The individual blacks out and the subconscious takes over. At that point the body does whatever it needs to in order to escape the situation it's in."

"It sounds like they become an animal," Kato says.

Oki nods. "Basically. And I'm afraid that's all I know about the condition at this point."

Samané sits back in his chair, trying to digest all the information. "Leave it to Metis to have a unique condition that hasn't been seen in hundreds of years."

"Eh, it's all right, kid," Kato says. "Don't let it discourage you."

"Discourage me?" Samané smiles. "It's just the opposite." A flicker of surprise from Kato and Oki. "That just means I have to get back to working hard so next time I fight Metis I'll beat him. If he can increase his power two-fold with that state, I'll just have to work and increase my power three-fold. If he has the Excessum to help him, I'll just put together a fighting team of my own. No matter what, the next time I fight Metis I will not lose!"

* * *

Lo sits in an all-white room, alone. Other than the table, the chair she sits on, and the one opposite her, the small room is empty. She stares at the reflective glass embedded in the wall, unsure if someone is watching her from the other side. Despite this, she critiques her appearance, straightening her bangs and tucking a lock of red hair behind her ear. The door creeks open and someone with the same crimson hair enters. "Were you going to keep me waiting all day?" Lo snaps.

"Just as loving as I remember, sis," Callisto says. He walks over and stands next to her chair with his palms up. Lo waits until he stops before standing up to hug him. Despite her frustration, their embrace is loving and warm.

Both take a seat and Lo looks around. "Is this your interrogation room? I feel like a criminal in here."

"Used to be," Callisto says. "It's the visiting room now. Anyway, what's new?"

Ground Zero immediately runs across Lo's mind, but she can already imagine Callisto's reaction after she tells him about honing her ryken powers, journeying miles from Centrum City through a mutant forest and a treacherous cavern, battling ryken all the while, just to meet the Excessum and behold their evil tournament in all its wicked glory. Instead, she carefully chooses another reply. "Just spending time with Samané and Gaudyme, really. Wondering why I put up with either of them." She rolls her eyes. "What about you? You're not dead yet, that's cool."

"Not yet. A couple close calls though." Lo stops, her eyes widening and nostrils flaring. Callisto chuckles. "I'm joking, I'm joking." *Well, kind of.*

"That's not funny!" she scolds.

"Oh, calm down. I'm in good hands here. I have a nice, solid team to support me and watch my back. I trust those guys with my life."

Lo gives Callisto a deadly serious look, compassion in her tone. "Just be careful."

"I will. How's Gaudyme doing?"

"That Stupid Virus is really taking its toll on him," Lo says, "but other than that, he's fine." She pauses. "Samané is doing fine too."

This time Callisto offers the serious look. "I didn't ask about him."

"You're really still mad?" Lo asks.

"Yes," he answers, tersely.

"It's been over three months."

"Good to know."

"Come on, are you going to be mad forever?"

Callisto frowns, hard. "Maybe you don't remember what he almost took from me. All because he *forgot.* As if my dream of changing the world is just some childish notion that will burn out by the week's end. This is what I've always wanted to do, Lo. Bring justice to an unwell Laevus. This is who I am." Callisto clenches his fist on the table. "I can still remember that sinking feeling I had when General Jove ordered me out that day. I felt so helpless, so insignificant. Like my whole life to that point had meant nothing."

Callisto has always been like this, Lo thinks. *Passionate beyond belief. It's so inspiring, captivating even...when things are going well. But because of that he's tunnel-sighted. He only sees his goals and it shadows his empathy.*

"I was lucky," Callisto continues, "and given another chance by General Nicon. Since then I haven't taken my opportunity for granted, not one second. I'll never again place my fate in someone else's hands when it can be controlled by my own. I'll use my power to change the world in any and every way I can. I *will* make a difference, I promise you that."

* * *

Two men and one child wait outside a stone building in the middle of a forest. One man frowns at the sky above, as if its blueness is a direct insult to him. The other man sits up against the building, sharpening a spear. The boy sits on a rock, his chin pressed into his right palm. "Waiting outside these stupid meetings is always so lame," the boy says. His long brown hair covers one of his large eyes. "I'm going to die from boredom!"

Nightshade looks at him, a sneer on his pale face. "You're going to die if you don't stop your complaining, Napalm, but it won't be from boredom." Napalm sticks his tongue out at Nightshade.

Hunter stands, stretching. His thick locks of hair move with great weight at every differing position. "Give the kid a break, Shade. He's only ten years old."

Nightshade keeps his eyes locked on Napalm. "You've been saying that for a year, Hunter. When is this brat going to grow up?"

"A year? Last year I told you to give him a break because he was nine, not ten." Hunter chuckles.

Nightshade shifts his scowl to Hunter just as a shadow crawls out from under his feet. "Zacata, stop!" The shadow stops its slithering immediately. "His blood isn't worth riling up Master Misery."

Hunter holds Nightshade's gaze with a smirk. "The prey's blood is always worth the hunt."

"Keep your hunting philosophies to yourself," Nightshade growls. "I'm not in the mood."

Napalm jumps off the rock. "Go Hunter! I bet you could take him! Give him the old one-two!"

Hunter returns to his seat, picking up his spear. "Now isn't the time for that, Napalm."

"You guys aren't any fun," Napalm whines. Someone else emerges from the trees, joining the three. "Especially him! He doesn't even talk."

"He's been like this ever since he joined us," Nightshade says. "I'm starting to think he's homesick."

"Based on my experiences with him at the Shack, I don't think he was ever much of a talker in the first place," Hunter offers.

"You all speak as if I am not in your presence." Metis regards each of the three for a moment.

"You talk as if I care, Sutari," Nightshade snaps back.

Metis shakes his head. "I can't fathom what you gain from bestowing that name upon me."

"We all get cool names when we join the Excessum," Napalm explains. "You're supposed to like it." Metis only squints at him in response.

On the inside of the stone building two Prime Excessum members sit around a long table, just as restless as those outside. Six torches are lit on opposite walls, with pictures of wealthy men between every two. At the head of the table a man impatiently fiddles with an unblemished golden coin. On one side an elaborately etched lotus plant is engraved; on the other, the letter *D*. The man speaks as he examines the coin with the same scrutiny as his prior thousand inspections. "Let's just get this meeting started already. It's obvious Apathetus isn't coming. She probably fell asleep."

Fulminate's company continues to stand with his back to him, looking at one of the paintings. Fulminate sighs. "You know we've been here for almost an hour and you haven't said one word. I've seen mysterious, but you're plain creepy." He is unsurprised when the only response he receives is the slight echoing of his voice in the empty meeting hall. Finally, he stands. "Not that I haven't had a blast, but I have things to do and money to make."

"Stop."

Fulminate pauses at the door and turns to see Misery facing him. Misery's cloak covers everything below his nose and is so black it seems the Excessum member discovered a way to fabricate a garment out of darkness itself. Fulminate can almost swear the torches closer to Misery are fainter than those farther away. What's most disturbing is that all have seemed to grow abnormally dimmer since he found Misery closed inside upon his arrival.

"I called us together because I have interest in the Amica Kingdom," Misery says, his voice low and powerful.

Fulminate strokes his immaculately trimmed beard. "Is that so? Well then, there's not much more that needs to be said. What do you need from me?"

"I initially planned to have our men take the kingdom, but without Apathetus' subordinates we can't still do that."

"Are you implying that we might have to get our own hands dirty? I don't know about your guys, but I'm sure Hunter and Napalm could take that entire kingdom down by themselves."

"I'm not so arrogant, Fulminate. But we won't need to involve ourselves, either."

"Using extra men on a job just wastes time, which in turn wastes money."

Misery turns back to the painting. "I won't waste any resource. True misery will always find the most efficient way to ravage the heart."

Fulminate smiles. "You're the creepiest genius I know. You get things done; that's what I love most about you. I'll leave my men in your hands."

* * *

Lo's lips turn downward as she frowns fiercely, her hands on her hips. She tilts her head as if the slightly different angle could grant her a remedy to her frustration. On the road to Centrum City High School she and Samané wait for Gaudyme. "I don't know why you always want to wait for him," she says. "He'll never learn to be on time if we don't leave him once or twice."

Samané shrugs. "Relax, there's no hurry to get to school anyway."

"That's not the point!" She turns, walking past Samané. "Do whatever you want, but I'm leaving."

It's then that Gaudyme stumbles out of his house, still putting his shoe on while galloping to the corner. "Wait, guys! Don't leave me!"

"Hold on, here he comes," Samané says.

Lo stops. "You both are so annoying."

Gaudyme reaches his friends and struggles to catch his breath as they walk away. He stumbles forward as if an invisible tether links them, still gasping for air. "Wait, you two! Let me catch my breath first."

Samané trails Lo a step. "I think if Lo waits any longer she might explode from anger."

"You got that right," she says, "so put a pep in your step, Gaudyme."

When Gaudyme stops his exaggerated laboring, Samané changes the subject. "I have to talk to you both about something."

Gaudyme offers a huge smile. "Whatever it is I'm all in."

Samané's brow furrows. "You don't even know what it is yet."

"Doesn't matter, it already sounds like fun!"

"Can you just let Samané talk?" Lo snarls.

"Okay. I've been thinking about starting my own ryken combat team," Samané says.

"I knew I wanted to do it!" Gaudyme exclaims.

Lo shoots him a glare, then regards Samané. "A combat team?"

"Yeah, something like a ryken squad," Samané says. "It was Kato's idea so he'll be helping us out, and considering he was a general, he has experience with this stuff."

Gaudyme bounces with excitement. "Let's do it! I'm all ready to go!"

Samané smiles, then looks over. "Lo?"

She bites her lip. "I just need help understanding this one thing. What's the point of the ryken squad and recruits like Callisto if we do this? Doesn't that compromise their actions and sacrifices?"

"I get your point," Samané says, scratching his head. "As the son of the Commander of the ryken squad I respect those guys a lot, but I also know there are matters that the ryken squad overlooks for political reasons or things like that. We'll just try to tie up the loose ends, nothing extreme."

"I guess I can see where you're coming from," Lo says, her doubt obvious.

A few seconds pass before Samané takes the leap. "So what do you say—you going to join me and Gaudyme?"

Lo sighs, then smiles. "What the heck? It might be fun."

Gaudyme throws a fist in the air. "All right, Lo! Way to go! And I already have the perfect name for us."

"Here we go," Lo says, rolling her eyes.

Samané puts a hand on Gaudyme's shoulder. "Why don't you let me and Lo worry about that part?"

"Aw, but you'll like it, I swear! I worked really hard on it. You ready? The Novice Pack! You get it? Because we're rookies."

"What happens when we get better and more experienced at this?" Lo asks.

"Well, you never really get good enough at these things, right? In a way, we'll always be rookies with lots to learn."

Samané and Lo look at one another. "I actually like it," Lo finds herself saying.

"Me too," Samané agrees. The teens enter through the front doors of Centrum City High School and start to make their way to their lockers. "That's actually not a bad name, Gaudyme. Has a bit of humility to it."

Gaudyme can't stop himself from grinning. "I figured a day like this would come sooner or later so I wanted to be prepared. This is so awesome! When do we start?"

Samané looks around as he reaches his locker. "Can you keep it down? I'd rather all of Laevus not know about this."

Gaudyme nudges Samané with his elbow and tries his best wink. "Not until we save the world at least, right?"

Samané blinks. "Anyway, you guys can head over to Kato's right after school. He'll be expecting you." He closes his locker, stepping away.

"Where are you going?" Lo asks.

"I've got to talk to this guy about a thing," Samané says, waving. "I'll catch up with you two in a bit."

* * *

"You ready, Callisto?" Jove asks.

Callisto slips his feet into his boots, laces them up, then stands, straightening his uniform. "Yes, sir."

He follows Jove out of his room to find Prix leaning against the wall a few steps ahead. "If it isn't the one and only Elastoman," Prix says.

"Hello, Prix," Callisto responds, grudgingly.

Jove proceeds down the hall and without a second thought his recruits follow suit. "I'm going to need cooperation from the two of you on this mission," Jove says. "Before we leave I want to go over our objective one last time, for absolute clarity. We are to rescue a hostage by the name of Acura. She is a seven-year-old girl who has been abducted by the ryken gang Mercury. We will venture to the Tario Mountains and subdue their leader Gregarious."

Jove stops at the exit of the Arena with his recruits close behind. He turns with a stern expression. "You are by no means to engage Gregarious in combat. He is a dangerous man whom I will handle—do I make myself clear?"

Both recruits nod. "Yes, General Jove."

Recruitment

Deep inside the Tario Mountains there is a fortress within the hollowed-out rock. The hideout Callisto creeps stealthily around is home to the violent ryken organization known as Mercury. The ceiling of the base is low, leaving only a few inches between the top of Callisto's head and smooth metal. That, along with the dim lighting, gives Callisto a cramped, claustrophobic feeling, further raising his anxiety. Despite this, he and Prix subdue a handful of watchmen as they infiltrate; all is going according to plan.

The two reach a red door. "This is the room the general mentioned," Callisto says, his heart thumping in his chest. It's always difficult for Callisto to calm his nerves before a hit, regardless of how he may appear on the outside.

"Obviously," Prix growls. "Now stand back. I don't need help from you, Elastoman. It'd be better if a rookie like you just stayed back and left it to the professionals." Without a second thought, Prix kicks the handle and barges through the door. He and Callisto enter an area far more spacious than the hallways leading to this point. Unfortunately, the large room allows for a number of Gregarious' men to congregate.

Callisto steps through the doorway after Prix, quickly noticing how outnumbered they are. "It's almost like they were waiting for us," Prix says with a smirk.

Callisto's eyes linger in the back of the room. "And General Jove was right. This is where they're keeping the hostage," he says, nodding toward the unconscious girl tied to a metal beam behind a wall of thugs.

A greasy man steps forward. "Too bad you won't be able to save her."

"What's worse is you won't be able to save yourselves," another follows up.

Prix tries his best leer. "The thing is, we're going to save her then take you lowlifes to prison. How's that sound?"

Callisto steps up, shoulder to shoulder with Prix. "But if you guys surrender now you might only have to serve a few centuries."

No one responds. Just snarls and glares. Then someone yells, "Get them!"

The men begin to converge on Callisto and Prix but before they can both recruits release the restraints on their spirit energy, allowing their power to spill forth in a controlled torrent. The criminals are battered back by Callisto's stretched fists. They fire forward and snap back in quick blows his opponents, dropping in heaps, can't keep pace with.

Prix displays an even more remarkable level of talent as he mows down the enemies in greater numbers. Conjuring up small disks of spirit energy, Prix launches dozens within seconds. Each disk dissipates after cutting an inch or so of flesh, to avoid cutting his opponents in half. *I cannot let that newbie take out more men than me,* Prix thinks. *I have to remind the general why I am his righthand!*

Prix's razor disk attacks are so fast, Callisto muses. *He creates them in fractions of a second. I've never seen someone manifest their energy so quickly.*

In a few minutes, Callisto and Prix turn Gregarious' army of henchmen into a horde of cut and bruised lackeys strewn throughout the room.

Ceremoniously, a tall, bald man walks through a door on the opposite side of the room. Callisto identifies the bearded man as Gregarious. *That means General Jove couldn't find him from his rear infiltration,* Callisto thinks.

"To believe you two lowly recruits could defeat me by yourselves is the biggest insult the government could've given me," Gregarious says. Prix and Callisto brace themselves. Gregarious continues across the room slowly. "No matter. I suppose your head on a stake with this little girl's will show them not to take me so lightly!"

Prix's spirit energy flares and Callisto places a hand on his shoulder, neither of them looking away from Gregarious. "Don't, Prix. The general gave us strict orders not to engage him. We should retreat while we still can."

"The general isn't here so you can stay there being scared if you want, but I'm fighting!" Prix shoots off two energy disks in one fluid motion.

I've got no choice but to back him up, Callisto concludes.

If I can take him down, it'll remind everyone back at the base just how strong I am! Prix thinks.

The disks hit their mark, cutting the man into fours. Prix smiles at the result as Callisto stands in disbelief at the ease of Gregarious' defeat. In that moment he turns to see Gregarious with his axe coming down on Prix's head. *A decoy!* Callisto thinks, already shooting his arm toward Gregarious, knowing he won't reach his target in time.

Gregarious' axe barely makes contact with Prix when Gregarious freezes impossibly still, mid-swing. It's then Callisto realizes he cannot move either, his body and extended arm frozen in the moment.

"Law 22- Blind Motion."

Gregarious struggles against the invisible force, muscles bulging, all of his might desperately trying to bring his axe down. "Why... can't I... move!"

General Jove approaches Gregarious with his eyes closed. *Where did the general come from?* Callisto thinks, a little more than shocked.

"So the government wasn't so foolish after all," Gregarious says, a hint of pride in his words. "They sent Jove the Legislator for me. I guess it couldn't be helped."

Just as Prix moves out from under Gregarious' axe to stand by Jove, Callisto realizes the situation. He closes his eyes just as Jove and Prix have done and immediately regains control of his body, retracting his limb.

"You boys disobeyed a direct order," Jove says, his voice low but harsh. "I'm sure you both are aware there will be consequences."

It's then that the realization dawns upon Gregarious. *Their eyes! I must close my—!* The thought is cut short when Jove's foot connects with the back of his head. Gregarious is sent spiraling into the wall of the chamber. The impact shakes the entire base with the force of an earthquake, causing Prix and Callisto to stumble to the nearest sturdy object for support. When the ryken-made tremor ceases, Callisto notices that section of the mountain has caved in, burying Gregarious in the process.

Jove steps forward. "And now to save the hostage."

* * *

A swift blow to the gut brings Metis to his knees. "Stand up," Nightshade hisses between his razor-sharp teeth. Metis gasps for air, his forehead pressed into the undergrowth of the forest floor. "Stand up!" Nightshade repeats, grabbing Metis' hair and forcing him to his feet. He is wobbly at first but wills himself stable. Nightshade steps away then turns back. The two regard one another, contempt in Nightshade's eyes and a stoic impassiveness in Metis'.

A dark blob separates itself from Nightshade's shadow and crawls to Metis with extreme quickness. Metis' eyes turn purple and a similarly colored light falls upon the darkness. The intensity of Metis' irises gradually increases as he exerts more spirit energy to hold the black force at bay. Before Metis realizes, Nightshade is on him with a two-piece combo, landing Metis on his back. The shadow wraps a lip of its blackness around Metis' neck, strangling him while pinning him down.

Metis claws at the physical darkness as Nightshade takes a seat on his torso. "You're not very good at this." Metis continues to scrape and claw for air. "Not so uncaring when you can't breathe, are you? Honestly, I don't know what Master Misery sees in you. Just another spoiled brat of a teenager if you ask me." Metis' struggle slows and Nightshade stands again, walking away. "That's enough, Zacata. We don't want to kill him."

With that Metis is freed. He sits up, coughing and sucking in huge gulps of air. Once his breathing settles he notices Nightshade has left. He goes to stand but his body protests with screams of the bumps and bruises all over his body.

Pain. The two have become quite well-acquainted recently.

A simple concept. Pain. Yet no one appreciates its majesty. It's contradictory in a sense, for how can we embrace that which we have been biologically tailored to shy away from? But that is the precise reason we should claim it. I'll be obsequious unto pain and face these minute afflictions to alleviate the true pain this world needs to remedy. Whether ryken or human, we adapt only when in pain, only to stop the anguish of the moment from happening again. The greater the pain, the more dramatic the adaptation. So I'll suffer this. I'll suffer whatever I must to become what rykenkind demands for change. Then... I'll be the world's pain.

Metis looks at his hand, noticing his dislocated forefinger. With his aura, he pops the joint back into place with nothing more than a grimace. *But I must first start with myself. How can I change others when I would not put myself through that same pain? I possess as many imperfections that need to be burned away as anyone else. Perhaps more. However, I am willing to seek judgment and take the punishment, to own that retribution until it has become me. And then put it under me. It's evolution. And I mandate that this world evolve with me.* Metis looks up to see Nightshade has returned. *In time pain will melt away all weakness.*

"As much as I would love to beat you down further, Master Misery has business to discuss with you," Nightshade says. "Looks like you're headed to the Amica Kingdom."

* * *

The hallways of Centrum City High School bustle with the nearly infinite energy of teenage youth. Subnuba leans up against his locker, talking to his sidekick Emmon. "Then I told her I don't do relationships because they cramp my style."

"Wow, you really told her that?" Emmon asks incredulously.

"Of course I did. I don't hold my tongue for any man, woman or beast. Heh." Much to Subnuba's surprise, Samané walks up. "Yeah? What do you want, you ryken scum? Don't you have some old ladies you want to beat over the head?"

"Good one, Subnuba," Emmon cheers. "All ryken are nothing but troublemakers."

Samané folds his arms across his chest. "I think Lo might still be at her locker, Emmon. If you're lucky you'll still be able to catch her." Emmon's eyes light up. He looks to Subnuba as if for permission, and with a tilt of Subnuba's head, Emmon flees to catch his crush. "You were laying it on a bit thick there, don't you think, Subnuba?"

"State your business or get out of my face, Lutrio." Subnuba scowls.

"Okay," Samané says, keeping his voice low. "I'll get right to the point. I'm starting a ryken group of sorts and I could use your help."

"No way. Now leave."

"Just hear me out first. We both could benefit from this, Subnuba. No matter how much you embrace this human life of yours, you know deep down inside it's a lie. I can help you take your first meaningful step as a ryken—controlling your spirit energy."

"I said no! Now stop pestering me you lowly ryken!"

Subnuba's voice garners the attention of everyone in the hallway. A ryken antagonizing a human is never a good thing. Samané tries to appear as disarming as possible as he eases away, his stride still confident in its nonchalance. "Don't worry, Subnuba. I won't give up that easily."

Later, in detention Samané sits in his normal ryken-assigned seat in the back. Diagonally forward from him, Subnuba takes his routine daily detention seat as well. "You ready to join yet?" Samané whispers.

Subnuba whispers back, "Stop asking me that! I wasn't ready to join in first period, I wasn't ready to join in study hall, I wasn't ready to join at lunch, I wasn't ready to join in gym and I'm not ready to join now!"

Samané shrugs. "You do realize that I'm just going to keep bugging you until you say yes, right?"

Subnuba puts his head on his desk, a headache pounding behind his eyes.

When detention lets out, Subnuba takes his time going home. *Lutrio is such a little sissy. It's so pathetic seeing him beg me to join his kiddy ryken team. Maybe I should do it just to show him who is really the strongest between us once and for all.*

Subnuba enters his house and his mom, Sheila, meets him at the door. "Subnuba, honey, why didn't you tell me you were having company over today?"

Subnuba frowns. "Company?"

He speed-walks into the dining room, and his jaw drops when he sees the guest in mid-conversation with his father. "Hello, friend!" Samané exclaims enthusiastically.

Once Subnuba stops gaping, he snaps, "Lutrio? What are–!"

"Subnuba, use your inside voice," Sheila interrupts. "You know better than that."

Subnuba shrinks. "You're right, Mother. I apologize."

"Your friend here was just telling us how you two are great buddies on your school's martial arts team," Subnuba's father, Subnuba Senior, explains.

Sheila smiles. "Yes. Honey, why have you never mentioned him before? He seems very fond of you and he has excellent manners as well."

Samané takes a sip of his tea and places his cup on its coaster with exaggerated carefulness. He then wipes his mouth ever so gently, the epitome of decorum. His smile is pleasant... well, to Subnuba's parents at least. Subnuba seethes on the inside, seeing the underlying smugness in Samané's every gesture. "You both are simply delightful,"

Samané says, meekly. "I truly am honored to be in your magnificent home."

Sheila blushes from the compliment and Subnuba Senior proudly sips his tea. "Mother, Father, if you would excuse us, Lu— I mean, Samané and I have important homework we have to get started on right away."

"Of course, honey," Sheila says.

"That's right, son," Subnuba Senior says. "Homework comes first. I'm proud of you."

Subnuba bows. "Thank you, Father."

Subnuba heads to his room and, after properly thanking the Gahoras, Samané follows. Just as Samané closes the door behind himself, Subnuba swings at him. "How dare you come into my house!"

Samané easily dodges, grabbing Subnuba's arm and forcing him down. He puts a knee into Subnuba's back, having him in a submission hold. "How does it feel getting beat by me once again?" Samané releases Subnuba and walks over to a chair, plopping down on it. "Have some pride as a ryken. I thought you were more of a man than to run from a life you are meant to live. It's been two months since we got back from Ground Zero and what have you done differently since?"

Subnuba sits up, sneering. "Don't lecture m—"

"No, shut up and listen! And do you know why you're going to do what I say? Because I'm stronger than you, that's why. That's the way it works, right? You look pathetic, Subnuba, and you aren't even going to do anything about it." Samané shakes his head. "It's a sad day when the bully gets bullied."

Subnuba glares at him, his disgust evident. "What point are you trying to make?"

"I'm trying to pull out the ryken inside you! The part of you that wants to fight. Embrace that, like you always have! Just because you're a ryken doesn't mean you're any less than the humans, and you're no more barbaric. You're just Subnuba, so be Subnuba." When he breaks eye contact Samané gets up and makes for the door. "Fine, just sit there then. Continue to be something you aren't, see how far it gets you."

"I asked my parents about our ryken heritage a of couple weeks ago," Subnuba starts, his voice introspective. "They didn't seem to know about it. Either that or one of them is in complete denial. In any case, I don't think they would want to hear about their son being a ryken." Subnuba looks at Samané, his face deadly serious. "So if you can ensure that my parents won't find out that I'm a ryken until I'm ready to tell them... then I'll join your team."

Samané and Subnuba make a pact and Samané takes his leave. He walks down the darkened streets of Centrum City, more than a little pleased. *Subnuba actually caved a lot quicker than I thought he would. I was sure convincing him would take at least a week. Okay, now the next destination is—*

"Freeze Xarnes!"

Samané halts, slightly startled by the command, but more disturbed by the term "Xarnes"— a derogatory term for ryken. Samané turns to a man pointing a gun at him from a couple houses down the road. He holds his hands up. "I don't want any trouble," Samané says.

The human grips the gun tighter. "Shut up, Xarnes! Did I say you could speak?"

"*Xarnes* is such a harsh term. A lot of ryken would kill you just for calling—"

Samané's sentence is cut short by the bullet shot into the air. The human points the gun back at Samané. "Do you think I'm joking? I will kill you!"

Samané suppresses a scowl. "There's a reason they say *never threaten a ryken.*"

The human shoots at Samané and with a simple step to the side Samané dodges the bullet. The man pulls the trigger again, but in that short time Samané stands in front of him with his hand also on the gun, aiming it toward the sky. "Sorry to do this... well, not really." Samané crushes the barrel of the gun in his fist, rendering it useless. It's then a flash is emitted from behind and Samané ducks reflexively. His reaction is just in time as the bullet whizzes over his head—so close, in fact, that it shoots through his hair. Samané wastes no time fleeing the scene.

The man is left alone holding his worthless pistol, but then is joined by the second shooter. "That one was fast even for a Xarnes," the second man says. "You've done well, Hontale. Dr. Killinger will be pleased. We didn't get the kill, but we have enough." He bends down and grabs a lock of hair severed when the bullet grazed Samané's hair.

Episode 4:

Scared

Callisto surveys the battlefield. "Nicon's unit will be here momentarily. Our main objective is Acura," Jove says, walking toward the little girl tied to a pole. At the sound of her name Acura begins to stir, most likely due to the absence of the ryken ability keeping her subdued. Once her vision clears she can make out the three ryken squad officials walking toward her and begins to recall what happened.

"Get away from me, you mean ryken! Get away!" She begins to struggle ineffectually against her restraint, straining against the ropes in a panic.

Prix approaches slowly, his ryken ability manifested in one hand. "Don't move. I can't cut you down if you keep squirming."

Acura has a stream of tears flowing down her cheeks. "No! Get away! Mommy, help me! I'm scared!"

Jove steps up, his voice gentle but authoritative. "Acura, we're here to save you, but we need you to cooperate with us." He stops when he notices that she's too riled up to listen.

"I have an idea, General," Callisto says, "but I'm going to have to ask you both to give me some space."

"Don't do anything too rash," Jove says as he steps away. Prix follows grudgingly.

Callisto faces Acura who has yet to settle down. "We're here to take you home. All the bad guys are gone now."

"No! Get away! Someone help me! I want Mommy!"

"Your mommy is the one who told us to come get you. She's worried about you. She wants you to come back home."

"M... Mommy sent you?"

Callisto nods. "She said that some of the bad ryken took you away so she found some good, strong ryken to get you back."

Acura breathes heavily, but the tears have stopped falling. "Good ryken? I didn't know there were good ryken."

Callisto smiles. "Well there are! And you're looking at them! We beat up all the bad ryken who were mean to you so we could take you back to your mommy." It seems Acura is just now noticing the men strewn throughout the room. "There's no reason to be scared anymore, Acura. The good guys are here."

"O...Okay," she manages.

"Now, a friend of mine is going to cut you free so you can see your mommy again. Don't move and don't be scared. Nothing bad will happen to you as long as I'm around." Another smile, then Callisto turns. "You can do your thing, Prix."

"Good work, Callisto," Jove acknowledges. "A gentle hand to complement a strong fist. I'm impressed."

With a scowl, Prix walks over and uses his energy disks to cut Acura down. *Darn Elastoman for stealing the show from right under my nose! His plan wasn't impressive. I could've come up with it if this brat wasn't yelling so loud. He just needed us back because she felt overwhelmed. Once we stepped away he was able to get through to her. It's not genius; it's just child's play!*

Prix finishes his cut and Acura immediately runs and clings to Callisto's pant leg. "Hey there," Callisto whispers. "There's no need to be afraid of those two. They're the good guys too." She buries her face into Callisto's hip, squeezing his pant leg tighter. "Acura, there's no need to be scared. You're with me now and I'll keep you safe. I will protect you. You'll see your mommy again. I promise."

With Callisto's words Acura smiles for the first time since her kidnapping. Her face is bright and joy seeps out of every pore. In that moment her purity seems tangible. "Okay. Since you promised, I won't be scared anymore!"

* * *

Appearance wise, Acura doesn't look anything like a five-year-old Lo. Her hair, dark brown flowing down her back, is longer and fuller than Lo's has ever been. Her innocent eyes are a light brown. She has an even tan where Lo has always been pale, and she is as solid as Lo is thin.

But their smiles are identical. The contour of their cheeks, the way their ears lift and eyes squint are all the same. Even how one side of the upper lip rises noticeably higher than the other, though the effect is mirrored on Acura, reflects kid Lo's warm smile. The current circumstances, however, aren't ideal for such childish bliss. "Mr. General, how much longer until we get home?" Acura asks.

Jove regards the sun at its apex. "It won't be until tomorrow morning."

Her head hangs. "Okay..."

Callisto catches a glimpse of Acura's disappointment. Much as he expected, this too reminds him of Lo. He rips his eyes away, trying to find something to smother the anger building up in him at Gregarious and his thugs. In the distance he spots a field of flowers. "Look Acura, up ahead there's flowers. Let's go get some!" Before she can even respond Callisto scoops her up over his head and sprints to the field. At first Acura's grip is deathly tight, but after a few strides he feels her relax and not long after the laughing follows. "Hold on tight!"

Callisto stops, snatching Acura off his shoulders. He stretches his arms, pushing Acura face-first through the field. "I'm like an airplane!" she shouts. A gentle slope upward and a sharp decline down, Acura soars through the air, her laughter a pleasant song in Callisto's ears.

She does a few circuits of the large garden before Jove calls out, "Callisto, come! We mustn't waste more time."

Another dive before the aircraft returns to base. "I guess we need to get going again," Callisto says.

"Aw, already?" Acura asks, flower petals and grass stuck in her hair and clinging to her clothes. "But I was just starting to have fun."

"Just think, the faster we leave the faster you can see your mommy."

"Can't we play just a little longer?"

Callisto's expression answers her question and she sighs. He picks up a flower. "My little sister loves flowers. I figured the quick stop here would make you happy like it would make her." He extends the flower to Acura. "Now let's catch back up!"

* * *

The day passes uneventfully, one long road after the other. There is an occasional waterway that needs to be waded through or a giant hill that must be climbed, but for the most part the journey is simple. The route to the Tario Mountains had been much more treacherous, yet faster considering time was of the essence. Acura was ultimately the deciding factor for the course and pace used both ways.

The group sets up camp just after the sun sets, having a small meal around a smaller fire. It isn't long before Jove and Prix are soon sound asleep, and Callisto is not too far behind. "Are you still up, Callisto?" Acura whispers.

Callisto lets loose a long growl before responding, his vocal cords appearing to be the first to slumber. "Mmmm. Yeah, kind of." He forces himself to turn over. "Don't be scared, Acura. Nothing's going to happen."

Acura shakes her head gently. "No, it's not that. I was just thinking about my mommy. I miss her."

"Yeah?" Acura nods and Callisto takes a deep breath before sitting up. "Tell me a little bit about her."

Acura curls into a ball, closing her eyes as if trying to relive a dream. "Well, for starters she's really smart. She owns this super huge business and wears suits all the time and talks to really important people! But even though she has her mean face on a lot she's a really nice person. We play when she's not working and she always tells me to do my best and shoot for the stars!"

"Wow. She sounds really cool."

"She is! She's my best friend! Even when she says I can't have snacks." Callisto laughs and even though Acura doesn't know why, she laughs too. "Uh, Callisto?"

Callisto stretches, then lies back down. "Yes?"

"I'm glad we're friends."

"Me too."

"It's just... when I'm with you I know I'm safe. I'm not scared at all..." Acura's voice trails off as she falls asleep. Callisto stares at her, smiling at both her peace of mind and her innocence.

* * *

"Pick up the pace, Elastoman," Prix says. "Centrum City is only an hour away."

Another successfully completed mission by the ryken squad's finest. But not much else was to be expected. Division 1a is arguably the strongest division the squad offers. There's no telling who the strongest general is, but Jove has the best leadership of the four, from Callisto's perspective, at least. And although Callisto has never seen the other generals' firsthands in action, it's widely assumed that Prix is the strongest. It has been said, however, that General Clamous' son Shivers could possibly rival him.

Jove had told Callisto one day after an intense training session that he has the strength of a firsthand and would most likely earn the rank at the first opening. And with Hontale and Abimael as skilled as most of the other recruits, Division 1a is very well rounded and versatile— the best men from the best division. A mission like this was guaranteed to succeed. *Logically, Acura really has no reason at all to be scared,* Callisto muses.

"Mr. Pricks, why are you always so mean to Callisto?" Acura asks.

Prix suppresses a scowl. "I'm not mean to him. It's just the way we talk to one another. And it's not 'Pricks', it's Prix."

Acura raises her eyebrows. "Well, you always call Callisto a different name from his real name too."

Prix grunts. *Another arrogant human. They must just come out that way.*

Suddenly Jove, who is leading the way, stops. Naturally, everyone else follows suit. "Wha—" Acura manages to get out prior to Callisto covering her mouth. Jove's eyes shift sightlessly, as his focus is on his sixth ryken sense.

"I thought whoever was left of Gregarious' men would retaliate sooner or later," he finally says after a minute of tension.

"They're here?" Prix asks.

Jove relaxes. "No, but I see signs of an ambush up ahead. Maybe as many as a hundred."

"Gregarious still has that many followers left?" Callisto gasps.

Jove nods. "And they're waiting for us up the road."

Callisto kneels down. "Acura, don't be scared."

"I'm not." She smiles Lo's smile. "I have faith in you, Callisto!"

Jove starts down the road again, his voice having the edge it always has before a fight. "I'm going ahead to put down the ambush. Both of you stay here with Acura until I return."

"You're going to engage all one hundred men alone?" Prix asks.

Jove stops, then half-turns. "Do you doubt that I can defeat them?"

"No, it's just—"

"Very well then. You have your orders. Stick to them."

When the general fades into the distance Acura moves toward a tree not too far off the road. Callisto goes to stop her, but then decides against it, instead joining her in the shade. Prix, however, doesn't budge, keeping his attention focused on the horizon. Although his eyes wander elsewhere, Callisto too finds it hard not to think about the matter at hand and the possible danger Jove faces.

Acura, on the other hand, seems unaffected by their anxiousness and falls sound asleep on the soft grass. Her peacefulness is as calming and reassuring as it has been the entire journey back. *This is what it was all for. All the work I've done to get to this point. The obstacle that was accepting my race. The struggle of joining the ryken squad. Though things aren't exactly how I pictured them as a child, it's still a dream realized. To make a difference, however big,* Callisto moves the hair from in front of Acura's face, *however small...*

"I'm going up ahead to find the general," Prix yells from the road, interrupting Callisto's thought.

Callisto shakes his head. "Why am I not surprised to hear you say that?"

"I'll be back. Just stay here and babysit the human until then."

Callisto stands, making his way back to the road. "The general gave us clear orders to wait for him here. Me and you. We haven't even received our punishment for disobeying his orders from yesterday and you're already going to do it again?"

"Look, I've known the general a lot longer than you, so remember that before you start lecturing me, rookie. General Jove will only give us a slap on the wrist, which will be well worth accomplishing this mission with flying colors. I've thought this through, Elastoman, so maybe you should think a little before challenging my intuition again." Prix turns for the road. "I'm the general's righthand for a reason."

Prix jogs off, leaving Callisto. He grits his teeth and returns to sit by Acura. He tries once again to distract himself with less worrisome thoughts, but to no avail. He looks toward the sky, noticing that a few dark clouds are starting to roll in. He sighs. There's a glimpse of movement on his periphery from the road behind, in the distant greenery outside the town of Baste. Callisto's brow furrows. *Was that actually something or just a trick of my mind? An animal, human... or ryken?* Callisto is still for a full minute, even his heart beat seeming to hush.

I'm probably just being paranoid. As Callisto exhales, a group of ryken emerges from the bushes and trees in the distance. Callisto's stomach sinks. Two dozen, maybe more, move in full pursuit. The option to stay and fight is hardly an option at all. General Jove would be able to put down the mob. Prix and Callisto could handle them together if the pursuers are untrained as those at Mercury's hideout. But neither of them is here. Just Callisto. Well, worse. Callisto and Acura.

He frantically scoops Acura and runs in the opposite direction, only to see half as many men pursuing from that direction as well. *An ambush! They lured the general away. And Prix with him.*

Callisto's head swivels as he racks his brain for a solution. But nothing comes to him... except the enemy. He sets Acura down and incidentally wakes her in the process. Callisto braces himself for a hopeless fight when he feels Acura clinging to his pant leg. "Stay as close to me as possible."

"Okay Callisto! I won't be scared. I believe in you!"

Callisto looks down at her despite Gregarious' men. With her words Callisto feels as if he's powered up—as if somehow he could conquer this impossible task after all. The odds are stacked against him, but Callisto steps forward. *I can do this! I have to do this for Acura. I made her a promise.*

When the thugs from Baste are thirty strides away Callisto extends his fist, taking out a handful. *Not good enough!* An extended leg sweep puts half of the remaining men on the ground. He sets his sights on the group blocking the road ahead.

"Lethal Binding!"

Callisto's arms and hands stretch, gathering the entire group of men. With the bundle between his palms, he swings them overhead with a roar and slams them into the rear pursuers.

Acura watches in awe. *Callisto is so strong! He's taking them all on at once!*

Suddenly, a man emerges from the ground beneath Callisto's feet, attempting an uppercut, but Callisto impressively evades. Spinning away from the burrowing ryken's blow, Callisto turns into another ryken with a war hammer already in mid-swing. He is able to jump backwards just as the hammer comes down with devastating power. It hits the ground so hard it creates a crater in the earth, blowing Callisto and Acura away with the shockwave. Callisto, flipping in the air, stretches his arm out, grabbing Acura, and they both land safely. Immediately after, Callisto is struck in the face, causing him to stumble back. He raises his head from the punch to see a dozen more ryken running toward him.

"Hand Barricade!"

Callisto's hand grows, widening and thickening to serve as a wall which fends off the incoming attacks. His face drips with sweat. *I can't keep this up. I have to find a way to the general.*

The criminal ryken begin to skirt the wall and Callisto makes a run for it, his Hand Barricade still behind him, protecting his six. A dozen strides later a sharp pain stings the center of Callisto's palm and it causes him to retract his defense, his hand pulsing with pain. When his hand returns to normal size, he sees a hole nearly through its center. He shrugs off the pain, Acura's safety his one and only priority. A few more steps then a pair of bolas entangle Callisto's legs and he falls, turning onto his back to protect Acura from the impact. He sets her to the side and tomahawks the bolas around his ankles. Once. Twice. Only three strikes before the rope snaps and the group is upon him, Acura cowering behind.

The first tries a punch that Callisto deflects, returning one of his own to the ryken's jaw. He catches another's fist, pulling him in and palming his chest, sending him back into two others. Callisto uses the slight break to stand, blocking a blow once upright, but receiving a punch from another ryken that curls him up. Then a kick to the temple sets his world spinning. He lifts his head, willing his body to fight on, but a strike to the face darkens the spinning earth.

When Callisto comes to his vision is blurred, seeing a hazy blob struggling with a smaller blob a few strides away. After blinking, he confirms a man with a horizontal scar from the bridge of his nose to his ear holds Acura by her hair. Tears flow down both her cheeks as she shrieks at the top of her lungs. Callisto feebly reaches out for her, his arm stretching slowly. *I've got... to save her!*

Callisto is yanked up by two men. He struggles but is so weak the men hardly notice. The scarred man holding Acura sneers as his fingernails all grow, combining into one sharp, spear-like point. "The boss was a man of winning," he says. "He constantly took precautions to make sure that if he didn't win, no one did. It was always a hassle in the past, but in light of his death, I'm glad he was that way."

The scarred man rears his hand back and Callisto's eyes widen as he realizes that the time for ransoms and negotiation is over. There will be no empty threat. No ultimatum forthcoming. No last chance. Strength flows into his body, not from some inner encouragement or blinding anger or some superior willpower, but from desperation.

Pathetic desperation. Desperation to stop the criminal. Desperation to maintain his promise. Desperation to save Acura.

The man thrusts his hand forward. The blade cuts the air violently.

"Acura!" Callisto shouts. The men grunt as they struggle to hold him at bay.

The blade cuts the air violently.

Callisto's mind revisits Acura's smile. *I'm not scared at all...*

The blade cuts the air violently.

Since you promised, I won't be scared anymore!

The man buries his hand wrist-deep, gore exploding from Acura's chest. The blood that runs out flows into the tearful dampness at her feet, pooling on the dusty road, a dark crimson puddle. Similarly to Acura, Callisto too stops breathing as if it is he who is stabbed. Acura attempts to remove the man's hand from her chest, but it only succeeds in draining the last bit of her strength, her arms falling limply by her sides. She sinks to her knees when he removes his hand, somehow mustering the energy to lift her head. Her eyes are so desperate in that moment that Callisto feels as if he is peering into her soul, and she into his. Acura's lips move slightly and despite the fact no sound comes out Callisto can her voice so loudly that the rest of the world is drowned out.

"Callisto, I'm scared."

Making a Difference

Life is full to bursting with innumerable actions and various events. Some are meaningful, but most aren't. Just a mundane flow, going through the motions, today being no more than yesterday was, and more of the same for tomorrow. Just a hamster on its wheel. Infinite circles of futility. That's what Callisto feared most, that he would not have made a difference when it was all said and done. To live a life in which he impacted no one. To him, nothing could be worse than a vain existence.

Now he can see just how foolish he has been.

Acura lies face-down in a pool of her own blood. Little Acura. Poor, innocent, little Acura. Struck down because Callisto had chosen to make a difference in her life. He would be the last difference in her life. The ultimate difference. She had to pay for his weakness. She had to pay for believing in a promise he couldn't keep.

Callisto's body slouches, as limp as Acura's. He rests on his knees, held up by two ryken. The world buzzes and murmurs in a slew of haziness. The murderer approaches, his mouth moving but issuing only noise. Fear suggests itself to Callisto, but it's swallowed in the ever-expanding hole of emptiness inside, right beside his anger. The two holding Callisto tighten their grip as the scarred man stops before them. He jerks his blade of a hand back, taking aim.

"Law 14: Dangerous Ground."

Suddenly, the ground beneath Callisto's feet gives way, causing him and the two men holding him to plummet into a deep hole. At the same time Jove and Prix arrive on the scene. By the time the men notice, Prix already has a dozen energy disks flying. Jove presses through the crowd, taking down the men easily, crumpling every challenger with a single blow.

Prix subdues the last of Gregarious' men. He looks up to find Callisto crawling out of the hole he fell into as a result of Jove's Law. Confusion causes Prix's scowl to flicker. *What's his problem?* He looks to Jove, who kneels over a bloody body. When Callisto stumbles over, Prix realizes the situation.

"General Jove!" Callisto shouts, frantic. "You've got to do something! We've got to do something, quick!"

Jove sighs despairingly. "Callisto..."

Tears start to form. "You have to hurry or she's going to die, General!"

"It's too late," Jove replies.

Callisto starts to tremble. "It can't be too late. I promised her I'd get her home." Prix watches his teammate and general, his throat exceedingly dry all of a sudden. He turns away when Callisto grabs Jove by the collar. "Please General, do something." Callisto begs. "There has to be a Law that can save her!"

"Prix, relax yourself," Jove says to his righthand, eyes still locked with Callisto's.

"Save her! She wants to see her mommy again. Let me take her home!"

"Law 3: Passionate Sleep."

"I can't take her to see her mommy like this." Callisto releases Jove, stumbling away. "She's counting on me. She needs me." He falls to his knees, tears dripping from his chin. "I made a promise... and I'm going to see it through. I have to." Callisto crashes to the ground, his eyelids crushingly heavy. "Acura, don't be scared. Please..."

* * *

When Metis initially joined the Excessum he figured everything about life would be different. Many things are, he can't deny, but not everything.

Metis examines the sweet bread in front of him, drenched in maple syrup. He still loves having a big breakfast in the morning as much as he always has. His fork and knife clatter on his plate. He sits back, pleased. *Not as delectable as Mom's, however.*

Metis cringes at the thought of Shine. The waitress walks over, interrupting his self-scolding. "Here is the check. If you need anything else please don't hesitate to ask." She offers a smile, walking away.

"Pardon me," Metis says. She stops, body still half-turned toward her destination. "Is it permissible to leave your recompense on the table?"

"The tip? Yes, that's fine. Have yourself a fantastic rest of the day," she says, zooming back into the kitchen.

Metis takes one last sip of water from his glass then stands. He moves through the busy diner, meeting every wandering eye with a face of stone. He reaches the front counter and grabs the pen resting on it. *Dad was an enormous proponent of leaving tips. For subpar service he'd still grant respectable compensation, and anything beyond was endowed accordingly. I always find myself replicating his customs.* Metis takes the bill and writes on the back: *Be mindful to accept ryken in a corresponding fashion to how I accepted your mediocre service. You will give thanks one day for it.*

Metis returns the unpaid check to the table and exits. The town of Pochada starts to come alive in the light of the rising sun. People bustle on the street, doing all they can to not shove the person in front of them, while simultaneously trying not to be toppled by the person bearing down on them from behind. Metis finds the tightly packed mob unbearably infuriating. *I'd wipe the road clean of these buzzing humans if the result didn't inevitably cause more of the insects to swarm to me shortly after.*

It seems that as every day passes, Metis' rage grows more and more. Years ago, after his father's death, his anger was intense but targeted—targeted for whoever cheated Thralle and took his life, because it was obvious no one could've defeated him on fair terms. Although, as time progressed and the ambiguity of the culprit grew, so did the target of Metis' rage. Soon, just the sight of humans made him scowl in anger.

In truth, the act could have been committed by human or ryken, but Metis doesn't care. Humans were the cause. They were the reason Thralle left home that day to never return. Thralle was summoned to fight *their* war. For *their* reasons. How could he stomach these arrogant, selfish creatures? Metis can't understand. Every single one sets his blood to boiling.

Even his own mother. That was when his rage first began to scare him. Metis loved Shine, still does. But her being a human makes him furious, and because of that he's unable to deal with her. So to remedy the situation Metis began spending less and less time at home. That was when he found the Shack. The regulars being a blend of human and ryken mitigated his rage on account of the uncertainty of a particular individual's race.

That isn't the case here. Metis would be willing to risk all his life's earnings on the fact that he is the only ryken walking these human-infested streets of Pochada. The knowledge of it stabs at him worse than he anticipated it would. It seems since joining the Excessum his growing hatred of humans hasn't changed either.

Metis continues to navigate his way out of the town's center and passes the train station. The crowd thins out quickly beyond that point, as to be expected. What isn't expected is the other crowd gathered by the town's gatehouse into the Pochada Mountains. Metis grits his teeth.

"Fate loves to test my patience."

* * *

"Acura!" Callisto yells, surging out of his sleep. He scans the room, chest heaving, in a cold sweat. He's back in the Arena's barracks. Jove sits at a small table not too far off, doing paperwork. He doesn't so much as flinch at Callisto's outburst. Callisto puts a hand to his face and forces himself to take a long, slow breath. He repeats the act a few times but his breathing only becomes shakier. He then puts another hand to his face and begins to weep. Jove continues his work quietly, only offering a single glance as Callisto's weeping evolves into sobbing.

A while passes before his tears dry up. "Don't be so hard on yourself," Jove says.

"That's easy for you to say, General," Callisto says, his voice hoarse. "You didn't make Acura a promise."

"I didn't?" Jove says, an edge to his voice. "Every mission I accept is a promise to the victim, the criminal, and the nation that I will do my best to see that task come to pass. But all we can do is give our best. At the end of the day not every mission will be successful and not every job handed out will be completed."

Callisto shakes his head. "No. No, I can't accept that."

"You have to or you will destroy yourself long before any enemy has the opportunity."

"If I don't have what it takes to rescue an innocent child, then maybe I deserve it!"

Jove stands. "Listen to me!" Callisto bites his cheek in an attempt to fight back more tears. "In life you *will* fail. Everyone does at some point. I've failed too, very recently, in fact." Jove mutters a curse. "I should've never let Prix and you out of my sight. There were a million and one strategies I could've implemented instead, but I wanted to test you and Prix again. See if you would follow my orders, but I miscalculated. I didn't expect Gregarious' men to have taken a foothold in Baste. It was my leadership that failed Acura and my leadership alone."

Callisto frowns. "You didn't see her face. You didn't hear her voice. She was afraid... The truth of the matter is Acura died because I wasn't strong enough to protect her."

"There will always come a situation where you need to be just a little faster or just a little stronger to succeed. You will fail, Callisto. And no matter how many times you've been deemed a hero in the past it will still hurt." Jove's eyes flicker away from Callisto's, then return with intensity. "But you have to learn to move past that, otherwise it won't be just Acura who died back there."

"Am I just supposed to move past the fact that I let a little girl die?" Callisto clenches his fist. "Right in front of me." A tear escapes. "How could I ever move past that? Her *mommy* never will."

Callisto sits back, then rises out of his bed. "I understand how foolish it is to think that I'll never fail again, but I plan to train like that's the case. No. I'll train because that is the case. 'Failure isn't an option' is an understatement. I'll train until it's no longer a possibility."

Callisto exits the room leaving Jove alone. "The unwritten Law of Loss," Jove says softly, "more powerful than any Law I could ever manipulate."

* * *

A couple hundred Pochadans gather at the south gate of the town, all talking of the desperate man who took a young woman hostage. From what Metis can glean from their chatter, the criminal demanded that some harsh suburban tax be lifted, as his family could not live under its weight. Apparently, he didn't care if he went to prison after this; he only desired change for his family. *How supremely noble.*

Metis manages to land himself close enough to the action to hear the police. The crowd presses against him worse than at the town's center. Metis tries to listen in on the police's strategy but the humans continue their talking, some about things as pointless as hair appointments. Metis calms his rising temper.

"Pardon me, Mr. Officer," Metis calls over to one of the handful of men giving orders. "How much longer do you estimate this endeavor will last? I have business on the better side of the Pochada Mountains."

The man stares at Metis until he finishes speaking, then looks away, without a word. Another officer comes over, roaring, "You be quiet!" He puts a hand to Metis chest, regarding the crowd. "We need you all back! We're in the midst of very important negotiations!"

Metis looks at the officer's hand. "Allow me to be that resolution."

The man's arm glows purple and with a crack the bone of his arm separates. Metis steps over the writhing man, the crowd falling away in terror. Metis continues forward, the other officers not noticing his presence until he is already between them and the hostage building. Acting out of reflex, the officers set their guns on Metis as he proceeds.

"Hold your fire!" Metis hears. *Hold, indeed. We couldn't possibly have your criminal misconstrue your salvo as a hazard to him. That might lead to the loss of your precious hostage. You humans aren't senseless, I recognize that much... you're just infuriating.*

Metis explodes the doors open with a purple flourish. He saunters through the front lobby and on his way to the rear lobby he is stopped by a hysterical voice. "Don't move or she gets it! I'll do it! I swear I will!"

Metis looks at the man, late twenties at the oldest. His blond hair is a mess and his long nose drips snot. *Odds are he's merely a man who feels he's exhausted all other options. I can respect him.*

"Help me!" the hostage cries. She is a dark-skinned girl with short, straight hair and tears soaking her face. *Her, not so much.*

"I'll be frank," Metis says, taking a step closer. The man cocks the gun. "I don't have a preference whether she survives or perishes. A homicide here would only grant me less drudgery taming the lot of you in the future."

"Do you think this is a joke?" the criminal snaps. "Take one more step and I will blow this woman's head off!"

Metis stops.

Then takes another step.

The man pulls back on the trigger. It doesn't move. When he glances down there is a soft purple glow around his weapon. A force slams into his side and sends him sprawling into the wall. Shaking it off, the man tries to stand but a sharp pain shooting the length of his left side prevents him. A broken rib. He lifts his head toward his captive, who is now crying in the corner.

Metis moves closer to the hostage and she shrieks at his first step. *More afraid of the ryken saving you than your own potential murderer.* Metis shakes his head. *Why save her?* Despite his question, a purple aura grabs the criminal by the collar, then he and Metis exit the building opposite where he entered. There, more officers are posted.

"Freeze ryken!"

"I have your criminal!" Metis responds. "Provide me no resistance and I will relinquish him to you!"

Silence. A bit of movement, then more silence. Finally an order is shouted. "Fire!"

Hundreds of bullets slam into a transiently lit purple curtain. Metis advances with the criminal floating before him, his barrier preceding them both. As he enters into the officers' midst the barrier bends around him, providing his flank with protection as well. A moving barrier in Metis' blind spot is a difficult maneuver, but he's confident enough he can protect himself from a few hundred rounds. A couple of men try to engage Metis directly, but their fists are walled out all the same.

When Metis crosses the officers they finally cease their barrage. The area is hazy with gun smoke. Metis lowers the criminal. "They refused my terms," he says. "Return home to your family. You won't be captured. Not today."

The criminal looks at the police behind him, hesitant. An officer tries another shot, but Metis' barrier rejects the bullet. The man's eyes snap to Metis, fear encompassing him. "Stay away! Stay away, you freak!" The criminal flees into the mountain pass. Metis starts forward as the police behind slam into his Wall of Lutrio in pursuit. "Freak! He's a freak!"

"Why do I still try?" Metis growls.

Episode 6:

A New Righthand

Callisto punches the air, his main focus on his form. A dozen other recruits work out around Callisto, each absorbed in their own routine, but none move with his intensity. Callisto kicks the air twice and punches again. He reestablishes his stance just as he hears quick, hard footsteps enter the gym.

"Hey Elastoman!" Prix shouts. "I need to talk to you!"

Callisto punches again. "Not now. I'm in the middle of something."

The terse response only angers Prix further. He grabs Callisto by the shoulder, turning him around. "No, we're going to talk about this right now." The tension between the two is quickly noticed by the other recruits in the room. Some even let their curiosity get the better of them, stopping their training. "Guess what I just got finished doing for the last four hours."

Callisto turns away. "I'm really not in the mood."

"I said guess!" Prix demands, forcing Callisto back around.

This time Callisto meets his stare, deadly serious. A small crowd begins to gather. "Don't touch me again," Callisto warns.

He starts to walk away and Prix calls out after him, "I just finished overnight guard duty! That's a rookie's job! And do you know why?" Prix waits for Callisto's rebuttal but he just continues toward the door. "Because you were too weak to save a little girl." Callisto freezes. Prix smiles, getting the reaction he sought. "Aw," he antagonizes, "you going to cry now?"

Callisto explodes toward Prix, who wards off a kick and a punch, returning a strike that is blocked. Callisto kicks again, connecting to Prix's ribs, but he accepts it to land a blow to Callisto's jaw, causing him to stumble backwards. Prix quickly fires a razor disk that Callisto barely evades, and another that he doesn't avoid, cutting just above his elbow. Callisto, not wavering, stretches his arm but Prix catches his fist. He then retracts his body to his arm, the maneuver catching Prix off guard, awarding Callisto a kick to the face. The crowd starts to get into the action, chanting, "Fight!" as loud as they can.

Prix rises from the ground with a scowl. "That's it, Elastoman!" He fires off a barrage of razor disks, his hands becoming a blur. Callisto dances around the volley, taking minor cuts only to avoid the bigger ones. As he focuses on dodging, Prix engages him directly. Before Callisto has a chance to establish a defense he is punched in the stomach. He immediately drops to his knees, his lungs craving the air his body can't seem to obtain.

Prix gets behind him and grabs a fistful of hair, jerking his head back. He manifests a razor disk, placing the edge of it a hair's breadth away from Callisto's neck. "And you know what?" Prix whispers. "You're still not strong enough."

The words send a tremor through Callisto's bones. Rage. At Prix, yes. But mostly himself. Why can't he be stronger?

"Are you going to kill him, Prix?" Jove says, his voice booming with authority as he crosses the room, Nicon at his hip. The moment Prix sees Jove his expression of bitter fury is replaced with stupefied guilt. He releases Callisto, who collapses to his hands and knees. A second passes before Callisto summons the will to stand. "Callisto, I did not give you the order to leave yet," Jove says when Callisto goes to exit.

Callisto continues, ignoring his general. Jove mutters something to himself before glaring at Prix. "Go to the barracks and don't move until I give you further instructions. If I hear that you left for any reason whatsoever you will answer to me."

Jove always has an edge to him, even in the most relaxing of settings. He's a kind man; there are few more selfless. But that does not make him a pushover. If one ever judged Jove in that way, he would ensure that misunderstanding would not occur again. Prix lowers his head and obeys, swallowing the words of his illogical, egocentric defense. "This crowd needs to be dealt with as well, Nicon," Jove says. "I trust that you will handle things."

"You can count on me. Am I right?" Nicon answers. Jove makes his way out as Nicon speaks to the crowd. "You should all be ashamed of yourselves! We are all headed toward the same goal; we needn't fight with one another, I mean, am I right?" Nicon watches Jove exit the room over his shoulder then faces the recruits with a completely different expression. "So, who won?"

* * *

"Doesn't it get annoying carrying that flower around?" Callisto asks.

Acura clutches the large daisy tighter, smiling. "Not really. I love flowers so I don't mind."

"Hmm. I have an idea." Callisto kneels down to Acura's level, takes the flower and places it in her hair. "There, it fits you well!"

"Won't it fall out?" She shakes her head.

Callisto catches the flower. "Yeah, if you do that." He stashes it back. "But it will stay if you act normally. I got the idea from my sister. You're really just like her."

Acura beams her innocent smile. "I've never had a big brother before!"

Slowly Acura's smiling face begins to fade. Her childish bliss grows dimmer and dimmer until it disappears into the background of Callisto's mind, a much less pleasing memory making its way to the forefront. Similar to the previous one, this image is Acura, but her face is covered in tears. Without sound, Acura's lips move. "Callisto, I'm scared. Callisto, I'm scared. Callisto, I'm scared." The scene replays until all Callisto can hear is his name being yelled. "Callisto! Callisto!"

"Callisto!" Jove yells. His voice snaps Callisto out of his daydream. He finds himself outside, on the stairs behind the Arena. His breath is quick and shallow and he sweats profusely despite the cool night air.

Callisto places his head in his hands. "I... I don't know what to do, General. I don't know what to do next."

Jove takes a seat on the steps next to Callisto. "You're a lot like me, believe it or not," Jove says, introspectively. "You have a strong sense of justice. You like to divide right and wrong clearly, profoundly. But life isn't always so clear-cut; in fact, in most cases it's not that way at all. You don't need to blame yourself for what happened. It's not your fault."

Callisto frowns. "No matter how many times you say that, it still hurts all the same."

"But that won't stop me from saying it. I'll continue to remind you of this until you believe it, even if you don't want to." Silence falls and Jove uses the opportunity to change the subject. "You do remember that you're assigned to escort Princess Isabella of Amica? Imani should be arriving tomorrow with her. You should rest until then."

Callisto broods for a moment, then, "I can't work with Prix anymore," he says. "After what just happened I refuse to fight beside him."

Jove nods. "Your feelings are understandable. Honestly, I don't blame you. I'm not sure what happened back there, but I know you well enough to recognize that if things escalated to violence, Prix had to have gone overboard. Yet, even with that said, I want you on my team."

Callisto shakes his head. "I don't think that can happen."

"Just take the day to think it over. When you report in tomorrow, if you still feel the same, I'll begin to push your paperwork for transferring to another division." Jove stands, making for the front of the Arena for reentry, but pauses before leaving Callisto's field of view. "Prix isn't really the guy you see. He's only this way because you threaten his position as my righthand. He's an upstanding person, normally. I think you two would get along under different circumstances."

* * *

Metis strolls down a road in the Amica Kingdom, in no hurry to reach his destination. He finds himself liking his surroundings and there is no surprise as to why.

The Amica Kingdom is a ryken reservation separate from the nation of Laevus, yet it rests within Laevus' borders. This is because Laevus invaded Amican territory a couple hundred years ago under the guise of peace. *The curriculum in school always seemed to conveniently leave this story untold.* After winning a small war, Laevus took over a vast portion of their land, forcing the Amicans to assimilate or get pushed closer to the waters. But the Amicans are a proud people and thus they resisted the Laevinians in the centuries that followed. Finally, an agreement of sorts was reached in which the Amica Kingdom accepted a very large territory inland from the Laevus Nation and their protection, in exchange for their remaining land bordering the ocean. The treaty put an end to the bitter, ongoing war between nations, netted Laevus a number of port cities, and had hoped to salvage the relationship between Laevinians and Amicans.

The treaty accomplished all its goals, except the last. Ever since the document was signed three decades ago the Laevus nation has abused their power in the negotiations that followed, demanding land as compensation for further protection. Under the thumb of Laevus, and now entirely surrounded, Amica has little choice but to comply.

An unfortunate fate, really. Metis continues his journey through Amica. The nation seems like a place Metis would enjoy, if for no other reason than the fact that ryken here aren't oppressed. Unlike Laevus, here, ryken and human live in peace, not one above the other. The epitome of what Metis strives for Laevus—and the world as a whole— to be one day. It shows that it's possible for the two races to dwell together despite their differences. It might even quiet the fury within Metis to see humans who aren't as oppressively arrogant as the Laevinians are. He can only hope.

The kingdom is gargantuan for a single city, triple the size of the Laevinian capital, Centrum City, and that's even including the military district. But it's painfully tiny for an entire nation. Metis continues his circuit of the kingdom, studying it. This is how he spent his entire day yesterday, as well. He rounds the corner and happens upon a playground occupied by a number of children. *It's rather ironic when you ponder it. The two largest territories within Laevinian borders are primarily occupied by ryken. A land like this is where I belong, a place that takes their ryken heritage seriously. Refusing to bow to huma—*

Metis' thoughts are cut short when he notices a child being picked on by two slightly older adolescent boys. "Excuse the cliché, but why don't you delinquents antagonize someone of similar stature?" Metis asks, intervening.

The bigger of the bullies turns, shorter than Metis by a few inches. He has spiky hair and wears sunglasses. "Why don't you just mind your own business?"

"Don't think that just because you're a little bigger than us we'll back down from you," the other bully adds. He has a long face with big ears to match. His scrawny build is lightly perfumed with the scent of cigarettes. "Go away before we get angry."

The child is held against the gate of the playground, each arm pinned by one of the bullies. "You can't take these guys alone, they're tough!"

"Shut up!" Sunglasses demands. He lowers his head and shoots a spike of his hair through the gate close to the boy.

"I'm not afraid of you!" the boy yells, his voice shaky. He looks to Metis. "Go get help! They'll be too busy with me to run after you."

Sunglasses shoots another spike. "I said shut—"

The bully's hair meets a barrier in front of the boy's leg. Confused by the event the bully tries another spike, with the same result. All three children stare, trying to understand what exactly is happening. "As a ryken, my dad always stressed, *Don't use it until you understand it.* That adage is in reference to a ryken's spirit energy, and I can see with minimal observation that you have little clue how to wield yours with any fluency." Metis' eyes flash purple. "Someone could get injured that way."

Suddenly, Sunglasses has a purple aura surrounding him. He starts toward his accomplice. "Hey man, what're you doing?" Long Face asks.

"I can't control my body! Move!" Sunglasses throws a punch that knocks Long Face out on contact. Metis relinquishes control and Sunglasses immediately drops to his friend's aid. Metis stands over the two of them. "How very disappointing."

* * *

I want you on my team. Jove's words replay in Callisto's head and, although he is pleased by them, he still can't seem to smile. General Jove is an amazing leader. Fierce, yet gentle. Firm, but kind. Callisto counts himself lucky to be under such tutelage. So lucky, in fact, that he wrestles with the idea of still being on the same team as Prix Hadlim.

It was all he could think about yesterday which, distressingly, is considered progress from the nonstop assault of Acura memories rewinding over and over in his mind. Be that as it may, Callisto still doesn't like it. He knew the ryken squad would be challenging when he first set the goal for himself, probably the hardest thing he'd ever do in his life. He knew he would sweat, bleed and ache, but even still, he never imagined he could hurt so badly. Callisto had prepared for the physical toll of the ryken squad, but not the emotional. He hadn't really considered it, to be honest. But even if he had such forethought, there wasn't much he could do to ready himself aside from simply experiencing trauma firsthand.

Now that he's here, will he run? What will it teach him to scurry from Prix because his feelings were hurt? It would make more sense to face his problems head-on and remove their power over him. That's what he told himself he would do after Acura. Fight. In every sense of the word. After all, rising to this challenge is the only way to ensure you're prepared for the next.

Callisto rounds the corner to report for the day's duties and finds the rest of his fellow recruits already present. He falls in line. Soon after, Jove emerges from his quarters. Division 1a's recruits stand straight and tall. Jove strides down the line of four, inspecting them closely. "At ease, gentlemen." The group relaxes slightly. "Abimael, what have you to report?"

"Nothing, sir. Sparring with Brinks went well."

Jove squints. "Did you win?"

Abimael shrinks. "No."

Jove moves on. "Hontale?"

"Afternoon and evening guard duty was uneventful yesterday."

Jove nods. "Spar with Abimael until noon today. Then you two are back to guard duty. Train seriously or I'll have you each go a round with Prix next time. Callisto, I hope you're feeling better."

"A bit, sir. I have nothing to report."

Jove stands in front of his last recruit. "Prix, you're to continue guard duty until Abimael and Brinks relieve you. Anything to add?"

"Nothing, sir."

Jove steps away. "Quiet morning. Allow me to liven it up, then. I have an announcement. I want to make an adjustment to the team. Prix, your punishment for your atrocious behavior recently is as follows." Jove regards Callisto. "It is with great honor that I bestow to you, Callisto Socius, the title as my righthand. From henceforth the duty and privileges of said title are revoked from Prix Hadlim and given to you."

Callisto looks to his right and the shock on Abimael's and Hontale's faces almost match his own. He turns back to Jove. "The responsibility is a heavy one," the general continues, "but I'm more than confident you can handle it. You have shown me that you have all the qualities of a great leader. Being my righthand means that you will be my second-in-command and many of my decisions will be brought to you for an additional point of view. The directive of my righthand adjustment is effective immediately. Congratulations, Callisto." Jove extends his hand and Callisto grabs it with eagerness, shaking firmly. "That is all for now."

Abimael and Hontale nearly trample Jove on their way to Callisto with congratulations. Prix starts down the hallway with his head down, although Callisto doesn't notice. For the first time since Acura's death, he finds himself smiling.

Invested

The starched stiffness of the ryken squad uniform still feels good, just as good as when he first put it on. Callisto examines the perfectly stitched cuffs, the sharp seams and the flawless golden buttons of his shirt as he walks. His mind continues to wander due to the lack of conversation of his traveling companions. The silence is welcomed as long as Acura doesn't find her way into his thoughts, a feat she always seems to accomplish.

The mute journey, in truth, isn't anyone's fault more than Callisto's. Imani Amano, General Gwen's righthand, isn't ever really much for conversation. Callisto could count on one hand the number of times he's heard the small man speak. Moreover, Imani isn't big on a lot of things, such as combing his long dry hair, or tying his boots, or replacing the missing temple of his glasses. However, he always manages to see his missions to completion and as far as Callisto is concerned, that's all that really matters.

The other person hiking along the military district of Centrum City with the ryken squad recruits is Amica Princess Isabella Vortane. Her smooth face and inviting blue eyes give her a look as coveted by women as her regal status. The golden curls of her hair bounce around her delicate shoulders with every step. She's a sight to make most men do a double-take. But with their destination of the Arena close, no eyes are on her, and even though she is more than fine with that, a little conversation after the long journey from Amica would be welcomed.

Callisto, however, is having none of that. Flipping the Acura ordeal in his head over and over, he has concluded two things. The first is that he must work harder to stop failure. As long as he stays truly diligent he can always keep failure at bay. Deep down, in his heart of hearts, Callisto doesn't quite believe in that theory unreservedly as of yet, but with enough hard work he hopes to prove himself wrong.

The second conclusion is that he shouldn't allow himself to get personally invested in the mission or close to the victims and perpetrators. An inability to do this could only spell disaster for him when it comes to critical decisions out in the line of duty or create a burdening feeling of emptiness thereafter. As a ryken squad recruit he only has one job and that's to see his mission completed; everything else is vain. Callisto looks to Imani. *Perhaps there's a bit to be learned from him beyond the surface.*

"I'll see you later, Imani," Callisto says, once they enter the Arena. Imani only nods in reply before taking his leave. Callisto catches Isabella nervously biting her lip. He starts to comment on her worried expression but catches himself. What good could come from it? A glimpse into her personality? The beginnings of a bond? *Don't get personally invested. Complete your mission, nothing more.*

Their eyes meet and Princess Isabella offers a weak smile. Callisto only blinks. "Let me show you where you'll stay."

* * *

Jove enters into the small auditorium of the Arena, finding Gwen seated on the edge of the stage, her legs dangling, and Nicon in a front row seat. "Would someone like to explain to me why we're meeting in here?" Jove says, coming down the aisle.

"Because Gwen loves to anger me," Clamous answers as he enters.

"You got to host the meeting last month with no complaints from me, Clamous," Gwen says. "I wanted to have the meeting here as a change of scenery. Keep things fun, interesting." Clamous grumbles his way over and Jove sits with a seat between him and Nicon. "Now, let's get down to business. This next month is going to be pretty quiet, like the last few. Jove, your division has city patrol. Nicon, your division has guard duty. Clamous' division is on operational standby. And my guys have team training. Also Nicon, you're up for supervising the ryken trenches."

"Already? It feels like I just did it," he whines.

"It's been three months, just like always. Anybody have anything important to mention?"

"There was a report of ryken activity over in Pochada Town," Clamous says. "Culprit apparently was moving south."

Gwen takes out a notebook and jots something down. "Got it. Anything else?"

"We recently discovered another participant name for the latest Excessum tournament," Jove says. "Yatori Onyshala. Unlike our last two names, we're pretty sure she survived, although tracking her whereabouts has been frustratingly unsuccessful."

"Hmm. I see," Gwen says, taking more notes. "Did she win the tournament then?"

"That has yet to be determined. However, I will find out everything I can as soon as I can."

"Anything else?"

"I got that growth cut off my thigh," Nicon says. "In case anyone was wondering. Am I right?"

"Nicon, please," Jove says harshly. Gwen scribbles something out in her notepad and Clamous shakes his head, nearly snarling.

Nicon shrugs. "Man, you all are way too uptight for me. Am I right?"

"You get any more information on those ryken hunters?" Gwen asks. "It's been a few months now since they started popping up."

"I don't know what the colonel expects out of this, I mean, am I right? We can't legally engage them. And we really can't defend ourselves if they attack us."

"Just answer the question!" Clamous barks.

Nicon flinches, over-exaggerated, then laughs. "Nah, I got nothing. Am I right?"

"Surprise, surprise," Gwen says. "All right, I'll update the colonels then. You're up next month, Jove."

Gwen hops off the stage and the generals all make for the exit. Jove pulls Gwen aside on the way out. "Are you free sometime today or tomorrow?"

Gwen's cheeks flush. "Jove, thi-this is so sudden."

"Perhaps we can schedule something this week, if you're free."

She puts her hands to her face, barely able to contain herself. "Jove, I'm married. I couldn't possibly... Don't get me wrong, I'd love to, I just couldn't!"

Jove's brow furrows a moment. "Oh. Surely next week you could spare an hour to spar then."

Gwen's face goes blank. "Sparring? You wanted to know when I was free to spar. Not when I was free for..." Jove tilts his head slightly, trying to piece together the misunderstanding. "Oh. Well, then..."

* * *

Metis' stare is blank yet menacing, like the expression a reaper might have when he comes to collect his prize. Neither happy nor sad. Not eager, sympathetic, hateful or excited. Just a being completing his everlasting task. The bully with sunglasses reacts accordingly, running away after scooping his friend over his shoulder.

With nothing more than a parting look, Metis sets off on his way. "Heya! I'm Rhys!" Metis continues, not giving the slightest indication of interest in the child. Annoyingly, the boy persists. "I thank you for saving me back there. You're really strong! Where'd you learn to fight like that?" No response. "I get it! You're one of those unsung heroes aren't you? The kind who work in the shadows and don't talk, right?"

Metis' impatience gets the better of him. "Get lost, child, I have no business with you."

"Come on, don't be that way," Rhys says. "We're pretty much friends now. There's no reason to be shy." Metis suppresses a scowl, his temper rising. "You should let me thank you the right way for saving me. My mom will cook you dinner if you want. Come by tonight and eat with us! Is that a yes? Because if it is, you're going the wrong way. My house is in this direction."

Rhys runs a couple of feet and turns back only to find Metis still walking in the same direction. Rhys catches back up to him, still smiling. "Not hungry, huh? I completely understand. Maybe some other time. Anyway, what are we going to do tonight?"

Metis breaks off the road and arrives at a building of apartments. Once he enters there is only a nod of familiarity from the clerk and Metis goes up the stairs. Infuriatingly, Rhys still rambles on at his hip. "Is this where you live? Have you always lived on the outskirts of the kingdom? My family and I just moved out here. I can't say I like it much, but there's not like I have much choice. My dad—"

Metis enters his room, slamming the door behind him. He walks over to a table with a lamp and telephone, placing his father's timepiece down. He polishes the metal casing with his thumb before he turns around, nearly startled.

"This is a pretty decent place you have here," Rhys says, looking around. Metis blinks as if doing so will remove the boy from his chamber. "Yeah, this place is awesome. I want a pad like this when I grow up."

Metis tilts his head. "I see; your ryken ability is that you can phase through solid objects."

"Huh? I wish. I'm a human."

"Then how were you—" Metis shakes his head. "Strange, to say the least. Though what's stranger still is your statement. Wishing you were a ryken is a pioneering declaration to these ears."

Rhys laughs. "You talk funny. I like it."

"Shouldn't you be going now, human?"

"Aw, don't call me that. I hate being a human. They're so lame."

Metis squints. *A human who genuinely longs to be a ryken? Intriguing.*

"We can't do anything spectacular like ryken can. We're so weak and ordinary. I hate it! It's not fair. What'd I do to deserve being human? I bet if I were a ryken, punks like those guys earlier wouldn't pick on me! I'd beat them up and become their leader. I'd be strong like my dad and change this kingdom for the better."

"You have ambition, and not the noxious ambition of oppression typical of your kind. I'll confess, you've piqued my interest to some degree. What change do you speak of for this kingdom?"

"Well, you know how the government of Laevus always takes our land? My dad says that they're greedy thieves, stealing what doesn't belong to them. So if I were a ryken I would raise a super strong army. Not just for defense, either! I'd take back what rightfully belongs to us."

"Is that a fact? Those who inhabit Amica Kingdom are people native to the land that Laevus has since deemed their own. You would be tasked with reconquering quite a copious portion of land, based upon your claim. Land that the strongest nation of the world now possesses. I share your fervor on the topic. The humans of the Laevus government for centuries have taken land from Amica by pulling the strings of the ryken they subdue. They do this because they feel they're more worthy, as Laevinian humans always have. Self-centered, egotistical creatures they are, makes my stomach lurch whenever I think on it."

"Wait. Are you a rabble rouser?"

"A what?"

Rhys' eyebrows raise. "You've never heard of a rabble rouser? I can tell you're new to Amica now! Rabble rousers are people who rebel against our government. My dad says their views aren't the problem, but the way they go about change is what may cause a civil war. He says we need to have faith in King Atrium."

"Your father sounds an awful lot like someone I know. Those who feel that the methods are more important than the results will never see change come to pass. That mindset can only breed peaceful theories and fairytale philosophies. Fruitless wishes. None of which ends in evolution, true adaptation." Metis speaks with an edge and for the first time Rhys is unnerved by him. "This is why the humans have power in Laevus, because they are ruthless when necessary. They wield what little power they have extraordinarily effectively. Unlike you, however, I have the heritage to bring about change and I won't let it collapse by the wayside. Whatever it may mean, I will usher in a new era. Alone if I must."

"You can't change everything by yourself. You'll need help at some point."

Metis glares at Rhys. "I don't remember requesting your consultation on the matter. Come to think of it, I don't recall asking for your presence altogether."

Metis' blank eyes fall on Rhys. "Uh," the child hesitates. "It's getting pretty late now, dinner should be ready soon and I'm getting hungry." He makes for the door, looking over his shoulder, smiling. "Come by tomorrow. I'll have my mom make an extra plate for you!"

Metis watches him exit, emotionless. "He reminds me of Samané."

* * *

"It's time, Princess," Callisto says, sticking his head into Princess Isabella's provisional room.

"Oh, of course." She stands then nervously starts to smooth the imaginary wrinkles from her skirt. Callisto leads her down a narrow hallway with paintings of old men on both sides. Some have long hair, some none at all. Their skin colors vary from pale white to midnight black. A small number of them are smiling, although most wear frowns. What they all have in common, however, is the great power they wielded in their time. The showcase has little value, as Isabella's eyes stay on the floor. "Tell me, Callisto. What is Colonel Calamity like?"

"This will only be my third time seeing him, and I have yet to hear him speak. Your guess is as good as mine." Isabella chews at her lip. *Not the answer she was hoping for,* Callisto muses.

"I need this to go well," she murmurs to herself, clenching her fists. "People are counting on me." Callisto pulls a set of keys out and slides one into the door. "You can do this, Isabella. You have to."

Don't get personally invested, Callisto thinks. *Complete your mission, nothing more.*

The two enter into a modest-sized courtroom. To either side of the aisle they walk down are five rows of chairs. Callisto escorts Princess Isabella through the waist-high gate to stand before the judge at his bench. Colonel Calamity.

He's a dark man, the whites of his eyes standing out in sharp contrast. His nose is normal-sized, but his nostrils are gaping holes, so big it almost seems as if you'd be able to see straight to his brain, given the right angle. Cloaked in the blue of the ryken squad, Colonel Calamity sits high and looks low on his visitors, his thick, black beard only allowing a line of exposure for his lips.

"This is the last of the day, correct, Mariova?" Colonel Calamity asks, placing his chin on his palm.

A man at a table by the wall quickly scribbles. "Yes, sir," he squeaks back, never raising his head. "This is Princess Isabella from Amica."

Isabella steps forward, bowing her head. "It is an honor."

"Mutual," Calamity says, flatly. He sifts through the documents on the bench. "Ah, yes, here it is. This is the day we're supposed to reinstate our treaty, but instead Amica sent you. Why is that?"

"It's because we cannot accept the terms of the treaty," Isabella says, her voice shaky.

"Oh?"

"The Laevus Nation is demanding fifty percent of Amican land and an implementation of a new tax, all in exchange for the same protection we were supposed to be guaranteed since our first signing. It is nothing new that Amica and Laevus have never seen eye to eye in the past, but we are willing to work and come to a new agreement."

Calamity smiles. "A new agreement? For what? If the terms are unacceptable then there will be no treaty." He lifts his gavel. "Case dismi—"

"No, please!" Isabella shouts, her voice cracking. She takes a breath to stop the tears she feels at the back of her face. "Amica cannot give that amount of land away and continue to house our citizens. If we accept these terms, our people will rebel again, just as they did ten years ago when we renewed the treaty last time. Amica is weaker now and if civil war breaks out... we will collapse.

"Of course, if we don't sign the treaty our nations will be outright enemies once again, and I don't have to state what kind of disaster that spells for Amica. Laevus has the power here. You always have, even when you Laevinians first came to our land centuries ago. We've admitted that and given you all we can, surviving on the scraps you left behind. But now, I'm begging you, please don't take our crumbs too."

The colonel raises a hand to his chin, clawing at his beard. He deliberates for what feels like an eternity to Isabella, then repositions himself in his seat. "I. Don't. Care. Case dismis—"

"Wait!"

Calamity, Isabella and Mariova all turn their heads, surprise plain on their faces. Callisto is the most shocked by far, almost not recognizing his own voice ringing in the court. He searches the faces of those staring at him as if hoping one of them will take blame for the outburst.

"Do you have something to say, recruit?" Calamity growls.

"Colonel Calamity, sir. With all due respect, maybe there is some good that can come out of working a new treaty with the Amicans."

Calamity's eyes are intense with disbelief. His beard shifts slightly as he repositions the scorn in his mouth. Just when it seems as if he will explode with anger, he erupts in laugher instead. He puts a hand to his forehead, then one to his stomach, doubling over in his high chair, laughing harder still. Callisto and Isabella share an uneasy glance at one another.

"Oh, this is good. Very good! It's been a long and tiring day. I needed a nice, hearty laugh. I'll tell you what. You can travel down to Amica and find something that you believe will be worth saving. If I agree, I'll only levy a tax on the kingdom henceforth. I disagree? We'll just leave them to rot for the good of humanity or whatever. Sounds good? Great! Court adjourned." He slams down his gavel. "Safe travels, recruit. Let me know how you like it there."

Calamity closes a book and stands, still chuckling. He wipes a tear from his eye as he steps down. When he exits Princess Isabella turns, her face slack with shock. "Why did you do that?"

Callisto mutters a curse under his breath. "I got invested."

Episode 8:
Right or Wrong

Metis stares at the giant structure in the distance with a face no different than if he were staring at a ruined, archaic cottage. The building covers five acres of land and, except for the center, rises up three stories from the green fields beneath. In the middle of the grand estate is a tower of a clock so tall it seems to stab the very sky with its Amican flag atop.

The Amica Castle, Metis muses. He turns his stoic eyes away from the architectural marvel, heading home from another day of sightseeing, if you could call it that. Aside from the mishap with the human boy on the previous day Metis can't find one thing he doesn't like about the Amica Kingdom.

What he most enjoys is the simple fact that ryken here aren't ashamed to be ryken. It wouldn't be unusual to walk down the street and see a man leap twenty feet to retrieve a kitten from a tree, or a girl fly down a road to make it to school on time. In a society like this, amazing feats aren't rare to stumble upon.

Though what infuriates Metis as much as any oppressing human is a ryken who fits the mindless, violent narrative the humans push in Laevus. Ryken who fall into that stereotype stymie the progress of mankind and rykenkind alike. They tell the tale that ryken can't be more than what history has shown.

But Metis is no hypocrite. Where he differs from the typical ryken delinquent is in his purpose. Although he may use violence, it is only when necessary. His sole objective is to achieve an end to the current era in Laevus. His efforts are anything but mindless.

Metis enters into the building where he's been staying the past week. He heads for the stairs but is stopped by the clerk. "Excuse me. Sorry for bothering you, but some mail arrived for you earlier."

Metis takes an envelope from his hand without a word, proceeding upstairs. *Who is aware of my presence in Amica?* Once in his quarters Metis carefully opens the envelope.

We have your precious little friend. If you ever want to see him again, bring ten thousand pines to the Stoney Hut on the village boarder. If you don't have the money, find it.

With a harsh purple light engulfing it, the letter deteriorates into nothingness. Metis' face remains impassive. *Simply infuriating.*

* * *

Here it comes, Callisto broods. Jove enters Princess Isabella's quarters with Prix close behind. Neither say a word to Callisto, who stands by her doorway on guard. After a short exchange inside, Isabella is led down the hall by Prix. She offers Callisto a regretful glance as she passes.

"Callisto," Jove's voice booms from inside. Callisto enters the room with his head lowered but his eyes locked with Jove's, as if to say he yields to Jove's command, yet isn't ashamed of his actions.

Despite Jove's shorter stature, somehow he still looms over Callisto. "The paperwork for your elevated status hasn't even been processed yet and you already do something foolish as this? What possessed you to speak out against Colonel Calamity in his own courtroom?"

"With all due respect, General Jove, I only did what I thought was right."

"Right? In what world is challenging your superior in open rebellion right? You're lucky the colonel was gracious enough to not snatch your status as recruit from you in one fell swoop."

"Sir, what would you have me do seeing corruption right in front of me?"

"Callisto, I'd choose my words a bit more wisely." Jove's voice is flat and that much more intimidating because of it. "You are merely a recruit. You have no authority to determine what is or isn't corruption. You've been here mere months and claim to understand the higher politics of the ryken squad?"

"Then what would you call our dealings with Amica, sir?"

"Laevus is a nation of justice and freedom. Our dealings with Amica only enhance our ability to provide that service to the world."

"Are you saying stealing their land is a service to them?"

Jove shakes his head. "You're greatly misunderstanding the terms of the treaty. But the point here isn't your understanding, it's your obedience. You don't publicly speak out against a superior, especially a colonel. That's unacceptable and I won't tolerate it." Callisto starts to rebut, then bites his tongue, his anger nearly overwhelming him.

Jove sighs empathetically at the silence, his expression softening. "A piece of advice for the future. Trust in our methods. They work. Believe in our system."

"At what point should this blind obedience stop?" Callisto asks, trying to control himself even as the words spill out. "Should I believe in a system—"

"Stop. Just stop. You won't challenge your higher-ups again. That's an order. Break it and there will be consequences."

Callisto stares into Jove's hard eyes nearly grinding his teeth. "Understood, sir."

"Prix and I will join you on your journey," Jove says, heading for the door. "We leave tomorrow morning. Let's hope this all isn't an utter waste of time."

* * *

In the Stoney Hut men and women alike throw dice, arm wrestle, dance—whatever pleases them—all in the name of fun. In the back room, however, there is only business. Sentinel, the owner, smiles at the papers on his desk. "This is all from just this week, Torrey?" The man beside him offers a servile nod. "Good work! Throwing in with the rabble rousers might just work out better than I planned." He laughs, slamming a fist to his desk. The dozen security men lining the walls offer smiles and small praises. "Today will be a very good day," Sentinel says, standing.

"You won't say that after my dad finds out you have me," Rhys yells from a cage in the corner of the large office.

Sentinel shrugs. "Your dad, brother—doesn't matter to me who pays for what was done to my kid. But the price will be paid."

"Brother?" Rhys questions. "He wasn't my brother! I don't even have a brother."

"I don't care, kid. Someone throw a blanket over that cage. Looking at him is starting to annoy me." A small tremor cascades throughout the building. "Ah. It appears he found the place."

Sentinel retakes his seat at his desk, folding his hands. He waits for a minute but the commotion outside the door only gets louder. Soon his impatience gets the better of him. "What's taking those halfwits so long to bring him in here?"

The door explodes off the hinges, a trail of purple light in its wake. Metis steps through smoothly. "Hey! Over here!" Rhys calls out. Metis pauses, surveying the room with meticulously.

"There's no way you made it back here alone," Sentinel says. "How many are with you?" A vein pops out on Sentinel's forehead when Metis doesn't respond. "Who do you think you are to challenge me in my domain? Get this straight: those up front were rookies, interns hoping to be in this room!" Sentinel's security men step forward, a line of ryken wall to wall. Torrey goes in the back corner to stand by Rhys' cage.

"Knowing this," Sentinel says, "I'll give you one more chance for redemption. If you bow before me, apologize, and agree to pay double for the return of your brother, I may consider letting you go with only a broken bone or two."

Metis puts his hands behind his back, one fist atop the other. "I'm not here to grovel at your feet. Nor did I come to bestow upon you any sum of money. I didn't come to rescue the boy from this disheveled excuse of a den." Metis pauses, his visage stone. "I'm here because you had the audacity to oppose me."

Without warning the first of Sentinel's men charges, colliding with Metis' Wall of Lutrio. The other men join him, all throwing their fists and ryken abilities at the wall. Nevertheless, the only thing that falls as a result is their morale. After minutes of the collective bombardment, Sentinel's men exhaust themselves nearly to the floor. *Whoa,* Rhys thinks, *he might be almost as strong as Dad!*

Toward the end of the attack Sentinel makes for the back door escape route of his office, but Metis catches him. With one punch he shatters Sentinel's jaw and hurls him back into his office, only stopping after he collides with Metis' Wall of Lutrio. The impact shakes the wall more than the feeble attacks of his subordinates.

Metis lowers his defense and stares around the room. After a moment he raises his hands expectantly. "Leave?" The men, including Sentinel's assistant, push and shove one another, barreling out of the room. After the last man has fled, Metis looks over at Rhys, who remains imprisoned.

"I suppose with my victory there is little reason your freedom should not subsequently follow."

* * *

"Are you guys always so dreary or are you only like this on beautiful days?" Isabella asks. The group of Jove, Callisto, Prix and Isabella trek toward the train station in the civilian district of Centrum City. The ryken squad officers sport casual clothes so as to not draw unwanted attention to themselves on their journey. "I can't handle another day of silence. It's driving me crazy."

Isabella's comments receive no response until Prix, out of pity, finally says something. "Sorry Princess, but the team is feeling a bit under the weather.

"I feel fine, Prix," Callisto says. "You shouldn't make assumptions."

Prix swallows his annoyance. "My mistake. I apologize."

Isabella sighs. "Well, this ought to be another fun day of travel."

The group boards the train and arrives at the town of Philips. From there they venture on foot toward Pochada town. The princess pushes out another sigh.

"That's the tenth sigh in the last hour, Princess. Are you feeling ill?" Jove inquires.

"Huh? Really? Oh, sorry. It's a bad habit of mine. I sigh a lot when I'm nervous."

"You sigh when you're nervous?" Callisto finds himself asking, smiling. "That's kind of weird."

Isabella hangs her head, blushing. "You wouldn't be the first to tell me that."

"Oh no, I didn't mean it as an insult. Being weird can be good in certain ways. Everyone is a little weird. If we weren't life would be pretty boring."

Isabella grins at Callisto's empathy. "Yeah, I guess you're right."

Her smile almost pulls a similar reaction out of Callisto, but remembering his place, he disengages eye contact with her. In the wake of Callisto's unwelcoming response Princess Isabella sighs again. Just as she exhales two large drops of white fall from the sky. One lands in her hair and the other hits the front of her shirt. She shrieks. "Gross! Bird poop!" She tilts her head so her long golden curls hang off to the side, away from her body.

"It might be best if we stopped," Jove says, an eyebrow raised.

"I have to wash up!" Isabella takes off at a jog toward a freshwater basin the group passed not long ago.

"Callisto, Prix, one of you needs to accompany her," Jove says.

Callisto's face immediately turns beet red. *Accompany the Princess to bathe? No! I could never! That would be an invasion of her privacy, even if it is for her own good. But... it's my duty. I must protect her. I'm not doing it because I want to, but because I have to. I cannot disobey an order. I have to protect her for the good of Amica and the reputation of the Laevus Nation.*

Prix bows low to hide his flushed complexion. "If I must, I'll escort the princess."

"No way you're doing it!" Callisto exclaims. "A gentleman like me is the only one fit for this task."

"I am a gentleman! I can handle this just fine."

"You just want to get a look at the princess. I know how your mind works!"

"The thought had never crossed my mind, but I can tell from your red cheeks that's all you can think about!"

"Did you say all you can think about is the princess' red cheeks?"

Jove just stares, his own cheeks growing red in embarrassment for his recruits. "Maybe it'll be safer if she just goes alone..."

* * *

"It's been a long time coming," Samané says, climbing the stairs, "but I finally found him." He observes a small sign on the door. *Runkurt Town Orphanage.* Samané raps on the door.

A caramel-complexioned lady with straight, dark hair answers the door with a smile. "Can I help you?"

"Hi. I'm looking for a friend of mine who lives here. Ventus Erubesco?"

Her smile melts away. "Uh. Sure. Right this way." Samané is led inside, taking a seat at a table to wait.

It has taken quite a bit of work to find Ventus' whereabouts, but at least the hunt bares fruit. Samané's search for Noctuama, the elegant woman of the Excessum tournament, has been far less productive, the main problem being the fact that Samané doesn't know anything about her—nothing, truly. For all he knows, even her name could be an alias. It would explain why no one, as far as he's traveled, has heard of her.

His lack of knowledge about her also nags at him for a different reason. Why is he searching for her in the first place? Is it because she's so strong? More than likely it's because she's attractive, despite his attempts to deny that as a factor, although it may be her mysteriousness that intrigues Samané most of all. Who is she, truly, and where did she come from? What is her goal and who does she spy for, or on, for that matter? For some reason, he needs these questions answered.

Samané hears activity behind the door. *Never mind her; I need to focus on accomplishing one miracle at a time.* Ventus enters, his long silver hair rippling in a ponytail behind him. Samané immediately takes note of Ventus' missing arm, the steep price for his journey to Ground Zero. Ventus nods toward Samané and Samané nods back. "It's been a while."

"Not as long as I thought it would be." Ventus takes a seat, then asks, not unkindly, "Why are you here?"

"I'll cut to the chase. I'm forming a ryken team and I could use your help."

Ventus tilts his head. "A ryken team? That's very illegal."

Samané's surprise is subtle. "I mean, I knew it was frowned upon, but..."

"Yes, illegal. Any organization of ryken forming outside of the ryken squad is illegal. Doesn't matter the cause or purpose. It's hardly fair, but fairness has never been a point of interest for Laevinian lawmakers."

Samané shrugs. "You and I both participated in a school sport. Illegal. You live outside of Centrum City as a ryken. Illegal. We ventured to Ground Zero and participated in the Excessum tournament. Very illegal. Why are we talking about this? Just being a ryken in itself in Laevus is pretty much illegal."

"You have a point."

"Join my team, Ventus. It could be beneficial for you too."

Ventus sits back and thinks a moment, then replies, "No. I appreciate your offer, but I'd rather not."

"Wait, seriously? You're denying me?"

"I must search for my purpose in life on my terms."

Samané's brow furrows. "I could be offering you the opportunity to discover that now. You won't know for sure unless you give it a shot."

Ventus stands. "No. I don't want to be your friend, Samané Lutrio. I'm not meant to be anyone's friend."

"Come on, at least think about it."

Ventus extends his hand. "I said no!" Suddenly a gust of wind sweeps through the room, flipping over the table and the papers on top. The gust knocks the chairs on Samané's side of the room over and lands him flat on his back. Ventus studies the wreckage before him. "You see, this is why I cannot join your team and could never be a friend. It's not my purpose in life. My purpose is destruction. These hands were meant to create chaos, not order. It's plain for anyone to see."

Samané stands back up and dusts himself off, calmly. "Is that it? That's a pretty poor excuse. Why don't you just create your own purpose or destiny or fate or whatever you want to call it? Take hold of it with your own two hands and mold it into what you want it to be. Stop letting this world tell you what you are and establish your purpose yourself."

Ventus moves his mouth as if he's going to reply but never does. His eyes fall, shifting as he ponders Samané's words. Finally, Ventus turns his back on Samané.

Episode 9:

Sacrifice

It was a long time ago, in a town even smaller than Runkurt. Looking back, it seems like another lifetime ago, maybe even someone else's life.

The town was called Maligonny, out in the middle of nowhere. Ventus was only a few days past his fifth birthday when school started. He had dreamed of this day for what seemed like an eternity. He would finally have the opportunity to meet children his age and have fun and play games with them. He wasn't sure what school games were like, but he was eager to find out. A dozen or so kids lived in Maligonny, but they were all at least twice Ventus' age. He didn't fit in with any of them. But today would be different. It had to be.

Ventus woke up excited. Multiple times. Every hour he would snap up out of his bed, checking the sky for the sun. It seemed to be running late this morning. Eventually, however, the shimmering orb found its way.

Ventus burst through the door. "Dad! Dad wake up! It's time for school!"

Ventus looked up to his dad like no other person. Literally. His father, James Erubesco, was a large man, just a few inches shorter than seven feet. The near-giant swung his pair of stilt-like legs over the edge of the bed to the floor. He used a knuckle to wipe the sleep from one eye. His hand then slid down his cheek, where he scratched at his freshly shaven black beard. Ventus had never seen his dad frazzled or unpresentable. Even early in the morning or late at night, when James took off his tailored suits and fancy shoes, his precisely squared hairline and chiseled jaw always made him look comely. It was almost as if his body's natural processes left him perpetually well-groomed.

James stood, his chocolate face coming into the moon's light. "I think you might be a bit early, champ."

"No," Ventus cried. "You said when the sun comes up. Look, it's hard to see from this window, but you still can."

Sure enough, in the distant sky, if you cocked your head at just the right angle, the first of the sun's rays were visible. "Well, you got me," James said. "But you might be the first one there. Start getting ready and I'll make breakfast."

"Yes!" Ventus hugged his father's leg, his face level with James' kneecap.

Before Ventus scurried to his room, Brenda, James' wife, rounded the bed, yawning. Her hair was wrapped above her head almost ritualistically, customary after a fresh hairstyle. She blinked the sleep from her eyes, her long lashes fluttering elegantly. "I'll have your clothes laid out on the sofa in the living room when you're done bathing."

Ventus nodded. "Thanks Brenda!"

With that Ventus shot from the room. He flew around the house, barely able to keep his excitement at bay. The morning dragged on, seeming to take even longer than the night had. Ventus scarfed down his usual breakfast of eggs, sausage, and toast, urging his father to do the same. Finally, Ventus got him out the house.

When James had told Ventus the walk to school would be long, he still didn't imagine it could be this long. It wasn't that Ventus was getting tired; he was just too anxious.

"How is it that my legs are so much longer than yours yet I'm the one having a hard time keeping up?" James asked.

"You're just slow," Ventus exclaimed. "Can't we just run there?"

"We'll get there soon enough. Try not to rush things in life. You'll find it's much more enjoyable when you value every second."

"I'll value life when we get there."

James picks up his pace, placing a massive hand on Ventus' shoulder. "Let's try this. We'll do some math to take your mind off things and practice so you can do your very best this year. Okay, what's one plus one?"

"That's easy! Two."

"Easy, huh? Five plus five?"

"Ten!"

James scratches his beard. "Man, you're good. Six plus three?"

Ventus counts on his fingers. "Yeah, nine."

"Very good. Now, what's a thousand plus a thousand?"

"Aww, that's not fair. No one can do that!"

James laughs. "It's two thousand. I'll teach you that one day too."

Ventus' eyebrows raise. "Wow. You really know the answer? What don't you know, Dad?"

"There's plenty I don't know. Ask Brenda when we get back. She swears I'm clueless."

"No way! You're like the smartest guy ever. That's why you were chosen to be the mayor."

"It's not because I'm the smartest," James said. "It's because I have purpose. And I take my purpose very seriously."

Ventus tilted his head. "Purpose? What do you mean?"

"Purpose. The reason someone or something exists. For example, the purpose of the book bag you're wearing is to carry books."

Ventus took a minute to think it over, his pace slowing to a near stop. "I think I get it. But we're not book bags. Our names don't just tell us what our purpose is. How are we supposed to find it? How'd you find yours?"

James smiled. "Fantastic question, Ventus. For me, it was the first day at a new junior high. The same exact school we're headed to now was new in the city so none of the kids were familiar with one another. The teacher was late, and the classroom was in chaos. So, I stood on the desk in the front of the class and said, 'Everyone clean up this mess of a classroom, sit down and wait for our teacher like students should!' I was just lucky that the principal saw my display of leadership and courage because the kids would've probably tried to beat me up right then and there." He laughed. "And they did take their shots at me throughout the school year, but I didn't care, because I love to be a leader. Bring order to chaos. That's what I'm meant to do.

"As for you, and anyone else for that matter, it's up to that individual to find out for themselves what their purpose is. You should be conscious of it, always. But that doesn't mean you need to worry about it. When the time comes to begin fulfilling your purpose you will know what it is because you will be happy just by doing it. In this world, we must discover our own purpose. No other person can dictate it for you. Remember that."

* * *

As excited about school as Ventus had been, a few hours later he was just as disappointed. He'd hoped the place he'd always remembered hearing of would make him feel normal, accepted even. But it had only proved to provide him more of the same. Now, there was no denying fact. Ventus was different.

Ventus didn't understand why he was the way he was. Whenever he met new people, he'd prefer to watch than to speak. Well, he'd like to associate it with meeting new people, but he was like this even with Brenda and she'd been around as far back as Ventus could remember. It wasn't so much that Ventus didn't know how to express himself around others—although that was definitely true—rather, he never had much to say. If anyone addressed him directly, he'd answer their inquiries as concisely as possible. He was this way with everyone.

Except for his father.

When Ventus was with James everything just seemed easier. His thoughts flowed more naturally and Ventus actually wanted to talk. He could talk to James all day, and sometimes he did.

"One of my classmates asked me why Dad and I looked so differently from one another," Ventus was explaining to James and Brenda in the kitchen. "I didn't know the answer, so I didn't say anything. She asked again. Then she started getting mad that I wasn't answering her. The other kids thought it was funny to join her in asking me over and over. The teacher tried to stop them, but they would just start again when she wasn't around.

"At lunch, another kid gave his own answer. He said you weren't my real dad. I told him to never say that again. He didn't listen. So I punched him in the mouth." Ventus shrugs. "Not much of a fight. He fell to the ground after that."

The room was quiet for a moment. Ventus studied his father, who appeared pained and in thought. James ventured a glance at Brenda, who wore another, entirely different expression—a combination of the judging look people often unknowingly wore around Ventus, and another expression completely foreign to him. Later Ventus would become quite accustomed to the expression of fear.

"Ventus," James started, slowly. "Sometimes life isn't fair. More often than not, it won't be. You *should* be able to live the normal life of a normal person. But you won't, because you aren't normal."

Ventus stopped breathing. The events of today had made Ventus believe something was wrong with him. With his Dad's last sentence, facts evolved into truth. Ventus wasn't normal.

"You're special," his father continued. "And not special in the way parents always think their child is. You're truly special. You are what they call a ryken." James cast a guilty look at Brenda. "I'm certain of it."

"What's a ryken?" Ventus asked.

"They're like humans, but stronger and with special abilities."

"Abilities..." Ventus echoed. "The wind. If it's so special why'd you tell me to never use it?"

Without a word, Brenda stormed out. James cringed slightly, then proceeded. "It's because humans don't understand ryken. They're scared of your powers and what they could mean for them. It's the exact reason you shouldn't hurt people with your strength. The kid today—let that be the last time you use violence to silence someone. Think beyond. Use your mind, not your fists.

"For your sake, I've researched ryken quite a bit over the last few years. Information that's hard to come by and dangerous to seek, thanks to our government. I learned that ryken don't normally develop their strength and abilities until just prior to puberty. Usually around eight or nine. Yet you've shown signs of rykenhood since you were an infant. One day you'd pick up a chair, the next you'd sneeze and blow half the room away. I'm saying this to show that, even among ryken, you are special. It sounds great and it is, I promise you. But with that specialness will come jealousy and misunderstanding. Bear it. You're destined for great things, Ventus. I know it. You have remarkable purpose."

* * *

Later that night, Ventus had somehow managed to get some rest after his heart seemed like it was trying to beat its way out of his chest. Unfortunately, his slumber didn't last long; he was awakened by the voices of James and Brenda.

"Why didn't you tell me?" Brenda yelled.

"Because you already knew!" James snapped. Ventus' heart gave another attempt at escape. He had never heard his father yell before. "All the signs were there. You chose to ignore them because you think there's something wrong with ryken. You think they're violent or diseased simply because they're different from me and you."

"James, they're animals," Brenda hissed back. "Wild animals in human form. Sure, they start out innocent enough. You bring a lion cub in this house and it'll be cute when it's at your knees. But once it matures, you'll see there's no taming it. The same hands you used to feed it hours ago will be its next meal."

"You're wrong. We aren't talking about a mindless beast. It's Ventus. The child *we* raised. What would you have me do? Hand him over to the government so he can end up who knows where, doing who knows what for the rest of his life? Or maybe you want me to put him back on the mountaintop where I found him?"

"You should've never brought him here in the first place."

There was silence after that. Ventus lay in his bed, the world spinning around him, nauseous enough to vomit. What did all of this mean? Could it be that James wasn't Ventus' father after all? The thought caused bile to climb up Ventus' throat. He forced it back down.

James' voice crept into the silence, like oil into water. "Please don't make me choose. I didn't the first time and I won't this time, either. I love you both. I can be a father to Ventus and a husband to you, at the same time. Allow me to do that. If you love me, please, give me that chance."

Brenda's voice replied shakily, as if she were fighting tears, "I do love you. It's the reason I came back. I need you, James."

It would seem the matter was settled because after those words, the two fell completely quiet. If only the same was true for Ventus' thoughts. *Dad found me. That's what he said. If that's true, then that means that someone else must have not wanted me. Is it because I'm a ryken, or is there more to it? Dad said I'm strange even to the ryken. Something is wrong with me. It's not specialness. I'm different and I'll never fit in, with humans or ryken or anyone. Even Brenda hates me. Dad—he's not even my dad! I don't have a dad. I don't have anyone… no one will ever want me. How could they? I'm not normal.*

Ventus didn't even realize he was crying until a voice brought him back to reality. It was Brenda's. She approached his bed slowly. "It's not your fault that you were born the way you are. I don't blame you. Actually, if I close my eyes, I can almost see us being a family. In a different world, at a different time, maybe it could have worked." She moved Ventus' hair from his face lovingly and kissed him on the forehead. "Maybe."

Ventus never saw her grab the pillow. Never had a chance to react before it was smothering him. Out of reflex he fought back, his short, five-year-old arms reaching for Brenda's face, eventually settling for her arms, clawing at them desperately. Soon, Ventus' lungs were vacant, and his thoughts cloudy.

If Ventus died here, the world would probably be better off. James and Brenda would be happier, without question. Perhaps he should just lie back and let fate take its course. It would be easier for everyone, Ventus included. There was only one problem with that.

Ventus was afraid to die.

All at once the fear crashed upon him. It seized his body until all he could think of was surviving. It was all that mattered. Not his abnormality, not the world's happiness, not James. Ventus didn't want to die. And so he hit Brenda with his full power. Power he didn't know he had surged out of him in an exhausting flurry. Ventus' will to survive, manifested as a gust, struck Brenda in the chest, driving her through several walls, deeper into the house.

Ventus snapped up, his lungs desperate for sustenance. When the ache in his chest subsided, he raised his eyes to the destroyed walls. Brenda hadn't just been knocked out of Ventus' room; she had also cleared both walls of the bathroom, finally crashing into the furniture in the living room before coming to a stop. Now she lay motionless, James crouched over her body.

After a moment to himself, James stood up. He made his way to Ventus' room through the conventional hallway, although the route Brenda's body carved out would've been quicker.

"Life isn't fair," James started half to himself, eyes hollow, voice raspy. "If you didn't realize it before today, you'll never forget it. Brenda did love you. I believe that, truly. It was what made her overlook the fact that you are a ryken all these years." James swallowed, hard. "But when I finally confirmed, and the knowledge was out in the open she didn't want to accept it. Couldn't accept it. All her life she had been told that ryken were bad. Her little experience with them showed the same. She lost a good friend to one early in life. It's only natural that she would foster some type of hate. She was only exposed to the worst of your kind.

"This is all my fault. I brought you here. Brought you to her. When I realized you were a ryken I selfishly tried to keep you both in my life. I thought my purpose was to love you both the best I could..." James' eyes bore into Ventus. "I had planned to tell you this when you were older... when I worked up the courage. Now I have no choice.

"I am not your biological father. Five years ago, on your birthday, I found you wrapped in blankets on Mount Ventus. From the moment I saw you, helpless and pure, I couldn't let you go. Not for Brenda, not for the world. I don't know who left you there. I wish I did so I could show them what a wonderful life they missed out on. I wish I could thank them in person for what they gifted me. Even after all that's happened today, my only regret is that I didn't do more for you and Brenda. As her husband. As your father.

"Well, there's nothing more I can do for Brenda. But you are different, Ventus. Listen to me. This was all my doing. The destroyed walls. Brenda's death. It was all me. I killed my wife. You had nothing to do with it. A life in prison is what awaits me because of this. But if the authorities find out you, a ryken were the cause, I fear what harsher punishment they'd choose. I'll take the blame. It's my punishment for failing so miserably as a husband and father."

James stopped when there was a booming knock on the door. He placed a hand on the doorframe to Ventus' room as if he was going to fall over. His hand shook violently. Fear of the fate soon to fall upon him was noticeable even to a child.

"I guess that's my cue," James croaked.

Episode 10:

Lost Princess

The sun just peaks over the taller buildings of Amica, providing a beautiful orange glow to the great expanse of land. Metis takes in the spectacular sight with just a hint of a smile, fair weather still a weakness of his.

Since the rescue neither Rhys nor Metis have spoken, but finally Rhys takes the leap. "To be honest, I didn't think you'd come save me. Why did you?"

Metis weighs the question in his mind for so long that Rhys figures he'll remain quiet. He silently chastises himself before Metis answers. "You remind me of my brother."

Rhys' eyes snap to him, his surprise irrepressible. "Really? What's his name? What's he like? Is he cool?"

"His name is Samané and his resounding tenacity is indeed cool. Not once have I encountered another individual who possesses more heart than he. Samané could accomplish anything he motivates himself to do."

Rhys smiles. "He sounds awesome!"

"The way you're most akin to him is in your naïve outlook on the world. Samané has such a right or wrong way of discerning society, he seldom notices the silver lining. In a sense, I covet such a resolute mentality. To view things so clear cut..." Metis stumbles from his thought, looking at Rhys. "At any rate, let's hurry to your abode; your mother must be quite perturbed by now."

Rhys nods, pointing. "It's not much farther after the bridge."

Over the bridge and at the end of the road, Metis and Rhys come upon the house. Rhys knocks and his mother, Reyna, comes to the door. "You're late," she says, frowning.

Rhys winces. "I ran into some trouble that he helped me out of," Rhys says, stepping into the house, motioning Metis to follow. Metis does so slowly, carefully.

"Trouble?" Reyna inquires.

Rhys tries a weak smile. "I sort of got kidnapped."

After explaining the story to his mother, Reyna hugs him tightly, crying. Metis stoically observes the exchange. Reyna backs off, grabbing Rhys' shoulders. "I'm so glad you're safe. I have to call your father right away." As Reyna goes to the phone, she almost runs Metis over, forgetting he was there. She bows her head. "I cannot thank you enough for what you did for my son. Without you he could have been..." She pauses for a moment, trying to stop more tears.

Rhys tugs at her arm, whispering, "Come on, Mom! You're being so uncool."

"I understand," Metis says. "There's no need to thank me. I did what needed to be done. Your gratitude is ill-deserved."

Reyna shakes her head. "No, you do. You're a hero to this family."

"Mom, cut it out. He's supposed to be mysterious. He can't accept praise from people. He's one of those super cool heroes like in the comic books!"

"A Hero?" Metis says, as if unfamiliar with the word.

Reyna bows her head again. "Allow me to thank you properly. Will you please stay for dinner, mister...?"

Metis regards Reyna, and from Rhys' perspective, it seems as if he struggles to find the correct word to respond. Finally, he answers.

"Sutari."

* * *

Outside the gates of Pochada Town Callisto and Prix bicker. "If you weren't such a pervert there wouldn't have been an issue with you watching her," Callisto says.

"I had pure intentions," Prix replies. "You were the one eyeing her the moment she talked about bathing!"

"Enough," Jove snaps. "You two are giving me a headache. The fact is we screwed up letting the princess out of our sight. I'll take the blame, but we must get her back. I don't need to tell you the consequences if we can't. Prix and I will retrace our route back to the basin. Callisto, you stay here and search. She may have thought this the best place to meet up if she couldn't locate us initially. We'll rendezvous here at sunset with or without her and decide our next course of action from there."

* * *

"There's no reason I shouldn't be able to have a little fun while I wait," Princess Isabella says as she makes her way out of Pochada Plaza. It's been three hours since she lost her entourage of ryken squad officers and an hour since she arrived in the bustling town of Pochada. Granted, she hasn't been here long, but from the little she's seen she likes it. She even bought a few trinkets from the local markets as souvenirs.

Initially, she thought losing the others was the worst thing that could happen, especially if something unfortunate had happened to her. Not for her sake, honestly, her wellbeing is far less significant to her than the wellbeing of Amica. If some ill fate had befallen her before reaching Pochada, disaster would be the only word to describe the remains of Amica after their retaliation on Laevus.

Isabella pushes the thoughts from her head. If she must wait to be found, she's going to enjoy herself in the meantime. There's no harm in that, right? After all, she has been more than patient with her mundane escorts. They left her too much time to think, to brood—something her father always told her wasn't good. So maybe the split-up was a good thing. Time to herself. Away from her problems and obligations. Even if only for a moment, she is going to make the most of it.

Isabella bounces from building to building, sight to sight, soaking up all that Pochada has to offer. Before long she stumbles upon a commotion on the street. She has to struggle her way through the gathering crowd to get a halfway decent view of what is happening. Three city policemen stand around a frightened old man.

"What's going on here?" Isabella asks in the cramped gathering.

A man beside her answers, "The police are demanding tax money again and the poor man doesn't have it."

A lady follows up. "This is the second time this week they've collected. I wonder what they'll do to the guy."

Another voice says, "Hopefully they'll only take a finger this time."

Laevus even treats its own citizens this badly? Isabella shudders.

All three of the policemen are carrying firearms; however, one of them also carries a sword. Two of the police bring the old man to his knees and the third puts the sword to his neck, yelling over the crowd. "This isn't something I enjoy doing, but if I don't return to the mayor with my quota then it'll be me that has to give up a body part as payment! I do hope you understand. What should it be today? An ear?

Or a foot? Maybe I should just take your head as a sign to our spectators.”

“Or maybe you should leave him alone, you bullies!” The attention of the crowd shifts completely to Isabella as she fearlessly speaks out. She doesn’t back down; instead she steps forward.

“Look what we have here. A hero?”

“A government is supposed to protect its people! You’re given your power to help those within your walls, not harm them!”

“Only people with money have the privilege of protection. How can we offer them something so valuable with nothing in return? That hardly seems fair.”

“So you threaten him because he’s poor? Where's the justice in that? People like you make me sick! You give authority all over the world a bad name and if your mayor is half as corrupt as you three then he must be stopped too! If Laevus as a whole is like this, then...”

The guard removes his blade from the old man’s neck and starts toward Isabella. “You might want to watch your pretty little mouth. Shouting things like that in a crowd this large can get you in quite a bit of trouble.”

Princess Isabella backs away, looking around for other citizens who share her feelings, but all avoid eye contact, afraid that the risk of consequences isn’t worth the chance of reward.

Not too far off, in Pochada Plaza Callisto desperately searches for his lost princess. He looks to the setting sun. *It's almost time to rendezvous with the others. Where could she have gone?* A flash of Acura's lifeless face races through Callisto's mind. *No, I'm sure she's fine. I just have to find her.*

In the distance there is yelling. “Let me go! Let go of me!”

Callisto’s head snaps around. “Princess Isabella?”

Callisto races over to find Isabella being cuffed. The sword policeman pushes the old man from earlier to the ground. “We'll let you go this time because we've got bigger fish to fry, but you better have the money next time around! As for you, you're going straight to the precinct and the chief will decide what to do with you.”

“Let her go!” The policemen all look at Callisto as he pulls out his ryken squad badge. “I'm a recruit of the Centrum City Ryken Squad and I said let her go! Now!”

The police shrug. "We're not ryken, boy. You have no authority here as far as I can see. Stand down; you're out of your jurisdiction, Xarnes."

The crowd becomes deathly quiet at the word. Callisto tenses, but nothing more. The policeman laughs then roughly grabs Isabella by the arm, forcing her along.

"Callisto, help!" Isabella's eyes are as desperate as her plea. The next thing Callisto knows his fist is cracking into the policeman's jaw. The other two policemen draw their guns. "Try me," Callisto snaps.

There is a moment of tension before Isabella intervenes, her cuffed hands raised. "Stop! Stop! I am Princess Isabella of Amica Kingdom. On behalf of my nation, please stand down. It would be a bi-national disaster should this continue to escalate. You have my word that we will leave immediately."

The two remaining police hesitate, clearly less experienced than the third. They lower their shaky weapons. "Leave now," one says. "And take the ryken with you," the other adds.

* * *

Reyna places a second bowl of chopped potatoes on the table and retakes her seat. Rhys wastes no time scooping two heaps out. He takes a bite, barely chewing before continuing his story. "So their leader tried to make a break for the back door, but Sutari stopped him easily! He hit him with that purple light and the guy flew across the room! Then Sutari stepped over him, all smooth like! It was so awesome!"

Reyna smiles at her son's excitement. "Seems like you're a pretty strong young man, Sutari."

Metis finishes his final bite of vegetables before placing his fork gently on his plate. "In certain circumstances, I suppose, but I still have quite a journey ahead of me."

"Are you new to Amica? What brings you here?" Metis tilts his head ever so slightly, looking at Reyna as though he reads a book. "I'm sorry, that was rude of me to ask."

"I told you, Mom," Rhys interjects, wiggling his fingers, "he's mysterious. It's so cool!"

"I'm here to return to my roots in a sense," Metis finally answers. "I feel I've become too eclectic, causing me to lose a grip on who I really am. I've found myself becoming someone… something I've despised for the preponderance of my life, progressing down a path that should never be trod. I figured if I could return to the pedigree of my being, revisit not just who I am but where we've come from as a ryken people, perhaps I could unveil some answers. After such a revelation it was evident there was no better venue to begin than the Amica Kingdom, home to one of the last peoples of the great ryken race who take their heritage seriously."

"I see," Reyna says. "That's very insightful of you."

"Sutari, I just had an awesome idea," Rhys exclaims. "My dad is supposed to come back from work in a couple of days and take me fishing. You should come too! It will be fun!"

"I appreciate the invitation, but I'm not overly confident that I would fit properly into that atmosphere."

"I'm sure Sutari has a very busy schedule to keep," Reyna says. "We should just be thankful he was able to join us for dinner."

Reyna smiles at Metis and he fails at an attempt of reproducing the expression. *In her eyes, is that distrust?*

"Pleaseee!" Rhys continues to beg.

Metis barely hears Rhys as he studies Reyna, and she him, under the ruse of a smile. When Metis realizes they're waiting on his rebuttal he recalls the question, acquiescing. "I imagine it could be beneficial in some manner."

"Awesome! Fishing with you and Dad. You both are so strong. If I were a ryken we'd be a super team! Nobody would stand a chance. Hey Sutari, all heroes are supposed to have a super-powered move, right? What's yours called?"

A peculiarly intrusive question. Metis analyzes Rhys' word choice, his face and demeanor, none of which betray the other in a contradiction. Just blissful innocence on all accounts. *Astutely speaking, I'm likely being paranoid.* Metis starts to ponder the question. "A super-powered move? Hmm, although I wouldn't use that phrase per se, I presume it is true that most ryken have a dependable technique to use in critical situations. I would have to say mine is called Memor Barrage."

Rhys beams. "Whoa! Memor Barrage? What's it like? What's it do? Tell me! Tell me! Tell me!"

"It's my most powerful technique. Its uniqueness lies in that I've effectively trained my mind to unleash one hundred and ninety-seven separate aura attacks in fifty-five point sixty-seven seconds exactly. While I subconsciously bombard my opponent, my conscious mind focuses on the finishing blow. I store my energy for the strongest attack my mind can conjure. At the exact moment my subconscious mind finishes its assault I deliver the concentrated blow."

"That's one of the most awesome attacks I've ever heard of! I want to see it. You should do it now!"

"This isn't the time for it. In addition, the attack leaves me rather fatigued."

"I just had another great idea! You and Dad should spar sometime. I wonder who'd win."

"Okay Rhys," Reyna says, standing, "that's enough excitement for one day. It's time for you to get ready for bed."

"Wait! I didn't even get to tell Metis about my dad's super-powered move."

Metis stands. "No, thank you. A ryken's signature attacks are somewhat sacred. It's not something one shares frivolously. If your father should choose to inform me, let it be from his own lips." Metis turns to Reyna, her prior judgmental expression replaced with confusion. His face remains stoic despite his subtle satisfaction. "I do appreciate your hospitality."

* * *

On the third floor of the Alair household the Novice Pack gathers. "You mean to tell me that you interrupted my workout for that?" Subnuba snaps.

"What do you mean?" Samané asks. "This is big news!"

"Not really," Lo says. "When you told us where you were going yesterday, I'd figured as much."

"Come on guys, I'm really pumped about it," Gaudyme exclaims.

"I'm glad someone is showing a little team spirit," Samané says.

"Whatever," Subnuba grunts, walking away. "I'm going back to my workout. Don't disturb me again unless you have something important to say."

Samané shrugs. "Well, it's not how I envisioned things to have happened, but do you have any opening words to your new teammates and friends?"

Everyone stares at the newest member of the Novice Pack. "I'm happy to be here... and... thank you all for accepting me as an ally, I suppose," Ventus says, awkwardly.

Gaudyme slaps him on the back. "No problem, Wind god!"

"I will be joining in on your training sessions soon, assuming my surgery goes well."

"Don't sweat it," Samané says. "You'll be getting worked on by the best of the best. No one knows more about ryken health than Oki. She'll take great care of you."

"I don't know," Gaudyme says, "attaching a phony limb sounds complicated, even for one of the best. So much could go wrong. She could mess up when connecting the muscles or he could get an infection after, or she could put the arm on upside down, or–"

Samané smiles pleasantly. "Gaudyme. Shut up."

"Regardless, I'll do it," Ventus says. "If the fates allow, I'll be made whole again. If not, I will suffer the consequences that come with my attempt. Whatever happens, so be it."

Episode 11:

Lone Wolf

"The gates are just around this bend," Princess Isabella says excitedly. Her pace quickens as she leads her protectors a step.

The incident in Pochada Town turned out amazingly well, considering how poorly it could have ended. Callisto, a ryken, struck a human policeman. As a regular citizen, the act could get him locked up indefinitely. Under typical circumstances, being a ryken squad officer would keep him out of prison, but his position as a recruit would have almost definitely been revoked. It seems Callisto has been close to that outcome a little too often recently. Thankfully, neither of those fates have fallen upon him.

Jove actually commended him on quick, decisive thinking and ultimately said he had done the right thing. Princess Isabella going into police custody would not have gone over well with the Amican King. With the catastrophe averted, Jove will probably take the brunt of the heat from the government for allowing the issue to escalate to that point, but he said he is willing to take the punishment if it meant a mission well completed.

"I was beginning to think that we'd never get here," Callisto says, finding himself a bit more talkative after leaving Pochada Town.

"We're still an hour behind schedule," Jove says, "but decent timing considering the circumstances."

Isabella smiles. "Don't worry about it, General Jove. You and your team have done more than enough."

The group finally reaches the eastern gate of the Amica Kingdom and passes through. Callisto takes in the large expanse of land, doing all he can to keep his jaw from dropping. "This place is a lot bigger than I thought it would be. It's massive."

Isabella giggles. "I get that reaction a lot from first-time visitors. Though if you think this is impressive, you should see maps and photographs of our kingdom before. When my father was a child, our land was ten times greater."

The joy in Isabella's tone completely fizzles out by the end of her reply. Callisto starts to respond but bites his lip, trying to swallow his empathy. *Don't get invested.*

Fortunately for Callisto his inner struggle ends when a frantic guard runs up to the group. "Your Highness! Word of your return precedes you! It has spread throughout the kingdom!"

Isabella grows pale. "We have to get to the castle as quickly as possible."

"What's the problem?" Prix asks. "Are you afraid of being mauled by clingy supporters or something?"

"Not exactly."

"Princess, you must find a different course," the guard exclaims. "A mob has reportedly formed on this road and blocks the castle."

Prix points toward the crowd coming into sight. "I don't really need a report to tell me we've got trouble ahead."

"What are we going to do?" Isabella cries.

"What do you mean what are we going to do?" Callisto rolls up his sleeve, stepping beside Prix. "It's pretty obvious what needs to be done."

"No, you can't!" Isabella shouts. Prix and Callisto turn to her. "I can't let you hurt the citizens of Amica Kingdom. Even if they are rioting, I can't have outsiders intervene to subdue them. Amica has to handle this."

"We aren't going to be able to form a proper defense in time, Your Highness!" the guard wails.

Isabella shakes her head helplessly. "It's not their fault. I created them. If I could just lead this nation better the citizens wouldn't feel so desperate for change. They're only doing what they feel is right, what they think is best for the kingdom."

"And attacking you is what's best?" Callisto snaps.

"In their eyes, yes. They feel that Father and I are the problem, and by ridding the kingdom of us they will fix the problem."

The guard grabs Isabella gently by the arm. "Your Highness, we must get you to safety!"

"This is nonsense, Princess!" Callisto exclaims. "It is our duty to protect you and we will do that." He turns back to the approaching mob, sizing them up. "Even if that means disobeying your wishes."

Jove steps forward. "We won't touch the citizens."

Everyone stops, waiting for Jove to elaborate on his order. He takes a moment to regard his company, his confidence palpable. "Our duty is to protect the princess. However, within these walls, her words are law, and I will not break the order that laws create." His gaze locks on Isabella. "Even when the order from that law is the cause of chaos."

Prix tilts his head. "What does that mean, General?"

Jove walks ahead of his team, staring down the mob as they charge forward. "Follow me." Hesitantly, Callisto, Prix and Isabella fall in behind Jove. "Law 2: Void Essence."

The dozens of rioters come upon the group in a herd, but their presence isn't felt. The weapons, fists and dozens of ryken abilities that rain down on Isabella and her escorts pass through with no effect. Despite the phenomenon, the rioters don't stop, continuing their assault, passing directly through their targets as if they were ghosts.

"This is so strange!" Callisto yells over the crowd.

"This law allows all those subjected to it to lose relative physical substance," Jove elaborates. "It's the ultimate defensive technique."

Prix examines his hands, intrigued. "This is the first time I've seen your second law, General. I've heard rumors about it, but it's so much better than the stories could ever be."

"Thank you!" Isabella exclaims. "Thank you so much for this!" Isabella runs up, attempting to hug Jove. She leaps forward with her arms widespread. To no surprise she passes through him, falling flat on her face. She spits dirt out of her mouth. "I guess I should've seen that one coming."

Jove frowns. "Let's go Princess, the effects of Void Essence won't last forever."

* * *

"Child's play," Hunter says, tossing a large boar from his shoulder onto the grass. He notices Metis sitting on a stump not too far away from their cabin. "Let me guess, you've been here since eleven." Metis nods slowly. "I don't understand people like you. The meeting time is twelve. You know no one will show until at least then and still you arrive early."

Metis looks to the rustling leaves all around him. "The tranquil setting relaxes me."

Hunter shakes his head. "Anyway, Shade should be here soon."

"Lucky guess," Nightshade hisses, walking onto the scene.

Hunter smiles. "Instinct, my friend. It's just the type of person you are, really."

"One day that intuition of yours is going to be the death of you. I just hope it's sooner than later."

"You're probably right."

"Whatttt?" Napalm exclaims, arriving. "I'm still the last one to show up? It's not even noon yet. I was trying to be early!"

"Try harder next time," Nightshade says.

"Try harder next time," Napalm mocks.

Nightshade scowls. "Let's just get this done. The quicker we ravage this crumbling kingdom, the quicker we can get back to our masters."

"Who died and put you in charge?"

"Quiet Napalm," Hunter says. "There's no harm in letting Shade run the show."

Nightshade does well to restrain his shadows as Napalm sucks his teeth at Hunter's order. Once Nightshade calms himself, he continues. "Sutari, what's the status of the Culminary family?"

Metis stands, walking closer to the group so he can speak in a more controlled tone. "The plan is going more smoothly than I could've hoped. The child has taken a liking to me and, although suspicion may be present, I'll have struck before their defense can be fortified."

"'Struck?' For someone with your vocabulary I'd expect a better word choice. Killed is what you meant." Nightshade studies Metis and he stares back with equal intensity.

"Of course. How very foolish of me. Killed."

"If you two are done admiring each other, I'll take my turn," Hunter says. "The connections I have with the rabble rousers are doing well. I have been able to pull strings and move men from the sidelines, all on a strict budget. Some of my best work, if I do say so myself. That said, I have some very bad news. It seems the Laevus Nation hasn't nixed their treaty with Amica quite yet. Instead, apparently, they have sent three ryken squad officers here, Jove the Legislator among them."

An eerie smile creeps across Nightshade's face. "Jove the Legislator, eh? That'd be a nice name to add to my resume."

"You don't think that particular prey might be a bit too ambitious for the cause?"

"Huh? I'd expect you of all to understand, Hunter. What is it you say? The hunt is always worth the prey's blood."

"It's the blood is always worth the hunt!" Napalm yells.

Nightshade waves his hand. "Quiet, brat."

Hunter shrugs. "I couldn't care less either way. But heed my warning, the most thrilling prey is certainly the most dangerous."

As Nightshade takes in Hunter's words of caution an unfamiliar knot forms in his stomach. *Fear?* It's then he realizes his smile has faded. "When it comes time, the Legislator is mine, and mine alone."

"You'll hear no argument from me." Hunter dramatically bows at the waist, his dreads touching the grass. "Let it be so."

"What about me?" Napalm asks, nearly bouncing from excitement. "Can I fight yet?"

"Soon," Hunter says. "Just focus on your training."

"Aww, still? Training all the time is so boring."

Nightshade seems to converse with himself for a moment, but the others know he speaks to his shadows within. When they reach a conclusion Hunter says, "I'll look into getting some solid information on what the reason is for the ryken squad. I'll get my guys into the castle and see what they can scrounge up."

"In light of the ryken squad's presence, should I refrain from executing until a more auspicious time?" Metis inquires.

Nightshade squints at Metis. "I've already told you to kill him. How many ways do I need to say it?"

Metis looks away. "Understood."

Hunter chuckles. "Some birds won't fly until they're pushed from the nest."

"If this one doesn't fly soon, I'll kill him myself," Nightshade hisses.

Hunter raises an eyebrow. "You're not one for analogies, are you?"

"Rest assured," Metis says. "When the time comes I will fly. Analogies aside, I will kill. I will murder. I will destroy. Whatever term you so choose, I'll be willing and able." He starts to walk away. "If we're finished here, I have a life to live. And another to take."

* * *

Isabella is followed by Jove, Callisto and Prix into the great Amica Castle. The ryken squad members enter the main corridor with Isabella now as their escort. "This place is enormous!" Prix's voice echoes through the hall.

"It's stunning," Callisto adds.

The intricately patterned marble floor stretches to the exceptionally detailed, hand carved walls. Beautiful pillars punctuate the open area, supporting the breathtaking glass-stained ceiling above. A gargantuan chandelier hangs in the middle of the hall, its slightly less massive siblings elegantly lighting the far corners of the room.

Isabella bites her lip. "To be honest it's a bit much for me. I'd prefer to just live in a normal house, but I guess that isn't a realistic request for a monarch."

"You should be more appreciative of the things you have, Isabella."

The king of Amica, Atrium Vortane, enters the room. His chubby face is decorated with bushy brows and a long, white mustache that droops off his face, meshing with a longer beard. Considering the size of his gut, he performs quite the feat with every step to not waddle. Atrium's stern expression almost demands enough attention to distract you from his thinning threads of hair atop his head.

As he approaches, Isabella whispers to Callisto. "I know I should've mentioned this earlier, but my father isn't too fond of Laevinians."

"There may come a day that these luxuries are no longer yours; be thankful," King Atrium finishes.

Isabella bows her head. "Father, don't talk that way. You know I'm grateful for everything I have."

Atrium embraces his daughter lovingly. "Oh, how I've missed you."

"I missed you too."

After their hug, Atrium sets his sights on the ryken squad officials. "You dogs are relieved of your duties. You can go."

Prix forms his lips to respond to the crude comment, but Isabella beats him to it. "Father, please behave! These men have done all they can to see that I made it here safely." Isabella looks to Callisto. "Some have even gone above and beyond their job requirements to help me. I am in their debt."

"Hold your tongue, Isabella," Atrium snaps. "We don't owe these Laevinian maggots a single thing!" Atrium turns on a heel, his stomach swinging like a wrecking ball. "Say your goodbyes to them and get cleaned up for dinner. That's when we'll discuss our plans going forward."

"I apologize for my father's comments," Isabella says once Atrium has exited. "He doesn't act like this normally."

"No harm done," Jove says.

"You all can stay in our guest rooms. We have enough for each of you to have your own, of course."

"That isn't necessary. A hotel will do just fine. Success or failure, we won't be in the kingdom long."

"Oh, I see."

"It has been a pleasure, Princess Isabella, and I wish you the best in all you do. If your assistance is needed during our time here I'll be sure to let you know. Laevus will be in contact with their final decision." Jove bows his head, then makes for the exit.

Prix offers Isabella a smile. "See you around, Princess. It was... entertaining."

Callisto just stands, looking at Isabella's dismayed expression. He curses to himself then says, "General, would it be okay if I stayed with Princess Isabella for the time being? It may help our mission for me to be guided by her."

Jove regards Callisto with his ever-intimidating, discerning gaze. "Very well."

* * *

Metis makes his way through the forest and eventually happens upon a large pond. He stands on the pond's edge, looking at his reflection. His hair has grown quite a bit since he last paid it any attention. It now reaches just past his shoulders. *When trying to reinvent a racist world typical adolescent concerns, like the length of one's hair, seem like moot points.*

The face of the person staring back at Metis is familiar; however, the feelings behind that stoic expression are anything but. Before his fight with Ventus Erubesco back at Ground Zero, Metis had honestly never thought much about killing. *So naïve.* And Ventus had called him out on it. Since then, the thought of being a killer, a murderer more accurately, has never left Metis' mind, and his new master made sure it stayed that way. In fact, it seemed to be Misery's sole objective to transform him into a heartless reaper. The biggest problem with said transformation has been how well it's working.

Misery's progress at reshaping Metis' mind shows him how wrong he had been to call himself a killer at Ground Zero. Maybe he could have taken a life at that time. Channeling his anger. Kneading his hatred. Thinking of his father. That was the recipe to killing before, when he had almost killed Ventus. Even then, he had figured Samané might intervene and save Ventus. And if he had not, maybe Metis might've even cushioned the fall at the last moment.

Now, however, things are different. There is no recipe needed. Although Metis has yet to kill, he knows he could if need be, without hesitation. There's no need to convince anyone anymore.

This foreign feeling of ruthlessness may be needed to create the world anew, but that doesn't mean Metis likes it. Quite the contrary— he hates it. He hates himself for being this way. He hates Misery for molding him this way. And he hates the world for requiring him to be this way. *All three will suffer greatly now that I am this way.*

There is movement from the trees behind Metis. He doesn't flinch; instead he smoothly raises his eyes from his reflection on the water. "Come out, or be forced out," Metis orders.

Hunter hops down off a tree limb. He brushes two leaves off himself as he approaches. "I trailed you all the way since the cabin. I'd hoped by now you'd be sharper."

Metis faces Hunter. "Do you have business with me?"

"Always so formal. So structured. I like that. Really, I do. Although the wilderness seems wild and chaotic, it is far from it. There's organization, rules even. A hierarchy called the food chain with no one truly on top. Some may claim it's the lion or the bear or the wolf, but they too return to the dirt to feed the trees and its undergrowth."

Metis squints. "I think I take your meaning, but your metaphors are notoriously difficult to follow."

A lock of hair falls over Hunter's face and he whips his head to throw it back over his shoulder. "Heh. I guess they are. What I'm trying to say is every man, creature, and deity plays their part. That's the way things are and always will be. There's no need to feel bad for it or try to be something you aren't. You're growing into a savage beast, a lone wolf, and the world needs that role. It doesn't make you better or worse than anyone, because you too will meet your end and provide your very being as nourishment to another to continue the chain."

"I see," Metis responds after a moment. "So, continuing with your analogy, I shouldn't force the issue. In time, I will mature into the lone wolf I'm destined to become and do that which only the wolf can."

"Yes. Should the wolf mourn for the ungulates he kills? Should he attempt to fly like the falcon because the sky is freer? Absolutely not. Humans and ryken are no different. People try to argue, but we are animals all the same." Hunter turns back toward the forest. "We're only more savage by nature."

A breeze skirts its way around the pond, rushing over and between the two. "I have yet to truly comprehend how your ryken ability functions, Hunter. How it is that you can read people so accurately?"

"It's instinct. Although it's not perfect. My initial judgment of you is proof of that. The first day you stumbled into the Shack I didn't think much of you. I told you about the Excessum and all its sins, expecting to scare you away. And now you're progressing far better than I could've ever anticipated with my ryken ability." Hunter stalks off into the forest, the inflection of his voice giving away the size of the smile on his face. "Yes, you're turning out to be quite the little heathen."

Episode 12:

Crossroads

The once-great kingdom of Amica lies spread out before her eyes. Atop the small, rocky mountain Isabella surveys much of her country. From the distance and grandness of the view, she can almost convince herself the kingdom isn't weeks, possibly days, from collapse.

Being up here always cheers her up. The free sky, the dazzling view, the fresh air are all so captivating, it never fails to make everything right. But not today.

Today, the sky isn't so free. Instead, the world is closed and cramped. Today, the view lacks its dazzle. Instead, apprehension dulls the scenery. Today, the air doesn't feel so fresh. Instead, it only suffocates.

A cluster of dots congregates down below for a few minutes, then disperses. *I can do nothing for them,* Isabella thinks. *My only job is to protect them, and I have failed miserably. I had no right to chastise those policemen. How am I any different? My citizens will be far worse off in the end.* A single tear rolls down her cheek.

She wipes it away angrily. *Crying won't change anything. I just need to come up with something. Callisto gave me another opportunity and I have to make good use of it.*

As if summoned from her thoughts, Callisto struggles past the boulder Isabella used to close her secret location off from the world. "You okay?" he asks, approaching the precipice.

"Didn't I tell you to wait for me?" Isabella asks, not unkindly.

Callisto pulls Isabella back from the cliff. "You shouldn't stand so close to the edge. Accidents happen." Isabella stares at Callisto for a moment before she bursts out in laughter. "What?"

She struggles to speak through her laughing. "No, no, I'm sorry. I'm just being silly is all."

Callisto finds his cheeks reddening. "Care to explain it, Princess?"

She wipes away a tear, this time from laughter. "Just call me Bella, please."

"Bella?"

"I'm really sorry about laughing but it's just you reminded me of my father. He has always been super protective of me. Growing up, he never wanted me to go anywhere alone and was always by my side if possible."

"Bella is daddy's little girl, huh?" Callisto teases.

Isabella lets out a contented sigh. "When I first met you, you were really distant. I could tell just from looking that you weren't normally so cold. I don't know why you wanted to come off that way, but I'm glad that I got a chance to meet the real you." She turns her back. "Now I can see that person I knew you were from the start. And I kind of like it."

"Let's get back to the kingdom," Callisto responds. "There's nothing more to do here, Princess."

* * *

In the Alair household the members of the Novice Pack gather for their daily training session. "Come on, guys," Samané taunts, "you've got to do better than that!"

Gaudyme swings his sword three swift times, cutting nothing but the air as Samané easily sidesteps. Subnuba throws a haymaker from Samané's blind spot, but he ducks. Another swing of Gaudyme's blade misses its target once again, Samané smiling all the while. Suddenly, a surge of wind nearly knocks Samané off balance, but he quickly recovers, evading the brunt of the whirlwind with his speed. While avoiding the gust Samané closes the gap in a blink, leaving Gaudyme and Subnuba in his wake.

"You can't do it all by yourself," Samané says, rearing his fist back. Ventus just barely dodges, then retaliates with two punches. Each of Ventus' blows are flicked off to the side as if his fists were nothing more than buzzing pests. Samané aims a kick at Ventus' stomach, but with a gust of wind Ventus pushes himself out of reach. At that moment Subnuba and Gaudyme return to the scene, both swinging at Samané from behind, but just as they're about to hit their mark Samané launches himself toward Ventus, evading again. Both pursue him, yet Samané still dodges their attacks all while primarily focused on combating Ventus.

Kato watches with droopy eyes, struggling to stay awake. "This is pathetic," he says to himself. "I'm not sure what's more embarrassing, their fighting techniques or the fact that the kid is so excited about beating them."

Samané misses a punch, and Ventus tries a kick, but Samané is too fast, catching his leg. He rotates on his heel, once, twice, ten times total, swinging Ventus round and round. Gaudyme just barely hops back, avoiding Ventus' whirl-a-round, though Subnuba, not as quick, is struck back by Ventus. "Subnuba!" Gaudyme laughs, pointing, as Subnuba is plucked off. Distracted, Samané releases Ventus at Gaudyme and the two collide, eliminating both opponents in one swoop.

Samané laughs with the same energy Gaudyme did. "You shouldn't get distracted so easily!"

"Neither should you!" Lo's voice rings out. She crashes a half-ton block of ice down where Samané stands. The mini-glacier hits hard, shaking the entire house. A few long seconds of silent anticipation pass as everyone leans forward, surprised. Finally, Lo smiles, jumping around, "I got him! I finally got that conceited jerk! One point for Team Lo!"

"I'm actually surprised to see you back up so soon after that last hit," Samané says from behind. His voice sends a cold shiver down her spine, freezing her completely. "This time I won't hold back."

As Samané's punch races forward Lo can only brace for the worst. Just before connecting he stops. The wind from his fist blows Lo's hair around wildly for a second. Samané takes a step back. "Okay everyone, let me go through what you all did wrong."

Kato rolls his neck trying to stay awake. "Is this really necessary, kid?"

"Of course it is. How else will they learn if I don't teach them? Anyway, Lo, you need to work on your physical combat skills. If your opponent can get in close, it's too easy to land a knockout strike on you. Subnuba, you obviously need more work and practice with your ryken ability. Gaudyme, you need to stay focused at all times during a fight. Even one mental lapse can cost you your life out in the real world. And Ventus, you're too hesitant with your new arm. Oki said the only way your body will ever really get used to it is if you use it like your natural arm. Test your boundaries and push your limits."

Except for Ventus, a look of aggravation creeps beneath the exhaustion of Samané's teammates. Still, he wears his smile. "Don't worry. I'm sure someday you'll all get to my level."

"Okay, that's enough," Kato says, stepping up. "Take a break everyone. Samané and I are going to go a round."

Samané's head snaps to Kato. "Huh? Why? What'd I do?"

"Heads up." Before Samané can react, Kato lunges, his fist slamming into Samané's chest. Samané staggers back, barely able to breathe. "Let's evaluate while we fight. Lesson number one: move faster."

* * *

Anything can be accomplished with enough willpower. That's what Callisto always told himself. Whatever the problem, if you truly believed you could conquer it and worked diligently, it would come to pass. His current predicament is no different. And he will continue to think it until he proves all the doubt within himself wrong.

Since leaving the mountainside view Isabella loves so much, Callisto has withdrawn, hardly saying a word. However, unlike when the two first met, Isabella doesn't hold her conversation back, continuing with the same cheerful disposition that forced Callisto into his current quandary. *She isn't going to make this easy.*

There is no easy solution. Callisto had agreed to go on a tour of the entire Amica Kingdom over the next few days, with the hopes of finding something that Colonel Calamity would deem worth saving. The tour would require ample time and communication with Isabella, both of which Callisto now finds problematic, not because it is uncomfortable or troublesome, but *because* it's neither.

"And here is the pond I was telling you about," Isabella says. "I used to come out here or farther down where the river is, with Uncle Grade when I was younger and go fishing. Grade isn't my blood uncle, by the way, but he's close as family. I've been wanting to go fishing again with him and his son, but I just can't find the time. The princess life isn't all it's cracked up to be."

Callisto only nods.

"You've been awfully quiet since we left the mountain," Isabella says, her voice small and fragile. Callisto turns away from her to eliminate the chance of eye contact. The maneuver draws his attention to a man with long hair on the other side of the large pond. The two study each other from afar. "If it was something I said or did, I apologize..."

The man from across the water starts to make his way around the pond. Likewise, Callisto starts around the pond toward him. "Stay here, Princess," he says, his voice hoarse from disuse.

Finally, Isabella notices the stranger, her heart sinking at his ominous presence. Callisto, however, finds himself smiling by the time he reaches the man. "Metis Lutrio. You're the last person I expected to run into."

Metis regards Callisto emotionlessly. "We're hardly ever cognizant of fate's workings. Callisto Socius, in the flesh. How are you?"

"A lot of good, a bit of bad," Callisto answers. "Can't complain overall, though. How about yourself? It's been years, man. What've you been up to?"

Metis takes a moment. "An assortment of different endeavors. Agonizingly busy. So much work, so little time."

Callisto nods. "Seems like no matter how much you work, fight, and sacrifice, there's always a bit more that needs to be done."

"But someone must tend to it lest the undertaking go perpetually neglected…"

"…And the corruption continue to grow. That's why I got this." Callisto reveals his ryken squad badge.

Surprise flashes across Metis' face. "Interesting. I wouldn't have imagined."

"Yeah, I'm a ryken. A lot has happened since I last saw you. I'm sure you can say the same. I wouldn't doubt that you're on the road to some greatness as we speak. I mean, what else would be your reason for being so far from Centrum City?"

"Greatness? One may refer to my efforts as such, though it all boils down to a matter of perspective."

Callisto chuckles. "You've gotten even more philosophical. I'm not surprised. But I am curious as to how much more you'll grow before our paths cross again."

Metis takes a long, slow breath. "Probably not much at all."

"You're too hard on yourself."

"Hmm."

"Well, I should probably get going. You know, got a world to change and all that."

"Before you depart, I can't help but inquire. How has Samané been doing?"

Callisto's mood darkens. "I don't know. And I can't say that I care. I take it you haven't talked to him recently."

"Not for a couple of months. I can only assume from your tone and disposition the same applies to you." Callisto nods. "I lament such news. In these dark times, a man's most valuable assets are his comrades."

"I really have to go," Callisto says. "Until next time. Take care of yourself."

"Work diligently," Metis responds.

"Always."

Callisto retreats to the woman he arrived with and they fade into the trail. Metis strides off in the opposite direction, the thought of a destination lost in his rumination. *How fitting. Fate loves to mock me; it revels in antagonizing me. It always has, long before my recognition of this fact. Just when my resolve feels it's most robust, the ways of the world long to test me...*

For that I am thankful. What greater gift can there be than being granted the tools required for evolution? Of course it hurts. It goes without saying that I wish it would cease, but my logical mind knows the quickest course to change will be the most painful. So the minuscule fire of my emotion that refuses to be smothered will shriek its complaints with my body. It will wail its protest in my head. It will cry for mercy in my heart, but fate will see to it that I evolve, nevertheless. Whether I desire it or not, fate will continue its work. There's no doubt in my mind that fate will ultimately create in me what this world requires.

Callisto Socius. A textbook, upstanding man. Samané's best friend, and quite possibly mine as well. Even still, if Callisto stands in my way he will be cut down all the same. Friend or enemy, favoritism and bias aren't luxuries that I will afford. If I can't suffer loss, it would be hypocritical of me to deliver it unto the world. I won't mourn, nor will I pine for some alternate destiny. I am the lone wolf and I must fulfill my niche.

* * *

Callisto and Princess Isabella make their way back to Amica castle, taking a route on the outskirts of the kingdom to avoid the public. Quietness separates the two despite Isabella's best efforts to eliminate it. Her brooding gets the better of her and she makes one last attempt. "This kingdom is in trouble."

"Huh?" Callisto says, off guard.

"The kingdom is in trouble and it's all my fault." A bird crows in the distance, but Callisto says nothing. "It was my job to repair the relationship between the Laevus Nation and the Amica Kingdom. No one told me to do it; the task was self-appointed. In fact, my father was adamantly against the idea. But that didn't make it any less important. Amica needs Laevus. That's no secret and it would be dumb to pretend it's not the case. My father knows this, and yet he seems to not care. It's almost like he's given up on Amica. But I won't... I can't."

Isabella pauses, but Callisto still doesn't respond; however, it doesn't matter. Vocalizing her thoughts somehow just works. "Maybe all my efforts are hopeless. That's what my father would have me believe. But I can't just stop. I love Amica Kingdom with all my being and I wish he still felt the same. There was a time when he fought for Amica, a time where he'd have given his life to protect our citizens. Now, that passion is gone.

"Regardless, whatever needs to be done I'll do if it gives us a chance at surviving this rough chapter. I know this isn't the end. I'll find a way to quiet the rabble rousers and keep Amica afloat so future generations might be able to get back what Laevus stole from us. I will find a way."

"Laevus is wrong for the way it has bullied Amica," Callisto says, his voice nearly startling Isabella. "Everyone knows it, but those doing nothing choose to ignore it. Laevus' lying and killing for land is disgraceful. Even if I don't have much power, how can I just sit by and allow it to continue? Something needs to be done."

Isabella offers a weak smile. "Thank you, Callisto."

"There's no reason to thank me. I joined the ryken squad to help people. All people, not just Laevinians. I want to help spread justice to a decaying world. I refuse to stand by idly and watch injustice like this. I don't know what I'm going to do, but I'll fight for Amica, no matter the cost to me."

"As much as I want Amica to get past this, I can't have you risking everything you've worked to get. You have your own life to live."

"I can't watch from the sidelines," Callisto says. "Doing that would make me a catalyst. I don't want to play any role in this corruption."

Before Callisto realizes, Isabella's arms are wrapped around him. "Are you always so virtuous, Callisto, or is it just for me? I'd find it hard to believe it if I weren't witnessing it." Callisto is so shocked by Isabella's sudden embrace that by the time he composes himself she is already releasing him. "Come on. We have to get back soon or we'll be late for dinner."

Episode 13:

Is It Just?

"Wait Dad, I didn't tell you the best part!" Rhys exclaims. "Then Sutari punches the guy across the room! It was so awesome!"

Rhys energetically bounces next to his father Grade as they approach the pond, barely able to contain himself. "It sounds like it was quite the experience," Grade says. "I'm just glad you're okay."

"It was all Sutari's doing."

"Of course. Thank you again." The three stop at the edge of the water. Grade extends his hand and Metis meets him halfway. He struggles to not grimace under the strength of Grade's grip.

"Your praises are unwarranted. The ordeal was only worth a modicum of concern," Metis says.

"Hey Rhys, why don't you go find some worms to put on the hooks while I get better acquainted with your friend here."

Rhys smiles, running away. "I'll be back with a hundred in a flash!"

Grade gently places his fishing pole on the grass. "I don't know what your reason is for coming here, but you need to stay away from my son."

Metis sets his pole down as well. "Hardly a quandary at this point; he's already delivered the prize I was pursuing. All that remains now is to seize it."

Grade shakes his head disappointedly. "I should've assumed moving Reyna and Rhys out of the castle wouldn't be a permanent fix. Very well. After I arrest you, I'll have to come up with a better way to keep them safe."

* * *

In the extravagant dining area of the Amica Castle, Callisto and Princess Isabella anxiously await the arrival of King Atrium. They sit across from one another at a table ten meters long, drastic overkill for the small party intended to dine. Finally, Atrium rolls into the room. "It's good to have you back home, Isabella. Your presence alone brightens my day!"

"I'm happy to be back home," Isabella says. "It felt like I was away for weeks."

Atrium takes his seat at the head of the table. "But you got back safe, a job well done for your first solo trip to that godforsaken country. Spending time with those Laevinians, ugh, makes me sick just thinking about it."

Isabella's eyes flicker to Callisto then back to her father. "Well, I'm home now so no need to fret over that."

Callisto stands, offering his hand. "Hello sir, I don't think I've had the opportunity to introduce myself yet. I am Callisto Socius."

Atrium looks back to Isabella, dumbfounded. "Has he been sitting there this entire time?"

"Since before you entered," she answers.

"Well, of course he has." Atrium squints. "I recognize you. The gardener?"

"No," Isabella says. "He's–"

"No, no. I've got it! The janitor."

"Colder."

"You sure? Hmm. Our bird whisperer, maybe?"

"Father, we don't even have one of those."

Atrium stops, a disgusted expression settling on his face. "...The Laevus dog."

"He's not a dog. Please, just listen. We've—"

"Listen? You want me to listen when you ignored me and invited this...this...this garbage to my dining table?"

"Excuse me, sir?" says Callisto.

"Father, stop it!" Isabella exclaims as Atrium rises from his chair.

"You heard me," he snaps. "You're nothing but garbage, boy."

Callisto swallows his anger. "What gives you the right to say something like that to me? You don't know anything about me aside from the fact I'm a Laevinian."

"I don't need to personally know garbage to identify it."

Isabella begins to plead one more time when Callisto holds his hand up, cutting her words short. "I want you to know that I agree with your standing on the treaty between our nations. The way Laevus has been treating Amica for the last century is corrupt—evil even."

Atrium tilts his head. "Is that it? Is that all you have to say? Do you actually believe feeling that way makes you any less garbage to me? A rodent can see that what the Laevus Nation is doing is evil. They have wronged this kingdom more times than I care to count. The nation itself is garbage, the decay of the world. Your feelings will neither help Amica nor hurt Laevus, so what does it do for me?"

Atrium's glare is intense, but Callisto meets it with meekness. "I'm sorry. I apologize for all the wrongdoings of my nation. It makes me sick to know such corruption exists right in front of me. I may not be able to now, but I strive to one day correct the wrongs of the older generations. I don't know how I will, and I know it won't be easy, but I won't stop until it's accomplished."

"Heh. Even garbage can have a pleasing aroma from time to time. I've lost my appetite. You aren't fooling anyone, boy."

Atrium heads for the exit but stops once he sees Callisto following. "I said I'm sorry, sir. As of now that's all I can offer you. I'll need time to change things, but for now, please accept my apology."

"My forgiveness is something I will never give you the satisfaction of having. I will go to my grave with hate toward you and your homeland. It was you who turned me into this monster and you who will feel my wrath."

Atrium spits and it lands on Callisto's shirt. He barely notices as he watches the king walk away with more disgust than he could ever have from simple saliva. When Callisto tunes back into the rest of the world around him he hears Isabella already mid-sentence, trying to ease his pain, cleaning his shirt with a cloth. "I'm so sorry! If I had known things would turn out like this there's no way I would've asked you to come here. I'm so sorry! This is just terrible!"

"It's okay, Isabella," Callisto manages, his mind already on his next destination.

* * *

Grade blocks an attack aimed at his temple, Metis' aura dissipating after slamming into his forearm. Another aura attack comes for his stomach, but the purple illumination meets the same fate. Grade roundhouse kicks Metis' Wall of Lutrio. The fortress of light barely shakes. Metis lands a quick shot to the face, as Grade backs off, evading Metis' follow-up strikes.

Grade wipes his lip, checking for blood, but the back of his hand remains dry. "My son doesn't lie, you're pretty good."

"I'm not befuddled as to why you've been deemed Amica's Protector," Metis says. "Your defense is quite formidable considering you aren't conversant with my ability."

"I wish I could say the same for you. How much longer do you think you can hide behind that wall? Not long enough, I guarantee you."

With that Grade takes off at a sprint but is slowed to a walk as he blocks everything Metis throws at him. Still he comes on, steadily. Step by step, foot by foot, as Metis' eyes flicker and shine with varying intensity, desperate to stop him. Eventually Grade is before Metis' Wall of Lutrio, defending without flaw. He draws his fist back, allowing spirit energy to flood his right arm. Immediately the arm begins to rotate at the shoulder, a drill made of flesh and bone. A dozen rotations a second, then faster by the time his knuckles spin against the barrier, carving Metis' wall away. A shot to the ribs curls Grade enough to end his strike, and another to the face lands the great Amican Protector on his back, but not before he can dig halfway through Metis' defense.

Grade lies on the ground for a moment, sucking the salty blood off his lip. He swallows his annoyance with the red fluid then sits up to see Metis, his eyes closed. *It's always the kids with the most promise that are the hardest to teach,* Grade broods. "A little repair work?" Metis' eyes remain closed. "That's a sturdy defense you have there. I'd be lying if I said I wasn't impressed. But impressed is far from defeated." Grade's arm starts its blinding rotation. "Let's try again."

Once more Grade approaches Metis' wall and once more Metis' futile attempts do little more than slow him. Once at the barrier, Grade only defends, making no attempt to attack the wall. Slightly, almost indistinguishably, Metis' onslaught begins to slow. When the timing is just right Grade plants his foot.

"Roto Punch!"

Grade's arm rotates so fast that the grass below leans away, pushed back by the centrifugal wind. His fist drills through the air quickly, although before he can make contact, Metis connects his aura to Grade's jaw. The blow, as strong as any Metis has thrown thus far, should make him stumble, but somehow Grade stands firm, delivering the strike. His fist penetrates the sturdy Wall of Lutrio, and by the time he makes it through, a one-foot diameter hole rests where there had just been impenetrable spirit energy. Metis has no time to balk as Grade's left hand slams into it next.

"Roto Punch!"

Again, Grade's fist rips through another portion of the barrier, Metis trying a multitude of quick, feeble attacks to keep Grade at bay. Unsurprisingly the result of the punch is the same. Grade rears his fist back a third time.

"Roto Punch!"

When Grade brings his fist forward this time he meets no resistance and nearly falls on his face because of it. He regains his balance, bemused, but when his eyes meet Metis' he understands the situation.

"What good is a defense that can't defend?" Metis asks. "I've reabsorbed the energy so that I may direct it more effectively." *What other choice do I have?*

"Smart," Grade replies. "Drilling through your wall was only warming me up. By the time we finished I would've barely broken a sweat and you would have been too exhausted to run away."

"I won't flee."

"A mistake, but one I'm thankful for. Makes my job that much easier. Know that, I don't take joy in this; quite the opposite, really."

Without warning, Metis' aura swirls around Grade, the light moving with increased speed. Grade quickly realizes the difference when a shot to the chest sends him stumbling backward. An overhead blow slams his head downward painfully, disorienting him enough for Metis to land two more shots to either side of Grade's ribs. Metis' aura is nearly at Grade's chin when he starts to rotate. His entire body spins so quickly that Metis' aura is deflected to the side before it can inflict any damage. After three tries, Metis accepts the defensive maneuver for what it is and desists. As a result, Grade winds to a halt.

Grade's shoulders rise and fall quickly. "Your strength continues to surprise me. I've fought more mature ryken who didn't give me this much trouble. I can't help but wonder... why have you come for me?"

"Such knowledge won't alter the outcome."

"Yes. I'm going to arrest you regardless." Blood from a blow to the forehead oozes into Grade's left eye. "But if it doesn't matter, humor me."

"No."

Grade sighs. "Stubborn brat, aren't you?"

He starts toward Metis, both arms rotating blurs. Metis' aura whizzes around him, but his spinning appendages dissipate the energy innocuously. As Grade closes the gap Metis realizes he can impede Grade's progress no longer and turns for the pond in a full sprint.

"You said you wouldn't flee!" Grade calls out.

Metis only takes a handful of steps before Grade is on him, grabbing his shoulder. Metis tries to shrug his hand off but instead Grade turns Metis, landing a clean blow to his jaw. Red and black pain burst into Metis' consciousness. Although pain has been a common theme in his life recently, one never gets used to the sensation. When Metis can focus on something other than the intense throbbing of his head and the sharp aching of his jaw, he hears Grade talking.

"I could've taken you out with that one blow. A sprinkle of spirit energy and your head would have split apart." Metis crawls for the pond, slowly moving forward. Inch by inch he squirms until he stops progressing. He desperately claws at the earth beneath him in his attempt, but the pond won't come closer. Just as Metis realizes why, a blow to the face seems to bring the stars of space closer instead.

Grade grunts in disgust. "I don't have my handcuffs, so I'll just have to take you back to the castle unconscious."

Metis can feel Grade's hands wrap around his throat.

* * *

"Would you like a drink?" Jove asks.

"No, thank you," Callisto answers reflexively. Jove retreats into the kitchen. Although Callisto has never had alcohol, on second thought, maybe it would be nice to have a sip before diving into this discussion. After all, he is of age now, so why shouldn't he enjoy a drink? Something to take the edge off.

Jove reenters the room with a cup of warm tea. "What did you want to talk about?"

Callisto contemplates how to phrase his question. He pondered his wording all the way from the Amica Castle to the hotel. From the hotel lobby to Jove's second floor room door. And from the moment Jove answered the door until now, yet he still isn't any closer to figuring out how to say what he wants to say.

So he just says it. "Do you believe the way Laevus treats Amica is just?"

Jove sighs. "Callisto, it's late. Can we not get into this again?"

"Please," Callisto says, desperately, "just answer, General."

Jove moves smoothly into the chair across from Callisto. He sits back, perhaps contemplating his own wording. He takes a sip of tea. "I do."

"How?" One word. An order masquerading as a request from student to teacher. Explain.

"In Laevus, we have rules and laws we obey, correct? Those who follow them are upstanding citizens. Though flawed on a fundamental level, as all people are, those citizens can still be just because they are within the law. The same holds true for any member of any society. If you are a part of a bigger entity, willingly or otherwise, you are subject to its laws, rules, and judgment. I'm saying all of this because people, human and ryken alike, fall into a natural law. A law of power."

Anger. But Callisto suppresses it. "So the strong should rule and the weak perish?"

"It's the way things have always been. I'm not a ruthless man. I do feel sorrow for the Amicans. But as a Laevinian, I am bound by the rules and laws of my nation and I will follow them to the best of my abilities."

"Without question?"

Jove nods, slowly. "Without protest."

Callisto hesitates then, when he's sure it's not the anger speaking, says, "That's blind obedience."

Jove cocks his head. Anger? "Explain."

"Under what circumstances would Laevus ever be unjust? Is there any order you would not carry out? Or would you just rationalize it under the pretense of some illogical law?"

"War happens. The conquering of nations happens. It's reality. It always has been. You can't change that, Callisto."

"But is it just?"

Jove's lips are a flat line. Anger. "I've already answered that."

"You said you believe it is because it's the nature of humans and ryken. But is it *just*?"

Jove sets his tea on the table next to him. "What else should one do? Disobey their superiors? Defy them in open court? Challenge him midway through his judgment?"

"This isn't about me, General. This is about Laevus and Amica. Is. It. Just?"

Rage. "We leave tomorrow, Callisto. I've had enough of this."

Callisto sits forward in his chair. "But I'm not ready yet. I've barely had an opportunity to explore Amica for what may be worth saving."

"This nation has lost. Let it go. The colonel sent you on this mission as punishment. It's not some heroic endeavor."

"You think I don't realize that? Still, I have to find a way to undo this injustice from Laevus."

"It's not injustice."

"It is."

"It isn't."

Somewhere along the conversation Callisto and Jove rose from their chairs, and now exchange glares inches from one another. Callisto is a tower, staring down on his superior with a scowl. Jove retaliates with a stern look, all his power, physical and authoritative, useless on the grounds that Callisto hasn't actually done anything wrong. Well, most of his power, anyway. "We leave tomorrow. End of discussion."

Thankfully Callisto has the self-control to mutter two words, and only two, past gritted teeth. "Yes sir."

Episode 14:

Pure Bloodshed

But everybody knows it's wrong, Callisto thinks. *This whole system. All the politics. Why hasn't anyone done anything? Why is no one trying to stop it? What I fear most is that this extends beyond even Amica. Where else is Laevus' corruption happening and ignored? How deep does this evil run? I was naïve to believe Laevinian hatred for ryken was limited to our country. I can't rule out the possibility that it may be worldwide, woven into every action, every interest Laevus has, as if the sole purpose of the government is to slowly whittle ryken out of existence. Why does no one fight back? Everyone knows it's wrong.*

The slamming of Jove's door behind Callisto snaps him from his thoughts. All of a sudden he feels exhausted. He heads for the stairwell, but his name is called before he descends. He barely has the energy to turn. What more could General Jove want? But when Callisto turns, he'd much rather continue his fruitless debate with his stubborn superior.

"For what it's worth, I actually agree with you," Prix says, walking toward Callisto. "I didn't mean to eavesdrop. The general and I have a shared suite and the walls are pretty thin."

Callisto tries a glare, but he's so tired the look probably comes off more as confusion. "Sorry," Prix says. Now Callisto's look of confusion is warranted. "Not for eavesdropping. Just for... you know, everything."

"What is *everything*?" Callisto asks.

Prix searches the floor for a second, then he takes a deep breath, looking Callisto in the eyes. "I'm sorry for giving you a hard time. It wasn't right, the way I acted." Callisto nods ever so slightly, expression still unsatisfied. "And I'm sorry for the little girl."

"Her name was Acura," Callisto snaps, struggling to keep his voice down.

"Yes, Acura Vale. I'm sorry for what happened to her."

The last thread of Callisto's patience breaks. "She was five, Prix. Five years old! She didn't have to die. But she did, because of us. Because of you. What is your sorrow going to do for her?"

Prix swallows. "Nothing."

"And it'll do less than that for me. Keep your sorries. My forgiveness is something you'll never..." Callisto's words trail off as he hears King Atrium Vortane's spiteful voice lacing his own.

This time it's Prix who offers the look of confusion. "I have to go," Callisto says, walking away. If Callisto felt exhausted before, dead would be a better description now. Dead on the inside, at least.

It's been a long day.

* * *

Metis struggles against the void. It isn't the first time darkness has tried to swallow him. Though the last time it fought so tenaciously to pull him under, all he could think of was Thralle. He originally believed the reason for that was because Samané was his opponent. This time, however, Samané is hundreds of miles away and still all Metis can think of is his father.

Thralle Lutrio. Cut down in his prime. Why? Well, the why is easy. Because of the humans. How? That is considerably trickier. Who could be strong enough to take down the strongest ryken in the world's most powerful nation? Metis doesn't know, but he will find out.

That is the reason he moves, the true reason for waking every morning. Changing the world is a byproduct birthed from that desire—to eliminate the possibility that humans would continue to puppeteer ryken. It wasn't Thralle's fault. No one would dare say Thralle's death was, not in front of Metis. He was a victim of honor. Loyalty, duty, justice, all ball and chain tethers binding Thralle's true power and influence. As a result, even in his prime, he was still under the humans' thumbs.

Not Metis. He won't make the same mistake. No, *mistake* is the wrong word... Thralle wasn't in error. Following that logic, Thralle's death must have been for some form of greater good. An abstract sort of good. A sacrifice to provide the pain needed to transform Metis into a catalyst willing to do what Thralle wouldn't. Metis will change the world for the better. That's why he must find his father's killer... so he can thank him properly.

But first, he must survive this.

Metis' eyes snap open, his irises royal blue, and Grade is sent spiraling backward. When Grade goes to sit up from the blow, his ears ringing, the world reels around him. He works to steady his thoughts, trying to process the scene. *What is happening?* Grade thinks. *He passed out. I'm sure he did.* Grade struggles to his feet. Metis floats toward him, encompassed in his own aura. Although Metis' irises shine with their new royal blue hue, his pupils are dull and dilated. "He's still unconscious."

The royal blue of Metis' eyes intensifies and there is a ton of force to Grade's chest. He slams into a tree, the century-old plant barely able to stay grounded from the impact. Grade hardly gives his body time to process the pain, rotating his upper body, arms straight out. The tree behind him is severed in two, its collapse appearing to occur in slow motion. Only after it rests on the ground does Grade stop rotating.

"This one is definitely unique," Grade says. "Boy, Rhys sure knows how to pick them." He grits his teeth. "I should've ended this when I had the chance."

Metis tries two simultaneous aura punches on each side of Grade. He is able to defend with his rotating arms, the power behind the blows causing his forearms to smart after. Grade never even sees the third punch to his stomach, only the blood he coughs up when he falls to his knees. He lifts his head, expecting the knockout blow, but instead sees Metis on his knees as well, hand to his head. Grade isn't exactly sure how, but he is able to muster the strength to rise once he can inhale again. Grade's knees buckle beneath him, but he wills them to do as they're told. He starts at a limp, then he walks, and by the time he reaches Metis he's in a full sprint. All the while Metis grimaces on his knees, his focus appearing to be locked on his pain.

"Roto Punch!"

The instant before contact Grade's arm is cloaked in purple and royal blue, the colors distinct and swirling. Grade balks at the sight of his halted attack, grunting as he pours his remaining energy into his punch. But his arm remains stilled in Metis' aura.

Metis' voice is a whisper, his face drenched with sweat.

"Mentum Barrage."

For nearly a minute straight Grade can't differentiate between himself and pain. Can't remember a time where pain wasn't all over him. His body moves, but only to the cadence of Metis' blows. And, as if the pain couldn't get worse, a final shot from Metis knocks the light out of Grade's world.

Metis struggles toward Grade, who lies meters off, defeated and unconscious. "It happened again," he says as he stumbles over. He pushes the thought from his mind, needing every ounce of his focus and energy on the here and now. When Metis reaches Grade, he begins regaining consciousness.

"You were more of a handful than I anticipated," Metis says.

Grade replies, his voice raspy and dry, "I could say the same about you."

"If you had fought with the intent to kill, this conclusion would have been vastly different."

"True, but that hardly matters now. What do you want from us? Money? Land? What is your gripe with the kingdom?"

Metis hardens his heart, an ability he has been getting disturbingly good with. "The only thing I've come here for is your head. Pure bloodshed."

Grade blanches. "Surely there must be something else that can satisfy you! Anything!"

Metis looks into the suffering eyes of his victim. Something deep within him begs for a show of mercy. A tiny voice, barely audible. But Metis takes a deep breath and just like that, it begs no longer. "Final words?"

"I have a family!" Grade pleads. "For their sake, please!"

"Valisious Slash."

A purple-blue crescent streaks out from Metis to Grade. Rhys, off in the distance, ducks behind a tree before the aura blade reaches his father, his eyes shut tightly. Why couldn't he help? Not that he would have been able to do much. Still, he should've intervened. It's not that he hadn't wanted to, his body just wouldn't move. Well, it would move away. That's what it wants more than anything, to turn and run away, never to return.

"It's normal to be scared." Rhys' heart sinks. "What I mean is it's understandable to be scared. I have no idea what normal people do or feel. I'm so far gone, it's probably better to say I was never normal."

A pale, slender man emerges from the darkness of the forest. His gait is slow, almost dramatic. Rhys tries to run but his feet can't move, literally. He looks down to see a shadow wrapped around his ankles. Tears start to fall. "Please don't kill me," Rhys begs.

"What kind of monster do you think I am? You haven't aggravated me. Not yet, anyway. Plus, you're more useful to me alive right now."

Nightshade looks toward the pond. "That brat actually did it. Maybe Master Misery was right. Only time will tell."

"Why?" Rhys cries.

"Why is exactly the right question. And make sure you answer this for anyone else who asks. The Excessum have reason to believe Amica possesses something of their interest. If it's here, we will find it. Amica hasn't the power to resist, but Laevus is a different story. Tell them to stand down before things get ugly."

Rhys' voice comes back weak and fragile. "But why Metis? He didn't have to do this. He's a good person, I know it."

Nightshade flashes his sharp smile. "There are no good people."

* * *

"Okay, gather around, kiddies," says Kato patronizingly, gesturing for everyone to sit on the floor. His voice returns to normal. "Let's get this out the way."

Samané, Lo, Gaudyme, Ventus and Subnuba all sit on the flawless white floor of the Alair household. "What's the topic for today, Kato?" Samané asks.

"Ah-ah-ah," Kato says, wagging a finger. "First we have to review. What'd we discuss yesterday?"

"I know!" Gaudyme exclaims, raising his hand.

"This isn't third grade, out with it, you goofball."

"We talked about ryken hunters." Gaudyme smiles, proudly.

"And..." Lo angrily prompts before Kato gets the chance.

"And... uh, and, hmm. I guess I can't remember."

Kato puts a hand to his forehead. "Why do I bother?"

"Ryken hunters are a group of humans who use specialized weapons to kill ryken," Subnuba says, in a bored tone. "Their most dangerous tactic for defeating ryken is by using akidiode, a chemical that can negate a ryken's sped healing."

Kato nods. "At least someone was paying attention."

"Ryken hunters are protected by law against ryken, as every human is. Because of that you recommend we don't engage them publicly. But if we find ourselves in an isolated spot, with no witnesses, we can use our own judgment."

"Very well done, Subnuba."

He shrugs. "Yeah, whatever."

"All right, today's lesson is ryken abilities. What do you know about ryken abilities so far?"

"All ryken abilities require spirit energy," Ventus says.

"Every ryken has only one ryken ability," Lo offers.

"Ryken abilities are hereditary," Subnuba adds.

"Ryken abilities are unique for every ryken," Samané says.

Everyone looks to Gaudyme. He scratches his head. "Yeahhh, I got nothing."

"I can always count on you, goofy." Kato shakes his head. "The only absolutely true statement you all made was the first one. So points for Ventus. Ryken abilities always require spirit energy to activate, no exceptions. Lo's point is true at face value, but I have heard of a ryken with multiple ryken abilities, although his original ability is more than likely the cause for that. I'm mentioning this to say be careful to not make too many assumptions out on the battlefield. Ryken are strange, dynamic creatures and can challenge some things thought to be fact.

"Subnuba's claim is true ninety percent of the time, though there are times when children spawn random abilities. And last, my star pupil, Samané, you're the most wrong of the bunch. Certain ryken abilities are actually very common. Before it was illegal to research and teach about ryken, there was a study that recorded the most common ryken abilities. Any guess as to what that ability was at the time?"

"Spirit energy manifestation?" Ventus asks.

"Close—that was the second most common," Kato says.

Gaudyme points his finger at Subnuba and laughs. "Ha-ha! Your ability is boring and common!"

"Well, Subnuba's energy attacks are second only to blade-using ryken abilities. Namely, your ability, goofy."

"No," Gaudyme whispers, eyes watering.

Subnuba chuckles. "What was that about boring and common, Admiratio?"

"That does include all blade users though: swords, axes, knives, what-have-you," Kato says. "Also, the study was conducted nearly a century ago, so the numbers have definitely fluctuated since, but that's just to give you a bit of perspective."

Oki emerges from the staircase. She greets the crew with her perfectly white teeth and a wave. "How's your arm, Ventus?"

He flexes. "It feels more like a natural part of me every day."

"Nice, nice." She grabs Kato's bicep with both hands. "You said you wouldn't be long," she purrs.

"Let me just make this last point," Kato says. "Not every ryken has a combative ability. I encountered a ryken once who could control his tear ducts, making it so he never had to blink."

"That's a pretty dumb ability," says Gaudyme frankly.

"Maybe, but he could've still kicked your butt—probably still can," Kato says. Lo sputters with laughter. "His ability may not have really been useful in a battle, but with spirit energy comes strength, stamina, speed, and healing. With that he was a decent recruit."

Subnuba stands. "Are we finished yet?"

Kato frowns. "I let you in my house, give you my time and knowledge. You think you all would be a bit more grateful."

"I appreciate you," Ventus says matter-of-factly.

"Kiss up," Subnuba grumbles.

"Atta boy, Ventus." Kato puts his arm around Oki. "Come on. Let's go downstairs."

"Just us, alone?" she asks, expectantly.

"I'll be busy, so make sure the front door is locked when you kiddies leave," says Kato, exiting with Oki.

"Those two are so perverse," Lo says, cringing.

Subnuba shudders. "And old—it's a nasty combination."

Episode 15:

The Books of Xenesis

She's late, Callisto thinks. Waiting on people has always been a pet peeve of Callisto's. It's simple, really. Be on time. It's just something you should do, the smallest of commitments to be kept. Things happen, however, and with every second that passes Callisto becomes less annoyed and more worried. From what he's seen, Isabella isn't the type of person to neglect a meeting. Not this one. A rendezvous that could hold Amica's future in the balance would be Isabella's number one priority. And a day alone with Callisto would be her second.

"Sorry I'm late," says Isabella, scuttling across the beautiful marble floor of the Amica Castle. "Something came up."

Isabella runs a hand over her ruffled hair, the blond locks refusing to be tamed in their usual curly fashion. As she approaches her distress becomes more obvious, despite her best efforts to appear casual. If her eyes weren't so red and puffy, maybe Callisto could wait until their tour to ask, "What's wrong?"

It's as if Callisto's question sucks out Isabella's remaining strength. She melts into his arms. "It's Grade," she cries. "He's dead."

Callisto says nothing, swallowing his shock. He just saw the man yesterday morning during Isabella's tour of the castle. He appeared as strong and healthy as one might expect from a person granted the title of Protector. Callisto continues to hold Isabella, comforting her. Her sadness seems to pulse from her heart, through bone, muscle, skin, and cloth into Callisto. "He was a good man," she says, after a while.

"How did it happen?" Callisto finally asks.

"He was murdered," she answers, her voice shaky.

Murdered. Could it be coincidence that he was killed while the Laevus Nation was here? Not that Prix or General Jove were the culprits; that wouldn't make sense. But perhaps someone else did it as a warning to Amica and Laevus. A warning for what, though? "Whoever did this did it for a reason. They'd want that reason to be known. Did they leave a message behind?"

Isabella tenses against Callisto's chest. It's weird how comforting it is simply being with him. How safe Isabella feels wrapped in his arms.

The sensation is reminiscent of being with her father when she was young, yet starkly different. "Everything is still being investigated, but as of right now nothing has been found. Maybe his wife or son will know something. His son Rhys was in the vicinity, but he's still shaken up and won't talk to anyone."

Callisto separates himself from Isabella. "I have to go talk to him."

Isabella nods. "I'll go with you."

"You can't. It's dangerous for you anywhere outside the castle at this point. We don't know who it is that's out there or what they want. The safest place for you right now is here."

"I'm safe with you, Callisto," Isabella insists.

Callisto... I'm scared.

He grits his teeth. "I can't keep you safe."

"I'm going, with or without you," Isabella says determinedly. "So please, just let me trust you."

* * *

Somewhere far from Centrum City—that's the best Samané can offer for his current location. That and someplace dark. He looks up the rocky precipice at a house on one of its lips. Hopefully the old man he'd spoken to was right and Noctuama is in there.

He has searched far and wide for the mysterious woman of the dark. Many leads from many different sources that knew someone, who knew someone that thought they might have heard of her. Weeks of searching had led Samané here, and even though all those weeks had only taught him that she was untraceable, he still hoped. Hoped against logic that she was in that house. Hoped against logic that she would be happy to see him. And hoped against logic that she would give him the opportunity to discover more about her. *It will work out. Things always do, one way or another.*

Finally, Samané makes it to the small hut. His heart quickens when he knocks. He allows a few seconds to pass before he raises his hand to try again. But then the door creaks open.

* * *

It happened again, Metis broods, eyes to the grass, the Excessum's cabin to his back. *But what is* it? Metis flexes his fingers, his normal purple aura encompassing his hand. Another fight Metis was on the brink of losing. Another fight he wanted to win so badly. Then the world goes black and when he can see again his opponent is on the ground, defeated. It makes no sense.

What happened to his opponent made sense. Somehow, someway he was able to drastically increase his spirit energy. It must have something to do with his desire to win, only triggered when his will is strong enough. Metis can hazily recall the events that happened during *it*. Something like a dream but at the same time... not. He can remember details, but it's as if he was watching from a third person's view, and that person could only see in black and white. The worst part of it all is that Metis has no control over what his body does. The entire time he struggles to come back to himself, the experience far more disturbing than the initial fear of defeat. Eventually, Metis regains control, but not without the same will it took to gain the sudden power in the first place.

In the wake of it, Metis can't help but wonder why. Why does this happen and why him? As far as he knows, from the bit he has researched and studied about ryken, no one has ever had a condition remotely resembling this phenomenon. Is there something different about him that causes his spirit energy to separate from his consciousness when he feels defeat is imminent? Maybe it's a deeper element of his own ryken ability he has yet to unfold to its fullest capacity. Metis has no idea. *One truth regarding my condition is undeniable. I'll never truly comprehend its parameters if I don't subject myself to it routinely. But how to go about effectively accomplishing that is an enigma in itself.*

"I was so excited I had to follow you back," Nightshade says, approaching Metis. He doesn't even try to conceal his sharp-toothed smile. "Well done for your first execution. I didn't think you were the decapitation type. One of my favorite methods, personally. A sure, quick kill and what could be better than that? Plus, it sends a great message to spectators, though the boy turned away before that highlight. Still, I enjoyed it."

"Why are you here so prematurely? Our rendezvous isn't until the morrow."

Nightshade cracks his neck. "You have a knack for ruining my mood. I'll pretend you didn't just question me. Anyway, how did the kill feel? Exhilarating?"

"Wrong," Metis says. Nightshade squints. "The kill I'm referring to; it felt wrong. Murdering another individual is wrong—you must be cognizant of that. However, let us not be naive. I knew when I joined the Excessum, since my father died—before that even—that abiding by laws, rules, morality or feelings of right and wrong wouldn't be the way the humans fell from grace. Only by force. I resigned myself to be that force. To overcome the darkness from the inside out, but not give in to it. That was how my father elucidated the concept and I can't delineate it a better way. Acc—"

"Shut up," Nightshade hisses. "Shut up before I kill you. You really, really know how to ruin my mood." Nightshade scowls and strides away.

* * *

"It all happened so fast," Rhys explains. "Like something out of a nightmare. First, we're heading to the pond and next thing I know Dad is on the ground bleeding. I wanted to help. I did, so badly. But my body just wouldn't move."

Rhys starts crying and Isabella offers a comforting hand. "It's okay, Rhys. No one blames you."

Callisto looks on with equal parts anger and sadness. *What monster would do this to a man and his family?*

"At the end I turned away," Rhys continues once he composes himself. "Then another man came up. He was really skinny and had sharp teeth. He said that Amica has something they want."

"They?" Isabella asks.

"Uh. The Exum, I think he said."

"The Excessum," Callisto corrects.

"Oh yeah. That was it."

"What could the Excessum want here?" Isabella asks.

"I don't know," Callisto replies.

"This is terrible timing for Amica."

"He said Laevus must stand down," Rhys adds.

Callisto suppresses a scowl. "There's no way we'll just ignore them while they pillage and destroy the kingdom."

"Callisto," Isabella says desperately, "without the treaty there's no reason for Laevus to get involved."

Silence moves into the Culminary living room. Rhys replays the events of the morning, critical of every decision he made. Isabella broods over the inevitable doom soon to befall her kingdom. And Callisto racks his brain for the answer to saving that same kingdom.

Then it hits him. "I need to get back to Laevus."

"What?" Isabella balks. "You can't leave. Not now."

"I have to talk to Colonel Calamity again. The chances are slim, but I think it's our best shot. Our only shot."

Isabella studies Callisto's face for a while, then tries her best smile. "I'll be waiting for you."

* * *

Noctuama is untraceable. Always has been and always will be. No one has ever seen her. Not the real her, anyway. Darkness incarnate. And who can find nothing?

Samané Lutrio apparently.

He has done what no one before him has. Tracked Noctuama. The two words themselves are an oxymoron. Not meant to solely exist in conjunction. An error. Misstated or misinformed. Surely it's not truth. If only Samané knew that.

Maybe she would tell him one day how she allowed him to find her. How there was something about him that intrigued her. That drew her to him. A certain light.

Perhaps that light is only the fact that he is so infatuated with her. It's for no reason other than her smooth skin and pretty smile. His fascination couldn't be based on anything deeper than that. He doesn't know her. No one does. And he'll never get the opportunity. Her heart is locked.

The door creaks open. "Samané Lutrio? What are you doing here?"

Samané tries a smug smile, but his genuine happiness gets the better of him. "I have my resources."

"Resources? So far away from Centrum City?" Noctuama sticks her head outside the door. "Are you absolutely certain you weren't followed?"

"Followed? By whom?"

Noctuama's voice falls to a whisper. "I've told you before, I'm a spy. I have met many people who can never know who I truly am. It's a miracle that you were able to track me down."

Samané shrugs. "I can do just about anything I want if I put enough effort into it."

"You shouldn't have come," says Noctuama. "This interaction is dangerous for us both. I have enemies who would kill you just for being associated with me."

"But I had to see you." There is a pause. "Well, I mean, I had to see you so I could ask you to join my team."

Noctuama shakes her head. "You have no idea who I am. How can you ask me something like that?"

"It's hard to explain, but I feel like I know more than enough about you, Noctuama."

"There is more to knowing a person than the emotions and beliefs they show you on the surface. Samané, you don't even know my last name."

Samané stops to think. "Well, come on. That's not fair. You never told me that."

"It won't work. It can't work."

Samané takes a step closer. "Listen, if you're running from the past then stop. Whatever it is, we can face it. Together." Another pause. It's now that he realizes how close he's gotten. He hops back, nervously laughing. "Together as in a member of the Novice Pack. Not together as like, a couple or anything. I mean, who said anything about a couple anyway? Two is such a weird number when you really thin—"

"I can't drag you into my situation. If you knew my life there's no way you'd be standing here asking me this. I'm sorry, but I decline your invitation." For a fraction of a second Samané sees fear in Noctuama's eyes, but when she blinks it disappears. "It's the way things have to be. It can't be helped. Who can change fate, after all?"

"So that's it? After all I've done to find you and travel here, you tell me no?"

"You're a good guy, Samané. You're smart, talented, and hardworking when motivated. I know more about you than you may think. This is why I came to you before the Excessum tournament in the first place. It's because I know you will do great things to change this world, I truly believe that. You have a light about you that draws people in. I wish I could describe it better than that." Noctuama bites her lip. "Believe me, you don't want to be mixed up in this mess I call life. You're destined for much bigger things."

"Let me make that choice myself," Samané says.

"You are adorable, I swear," Noctuama says, smiling. She retreats into the house, re-emerging a moment later with two books. "If you insist on entangling our fates, this might help."

Noctuama extends the tomes to Samané. The hardened, gray covers of the books are barely worn despite their evident age. The metal clasps that lock each book appear to be wielded directly to the front and back covers, a thick strap binding the book shut. When Noctuama drops the tomes into Samané's hands he can feel their weight. Physically, of course, but there is something else too, as if the value and importance of the books are a tangible force bearing down upon them.

"What are these?" Samané asks, bemused.

"Two Books of Xenesis. An unimaginably valued treasure. The best I can do right now is entrust you with these and promise that because of them our paths will cross again. And when that time comes, I will protect you."

Noctuama touches Samané's cheek with the back of her hand, gently. Despite his fluttering heart, he manages to speak coolly. "I think you have it backwards. I'll protect you."

"Of course. You're right." She offers Samané a heart-melting smile. "My mistake. Forgive me."

* * *

"This works out for the best," Callisto says to Princess Isabella. Prix and General Jove wait a few strides away at the Amica Castle gates. "The general was planning to head home today, anyway."

Isabella hesitates. "Promise me you will come back, Callisto."

You will see your mommy again. I promise.

Callisto takes a breath. "I can't. But what I will promise is that I'll try my best to make it back."

Isabella nods. "What more can I ask for? That will have to do."

"Callisto!" Jove calls. "We're done here. Let's get moving."

"Yes sir." Callisto turns and starts to take a step but a pair of smooth, slim arms wraps around him.

"Please come back," Isabella whispers.

<u>Episode 16:</u>

Life Goes On

"Lo!" Gaudyme yells down the street. "Lo! Wait for me!"

"You think the guy would learn to be on time," Lo grumbles to herself. "Every day he's late. Every day! No matter how many times I leave him, he's always late. I don't get it."

Lo continues, without a backwards glance. Gaudyme calls after her as he runs. She approaches the school gate, picking up her pace as it becomes apparent that Gaudyme will reach her before she crosses the threshold. For some reason she needs this small victory. Her steps come quicker, until she's nearly jogging. Still, Gaudyme catches her just before she passes the gate.

"You used your spirit energy!" Lo snaps.

"I had to catch you," he exclaims. "You were walking so fast! Why didn't you wait for me? I would've waited for you."

"Every day, Gaudyme! Every day you ask that and every day I tell you the same thing! I don't care! Be on time!"

Lo storms into the school, Gaudyme on her heels. "That's not nice! You told Principal Uricine that you would be nice from now on, remember?"

Lo takes a breath, trying to control her anger. "I didn't tell him I would be nice, I told him I wouldn't be mean. There's a difference."

"Well, leaving me is very mean!"

Lo reaches her locker, taking out her books and folders. "It was a dumb agreement, anyway. Just because you so happened to fall down the stairs after saying something stupid doesn't mean I pushed you."

"But you did push me," Gaudyme says innocently.

"But Principal Uricine doesn't know that! It's so unfair that he wants me to take anger management classes."

Lo finishes at her locker and the two reach a fork, diverging a step before Gaudyme stops. "Where are you going?" he asks. Breakfast is this way."

"Skipping breakfast today," Lo says. "I have to go finish my homework for history."

"Oh. I would help but, you know. Food." With that, Gaudyme heads toward the cafeteria. After snagging all the food the cafeteria staff will let him get away with, he spots a classmate. "You dropped something, Hugo," Gaudyme says, taking a seat beside him.

Hugo cocks his giant head to look beneath the table, searching the area. As his attention is diverted Gaudyme pilfers the breakfast pastry off his tray. "Where?" Hugo asks.

"Oh, must've been nothing," Gaudyme says, mouth full of pastry.

"Ugh. Why do you always do that?"

"Do what?"

"Whatever." Hugo takes a bite of his apple. His voice drops to a whisper. "Hey, can I ask you something? Is it cool eating in the ryken lunchroom?"

"What do you mean? There's food there, so yeah."

"No. I mean, what's it like? Do the ryken use their powers and stuff? It has to be awesome. I've always wanted to eat in there, but I can't because ryken are awful and everything."

"Ryken aren't really all that awful," Gaudyme says. "Take Samané, for instance—he's a cool guy. Just because we all know he's a ryken doesn't instantly make him bad."

"Maybe not. I don't want to take the chance, though. If he does turn out to be super violent like the rest of them, I wouldn't want him breaking my arm or even killing me because I made him angry."

"Ryken aren't anything like that."

"Of course they are. Actually, you should be more careful. You keep hanging around Samané, it's only a matter of time before you pay for it." Gaudyme gets up, his food only half eaten. "Hey! Where're you going?"

"I've lost my appetite."

* * *

"The bell doesn't dismiss you!" Mr. Lache snaps. "I dismiss you!" The teacher stares at the class for a minute, the room silent. "Okay, go ahead."

The students rush to the doorway, squeezing through the wooden frame two at a time. Lo is in no rush since her next class is in the adjacent room. She approaches her teacher's desk. "Mr. Lache, I have a question about number twenty-one on the test. Can't the answer also be C?"

"For my test it says to choose the most correct answer. Although C is correct, D is more correct."

Lo's eyebrows knit. "I got the question wrong because I chose a right answer?"

"You got the question wrong for not choosing the most correct answer."

"That's stupid."

"I beg your pardon?"

"That's stupid," Lo snaps again, walking away. "If I'm going to fail a test, I could at least get the questions wrong." Mr. Lache says something in response, but Lo is already out of the door. *Why does everyone around me have to be an idiot? Even the teachers!* Lo bumps into another student, falling down. "Hey! Watch where you're—"

The handsome face of the culprit stops Lo's rage in her throat. It's the foreign exchange student from Tobble. His strong jawline and trimmed mustache give him an older, masculine look. His height and slender physique are just icing on the attractive cake.

"I'm so sorry," Fred says, extending his hand, scooping Lo up. "I didn't mean to knock you over. I'm just in a bit of a hurry. I'm still learning the school's layout."

"No. It's fine," Lo says, her face turning as red as her hair. "I should've been paying more attention."

"Are you okay?"

"I'm perfect now."

Fred hardly notices Lo's best smile as he starts back down the hall. "That's good. Sorry again."

Lo finds herself smiling at Fred's back. Maribel finds her too. "He's never going to give you the time of day with a smile like that," Maribel says.

Lo walks right by her. "Your shirt's on fire." Maribel looks down, noticing the bottom half of her shirt engulfed in flames. She shrieks, running down the hall.

Lo enters her class, a different sort of smile forming.

* * *

Gaudyme enters the room as the bell sounds. "Just in time, Mr. Admiratio," Mr. Trela says. "Take your seat."

Gaudyme looks to the only seat in the room available, the chair next to his arch-rival Emmon. The two squint at each other. To get him as a partner for dissection was the unluckiest thing ever. Gaudyme looks to Lo, who sits across the room.

To get Fred as a dissection partner was the luckiest thing ever. Stuff like this never worked out for Lo. As soon as the dissection topic was brought up she just knew she would get lumped up with Gaudyme. Or worse, Emmon. She steals a glance toward them, and both have their eyes set on her.

"Why did my love have to get grouped with that ugly foreign exchange kid?" Emmon asks himself aloud. "Because she's so kindhearted, she's acting as if she doesn't mind. But I know she wanted to be partnered with me."

"Stop calling her your love," Gaudyme says. "She's not yours."

"Well, she's definitely not yours."

"I never said she was. But at least I don't live in some kind of fantasy land where I think I'm with a girl who obviously hates me."

"Lo doesn't hate me! She just hasn't understood her love for me yet. But she will."

"Not if I have anything to say about it," Gaudyme mutters to himself.

Across the room Lo reads the instructions. "Make an incision where the X is marked on the frog's belly."

Fred cuts the amphibian open. "Poor frog," he says. "It's so tragic that we have to experiment on these creatures. It just doesn't seem right."

Lo nods. "I completely agree! It's not nice. And I always try to be nice."

"I get why," Fred continues. "We have to experiment to get information, but is it really worth it?"

"Of course not! People are so self-centered. Just worried about themselves. Not me, though—I only care for others."

Fred smiles at her and she can't help but stare at his perfect face.

"Why are they just staring at each other?" Gaudyme asks Emmon. When he doesn't answer, Gaudyme turns to discover he's no longer beside him.

"I'll tell you what, foreign boy," Emmon says. "Swap partners with me and I won't have to beat you up." *Nailed it! This is exactly what Subnuba would do.*

Lo speaks through gritted teeth. "Emmon. Go sit down."

"Don't worry, my love. I'll take care of him." Emmon puts a hand on Fred's shoulder. "I warned you once; I'm not going to do it again."

"Could you not touch me, please?" Fred asks. "I'm trying to work."

"Maybe you didn't hear me. I said—" Emmon tries to turn Fred around, but he counters, slamming Emmon face-first into frog guts.

"No rough-housing!" Mr. Trela yells. "Emmon, sit down before I send you to the principal's office."

Fred releases Emmon as he spits out frog intestines, then slogs back to his chair, his head hanging. Fred returns to his seat as well.

"Marry me," Lo blurts.

"Huh?" Fred replies.

"What?"

Across the room Gaudyme laughs uncontrollably. Emmon scowls at him. "Well, at least I tried! You're just going to sit here and let Lo fall for another man?"

"Emmon," Gaudyme says, "my poor sap. You don't understand women at all. You have to relax. Don't let women know you're into them. Just become what they like."

"Become what they like?"

"Yeah. Some women like books. So become the book. Others like kittens, so become the kitten."

"Just like... transform into a... a kitten? How the heck do I do that?"

"*That* is the real question." Gaudyme winks and sits back proudly.

Emmon pauses, staring at Gaudyme blankly. "That's the smartest thing I've ever heard."

"I know, right?"

"Stop goofing off, you two!" Mr. Trela demands in passing. "Class is almost over and you haven't even started on your dissection."

"Oh crap, he's right!" Emmon exclaims.

"Quick," Gaudyme says, "you grab the notes and read them off. I'll do the cutting."

Emmon does as he's told, reading off the entire sheet in a minute. "There's no way we can do all this before class is over."

Gaudyme picks up the scalpel. He simply pokes the frog and all the pieces fall away just as the instructions directed—a flawless dissection. "H-How did you do that?" Emmon gapes.

Gaudyme pauses. He hadn't thought about explaining the maneuver. *Think, Gaudyme. Think! There has to be some realistic explanation for this that doesn't have to do with spirit energy. Come up with something. No matter what, don't say it's your ryken ability. Don't say it's your ryken ability. DON'T SAY IT'S YOUR RYKEN ABILITY!*

"It's my ryken ability."

Emmon tilts his head. "Huh?"

"What?"

* * *

On the second floor of the Alair household, Ventus and Subnuba spar. Subnuba tries a series of blows, but Ventus flows around his punches and kicks, evading in the ever-graceful, ever-infuriating way he always does. Ventus delivers a pump of wind to Subnuba's chest, sending him back into the wall, then to the floor. Subnuba's arm buckles under his weight as he tries to lift himself. Exhausted, he sags back to the floor.

"You're forcing things rather than allowing them to flow to you naturally," Ventus says.

"I don't need your lecturing," Subnuba snarls. "Just keep coming at me. That's the only way I'll get better."

"I respect your tenacity. It's how you've grown so quickly. Before much longer you'll be a powerful asset to Samané and the team."

"An asset to Lutrio is the last thing I want to be," Subnuba says, summoning the strength to rise to his feet.

"Well then, what is your reason for joining, if not that? Why have you chosen to fight beside Samané and the rest of us?"

To Ventus' surprise Subnuba doesn't already have an answer loaded. Instead, he thinks on the matter for a moment, then whips out a comb from his pocket, stroking it through his hair. "I joined to become stronger than Lutrio. He's had a head start with this whole ryken thing by a few years. But I'll catch and surpass him. I won't stop until I do."

Ventus frowns. "Do you want to kill Samané?"

"What? No! Well, I have thought about it once or twice." Ventus just stares at Subnuba. "It was a joke! Man, where's your sense of humor?"

"I don't joke about those kinds of things."

"You need to lighten up," Subnuba says, stashing his comb away. "Life has to be pretty boring being so serious all the time. Anyway, why did you join? You have to have something you're fighting for too."

Ventus takes a moment, but unlike Subnuba, it's to contemplate if he'll answer the question. He decides to oblige. "Initially, I was unsure of why I joined, or better yet, why I had the urge to do so. The feeling was unfamiliar, but when Samané came to me I knew I had to join. Something in my head just told me it was right, but I was so used to that same voice telling me otherwise that I rejected his offer at first. Luckily for me he insisted and despite my own feelings, I finally agreed. Since then I've developed a camaraderie with you all that I would've never gained otherwise."

Subnuba surprises himself with his interest in Ventus' vulnerability, although Ventus is so engrossed in his response that he seems to forget Subnuba is even there. "For that reason, I'm very grateful to have met Samané," Ventus continues. "I cannot thank him enough for the purpose he's given me. I'm honored to fight beside him in whatever way he asks."

Subnuba rolls his eyes. "What a bummer. You had me until all that Lutrio mushy crap."

Ventus takes his stance. "If that's the case, perhaps we should start again. Are you ready for another round?"

"See, that's why I like you," Subnuba says, smiling. "You're always there when I need a sparring partner."

Just as Subnuba takes his stance, someone emerges from the staircase.

"Did you skip school again to train, Subnuba?" Lo snaps.

"Great. Exactly who we needed to ruin our session. And why do you care if I'm in school or not? I didn't realize I had two mothers."

"Because when you aren't there, Emmon practically stalks me! You should've seen the stunt he pulled in lab. Keep that kid on a leash."

Subnuba chuckles. "Ah, Emmon. The kid is hopeless."

"I figured you two would take the day off since training is cancelled," Ventus says.

"What?" Gaudyme cries. "Training is cancelled today? I could've gone to Taco House with Hugo! His uncle's the owner and on Taco Tuesdays we can eat for free!"

"Don't you think you're being a bit dramatic?" Ventus asks once Gaudyme starts crying. In response, Gaudyme throws his arms up and starts running in circles.

"Socius, do something about your boyfriend," Subnuba says. "He's distracting me and Erubesco."

"He's not my boyfriend," Lo scowls.

Ventus is bemused. "Oh? Subnuba told me you two were lovers. Unless that is the case and you both are still open to meeting others."

"No!" Lo yelps, red-faced. Subnuba explodes with laughter. His bliss is cut short, however, when he becomes frozen in a giant block of ice. "There! That ought to teach him about spreading rumors."

Ventus scratches his head. "It wasn't true?"

"No! None of it! All lies!" Lo takes a breath. "Word of advice, Ventus. Never listen to Subnuba."

Gaudyme finally stops running. He puts his hands on his knees, panting. "Taco. Tuesday."

Suddenly, a huge crack appears down the center of Lo's capturing ice. After another second the ice explodes, sending icicles and shards everywhere. Gaudyme is cut by two bits, Lo melts another four and Ventus uses a gust of wind to disperse the shards headed toward him.

"I hate it when you do that," Subnuba growls.

She smiles. "Don't even think about it. We're still on different levels. Don't make me actually hurt you." Subnuba extends his arm toward her, palm glowing. "Is that supposed to scare me?"

"Baneful Blast!"

Ryken Hunters

Samané sits up, yawning and stretching after a decent night's rest. Once he wipes the sleep from his eyes he looks around, remembering he's not home. *That's right. Noctuama let me stay the night. Still doesn't make up for her refusing to join us. But this couch is comfy, at least.*

Samané makes his way toward Noctuama's room. He moves slowly, unfamiliar with the house, faintly lit by the dawning sun. When he reaches her room, he finds it vacant. He navigates his way back through the entire house until he confirms that she's gone. "What a hostess," Samané thinks aloud. "She didn't even offer me breakfast."

After gathering the valued books of Xenesis, Samané begins his trek to Centrum City, hiking back down the rocky hillside. The light of the morning sun makes his descent much easier than his trip up a dozen hours earlier. Soon Samané is off the giant hill and back on a level road.

I don't know what I should make of this situation, Samané thinks. *She kind of seems like she's into me. But at the same time, it's hard to tell. I mean, she denied my request to join the Novice Pack and then left without even waking me. I can't figure her out. I wonder if all women are this mysterious. Maybe she's just playing hard to get.* Samané's brows knit. *I don't have time for games! Come on, let's grow up. I'm almost out of high school and she must be older than I am; we should be past that. Maybe I'm just overreacting. She might just genuinely not be into me.* Samané sighs. "What a bummer."

"I can tell by your sigh that you're having girl issues, aren't you?"

Samané snaps around, his defenses up. There stands a man. Samané studies him, vaguely cognizant that he's seen him somewhere prior. Regardless of where their last engagement was, the man can't be here on good terms. "Who are you?" Samané asks nonchalantly.

"You don't recognize me?" he asks. "How soon you Xarnes forget."

Samané frowns. "Hmm. I think I do remember you." The man smirks, stashing a lock of his stringy blonde hair behind his ear. He then swings his arm around, loosening his rotator cuff. The stranger's relaxed disposition gives Samané a bit of unease. "No gun this time?"

The man's smirk widens into a smile with a set of teeth more yellow than his hair. "No. We've got something a bit more effective this time around."

"We?"

"Go ahead, forfeit our element of surprise," another man says, emerging from Samané's flank. He's a heavy-set man with the shadow of hair on the lower half of his face, but nothing atop his head. He has a colorful assortment of tattoos circling down his left arm and a large ring embedded in his right ear lobe. "Real smart, Hontale."

Ryken hunters, Samané thinks, repositioning himself for a better defense. *Two of them, like last time. I can't rule out the possibility there may be more, though. I don't like it. These guys are way too confident. What're they hiding?*

Hontale shrugs. "We did that last time and you see how far it got us, Rusco. Things are different now, we have—"

"No-no-no!" Rusco shouts. "Don't say it. We don't need to reveal our entire hand."

"Relax. You're too high-strung. All I was going to say is we have spirit energy."

Rusco slaps a hand to his forehead. "Why can nothing stay a secret with you?"

"What do you mean, you have spirit energy?" Samané asks. "If that's the case, you must be some pretty confused ryken to call me a Xarnes."

"We're not ryken," Hontale says. "We just have spirit energy."

Samané flips the idea over in his head a few times, their claim making less and less sense each time. "Humans with spirit energy? Sounds like ryken to me."

"A foolish analysis. There're bigger differences between ryken and humans aside from spirit energy. According to Dr. Killinger there's a fundamental DNA difference that separates the two of us."

Okay, Samané reasons. *I have two choices. I can leave right now and get home safely, or I can stay and fight. Something tells me if they found me a second time out here, nothing will stop them from coming back a third. Plus, what better place could I find to beat up alleged humans without the consequence of witnesses and law enforcement?* Samané takes his stance. "Let's get to the bottom of this spirit energy thing."

"That's what I like to see," Rusco says. "You ready, Hontale?"

"You're actually going to let me give it a shot alone first?" Hontale asks, incredulously.

"It was the doctor's call. Claims it's a valuable opportunity for data."

"Can't argue with the doc. You'll have to excuse me if I'm a bit sloppy, Xarnes. All of this speed and strength is still new to me."

If Samané had any doubts about the ryken hunters' claim to spirit energy, Hontale's power up puts them to rest. Hontale clenches his fists and flexes his muscles, and his spirit energy flashes into existence. The foreboding sensation is familiar and, at the same time, totally new. To Samané, it feels wrong, like being able to see with your tongue or smelling with your ears. It's as if Samané's sixth ryken sense is attempting to convey how unnatural the presence of spirit energy is in a human.

Suddenly, Hontale is on him, his punches and kicks driving Samané back. Spirit energy may grant a person greater abilities, but technique isn't one of them. Hontale moves with the fluency, accuracy and confidence of a veteran fighter. When Samané's back touches the rocky hill, a spin saves him from having his head embedded in the stone. Instead, Hontale's fist demolishes a small section of the hill's foundation, causing a miniature rockslide. Hontale retreats to avoid the falling boulders and smaller stones. Samané observes the destruction, unable to believe his eyes. *A human caused that with his bare fists.*

"This all feels so incredible," Hontale says, examining his own hands. "The power. If this is how you Xarnes feel all the time I almost don't blame you for being the animals you are. Of course you will resort to violence to solve all your problems; it's what you do best. It's what you were designed to do by Nature. But now we have the blueprints and we're going to use them for humankind's sake. We should thank you. If not for your DNA sample, none of this would be possible."

"You're monologuing again," Rusco cuts in.

"Can you blame me? This is our debut, the beginning of a new era! Let me have some fun."

"This shouldn't be possible," Samané hears himself thinking aloud.

"This wouldn't be the first time Dr. Killinger redefined what the world deems possible. To reverse-engineer a ryken's ability is something straight out of science fiction. Yet here we are."

Hontale lunges, causing Samané to backpedal. His hands are a blur, stinging Samané's palm with every block and smarting his forearm with every deflection. Hontale's attack ends when a backhanded blow creates an opening and he drives his fist into Samané's chest. Samané is thrown backwards and tumbles on the barren ground, kicking up a cloud of dust behind him.

Hontale looks at his fist in disbelief. "The power!" He tips his head back, reveling in the moment.

Rusco doesn't share his friend's excitement. *The ryken has yet to throw one punch,* he thinks.

The shot to his chest hurts; there is no reason to deny it. In fact, it hurts more than Samané anticipated. But it's far from what Kato can dish out.

A human with spirit energy. Bizarre is a gross understatement of the phenomenon. Data, information, experience—it's important that Samané use this precious opportunity to glean all he can from the humans to take back to Kato and get his thoughts on the situation. Unfortunately for the ryken hunters, however, Samané has analyzed enough.

He rises to his feet.

* * *

Four hours Callisto has been waiting. And he will wait many more if he must, as many as it takes. Colonel Calamity arrived late to his office this morning and even though Callisto managed to crowbar himself into Calamity's appointments, it doesn't seem he is as anxious to discuss Amica as Callisto. In all fairness, there's almost no way he could be as anxious. Even exhausted from the day-long trip yesterday, Callisto couldn't sleep much. He tried lying down for a few hours, but when sleep eluded him, he walked. He rehearsed his pitch to Colonel Calamity until he felt it was perfect. Over and over, anticipating a variety of his responses, until he felt confident. Or at least confident enough to sleep. And so he finally did.

When Callisto closed his eyes, he figured he'd dream of his impending conversation with Calamity that weighed so heavily on his mind. Or even the potential Excessum battle on the horizon. But instead, Callisto dreamt of Prix and King Atrium. Callisto dreamt that Prix was following him around everywhere repeating, "Sorry." Callisto ignored him, of course. Time sped by, years in a matter of seconds, but still Prix never stopped. That only made Callisto angrier because it was considerably harder to condemn him for something he was sincerely remorseful about. Eventually, the years took their toll and Callisto's appearance changed. When he looked in the mirror it was King Atrium who stared back at him. Callisto started to apologize, but when he opened his mouth, it was Samané's voice he heard expressing regret. The reflection spit on him in response. It was then that Callisto woke up.

Finally, after five hours Callisto is invited into Calamity's office. He nearly knocks the secretary over in his haste to enter. "Sir," Callisto says, forcing himself still despite his jittery nerves.

Calamity's feet are on his desk and a newspaper in his hands. "What can you do for me?"

"I'm Callisto Socius. Righthand recruit from division 1a. I've returned from Amica."

"Uh-huh," Calamity says inattentively, turning the page of his newspaper. "And what were you doing there?"

Callisto had hoped for a better opening to the conversation, but that didn't mean he hadn't planned for a bad one. "Sir, you sent me on the mission to find out if Amica is worth saving. I'm the recruit who challenged you in court."

Calamity folds his newspaper down. "Ah yes. You're the spunky one. I respect you. I couldn't tell you at the time because there were too many witnesses, but to speak out like you did took guts. Of course, if you ever do it again I'll have your badge stripped and you'll be thrown in prison for contempt of court, but that's a minor detail. Anyway, Amica trip. What about it?"

"Nothing, sir. You were right. There's nothing Amica offers that Laevus doesn't already have or can't take if they wanted. The treaty would be a liability."

"My thoughts exactly. You're a smart man to agree with me. Especially since I was planning to let the kingdom rot, regardless."

"Clearly it's the best move for Laevus," Callisto says.

"And what could be more important than that? You've done well, Mamisto."

"Uh, it's Callisto, sir."

"That's what I said." Calamity picks his newspaper back up. "Is that all?"

Callisto bows. "Yes sir."

"Very well, you're dismissed."

Callisto rotates on his heel, taking a step before stopping. "Oh, there is this small thing I forgot to mention."

"Hmm?"

"During my time in Amica, there was an incident with the Excessum."

Calamity folds his newspaper back down. "Go on."

"They killed the Amican Protector, Grade, and left a message behind. In short, they plan to ravage the kingdom and advised that Laevus stand down if we don't want trouble as well."

"Advised? Stand down? Trouble?" Calamity growls, his voice becoming hoarser after every word.

"That's correct, sir."

Calamity's feet come off his desk and he sits up. "The Excessum," he spits. "You give them an inch and they take a mile! Who do those punks think they are, threatening the most powerful nation on the planet? They've forgotten the power of our commander. The power of Colonel Calamity! Who issued the threat?" he barks, all but slobbering.

Callisto does well to not turn and flee from his fury. "I didn't see him myself, but apparently it was a slender, pale man with sharp teeth."

"Doesn't sound like one of the Prime Excessum." Calamity frowns. "If that's the case there's no reason for me to go down. Take whomever your commanding general is and get back there ASAP. Remind the Excessum that we control the world. If there's trouble, it's because we have caused it. They won't get their hands on Amica as long as I'm a colonel of Laevus."

"Yes sir." Callisto turns, unable to control his smile. He is stopped by the colonel before exiting.

"Don't you dare lose."

Callisto had almost forgotten. This was the easy part.

* * *

Hontale and Samané stare one another down. Hontale opens and closes his fingers in his excitement. "Let's try this again," Hontale says, engaging.

"Sloppy," Samané observes. He sidesteps Hontale's punch and delivers one of his own, hard to the stomach. A two-handed, overhead blow to Hontale's back slams him into the ground with devastating force. A few more boulders tumble in the background, adding to the rockslide from earlier. Samané waits until all is quiet again before he speaks. "You can't win."

"Don't be too sure," Rusco says, swinging from Samané's blind spot. Though expected, his approach is quicker than Samané anticipates and the only way to defend himself is to back away from Hontale. When Rusco is satisfied he stops throwing punches, retreating. Once beside his comrade, he kneels. Samané looks for an opening in his guard, but Rusco never takes his eyes off him.

Soon, Rusco and Hontale are back on their feet. Samané's blow was strong, but he held back; after all, he doesn't want to kill them. He notices the ease Hontale moves with as he flexes his arms and stretches, trying to work out the pain in his back. *I shouldn't have held back so much,* Samané concludes.

"I love this," Hontale says. "He punches a lot harder than you, Rusco, but my body just bounces back like it's nothing."

"Not if I punch you hard enough," Samané comments.

"No more one-on-ones, Hontale," Rusco says. "He held back. You're lucky he didn't bury you six feet under with one swing. We can't afford to take this Xarnes lightly."

Samané shrugs. "I'm glad at least one of you is perceptive."

Hontale's expression grows more serious. "You talk too much."

Both men lunge simultaneously, Rusco reaching Samané first. Although Rusco is quicker in foot speed, Hontale's punches come quicker. It becomes evident within a few seconds that the two are accustomed to fighting together. Samané tries a few defensive maneuvers that would tangle the two up, allowing him to take the offensive, but the hunters dance around each other with impressive chemistry.

The first punch Samané throws is a jab that hits Rusco's left eye. Samané is then taken down by a leg sweep a moment later, landing on his face. A roll, then Samané tries a backhanded blow that smashes into Hontale's chest despite his forearms held up in defense. He gets back to his feet, but Rusco is ready, landing four punches. By the fifth strike Samané reestablishes his footing, but Hontale comes from behind, locking Samané's arms. A hook to the face is the first blow of the hunters to draw blood. Before Rusco's next strike lands, a backwards headbutt to the nose causes Hontale to release Samané. He follows up with an elbow to the side that breaks a rib. Samané turns his attention back to Rusco, mid-punch. In a flash, Samané catches his fist and pulls him. This time Samané doesn't hold back.

The crack Rusco's jaw makes when struck is louder than Samané wanted. The speed at which he flies away is faster than Samané intended. And the impact he makes with the sheer hillside is enough to make Samané nervous. When the rocks that bury Rusco don't move after a minute, Samané is genuinely scared. To rough up a pair of ryken hunters outside the city with no witnesses is one thing. But a ryken killing a human anywhere in Laevus, under any circumstance, is a different matter altogether. As well it should be. Samané shouldn't have released his restraints so foolishly.

Suddenly, a sharp pain explodes down the back of Samané's leg. His vision wavers the hurt is so intense. He gasps as he falls to a knee. He sees Hontale clutching his side on the ground, attempting to stab again. This time Samané catches his hand and fires three controlled punches until Hontale's eyes roll to the back of his head. He sags to the earth as Samané releases him and tries to stand. The pain is too great. In a matter of seconds, the pulsing wound begins to make the world dance. Samané must get away, and quick, lest he pass out. Somewhere. Anywhere but here. He grits his teeth, summoning all his spirit energy.

"Hypersonic Dash."

One moment Samané is there, and the next he isn't.

<u>Episode 18:</u>

Blossoming Love

It feels like Samané is in a cramped box, even though it's just his leg that can't move. If he does try to reposition, an explosively sharp pain sets the lower quarter of his body aflame. So he stays still. Even asleep, his body knows to remain unmoving.

But eventually, Samané wakes.

"Hi there!" a girl greets him as soon as he opens his eyes. Samané rears back, startled, and immediately regrets it. He grunts through gritted teeth, wanting nothing more than the pain of his leg to subside. "Oh no, oh no, oh no," the girl repeats, running around the bedside.

Far too slowly, the mind-numbing pain dwindles enough for Samané to say, "Who are you?"

The girl retakes her seat by the bedside, her worried expression giving way to excitement. She sits upright, so much so that her back is arched. She is slender but curvaceous. Her skin is a perfect shade of brown, appearing golden in the areas where the sun peeks through the blinds. She tucks her dark brown hair behind an ear and flutters her eyelashes. "My name is Serena. And you are handsome."

Samané tilts his head. "I'm sorry?"

Serena coughs. "Had a tickle in my throat. What I meant to say was, and you are...?"

"Samané Lutrio." He goes to sit up in a more comfortable position but recalls the spasm of agony a minute prior and decides against it. "Thank you for your hospitality. I'm indebted to you."

Serena blushes. "Anything for my future husband."

"Your future what?"

Serena coughs again. She grabs a bottle of water from the nightstand and takes a sip. "Ah. Much better."

Samané offers Serena a suspicious look then relaxes his head back on his pillow. He tries to remember the events of yesterday, but his thoughts always come back to the pain of his leg. The knife used to cut him was undoubtedly drenched in akidiode. Never has Samané experienced pain so intense. Even when struck by Kato, who unarguably holds the record for the hardest punch landed on him, Samané didn't hurt nearly as bad as now. When he is still there is only a dull throb, but should Samané move his leg at all, it feels as if his entire thigh is skinless, naked and tender before the world.

Samané manages to get a hand down to the bandages wrapping his leg. A fine job from what he can tell. "I've changed your bandages twice already, applying a disinfecting ointment both times," Serena says, watching him. "I'm not an expert at stuff like this, but your bleeding has slowed down since. Plus, you don't have a fever, so I must be doing something right."

Samané smiles. "Thank you. I can't say it enough. I'm not sure what would have happened to me had you not come along."

"Tell me, are you a ryken?"

There's a hint of worry in Serena's expression. A part of Samané wants to spare her any headache from the implications of helping a ryken. But a larger part of him knows he should tell her the truth. He owes her that much. "Yes. I'm a ryken."

She puts her hands to her face. "I can't believe I've fallen in love with a ryken."

"What do you keep mumbling?" Samané exclaims.

"I love you," Serena replies, flatly.

"Uh..."

"I know it sounds crazy, but it's true! You're so darn adorable. And you've already thanked me twice for helping you. Plus, you're so darn adorable! How could I not be head over heels in love with you?"

Samané blinks twice. "...I'm uncomfortable."

* * *

"It's been over a day, Hunter," Nightshade hisses. "How much longer until we make our move?"

Hunter slings his head around, the black ropes of hair falling back over his shoulder. Nightshade, Metis and Napalm sit around the large table in the wooden cabin of the Excessum awaiting his response. "You're more restless than the rabble rousers. Why leave me in charge of timing this attack if you're going to try and rush my decision?"

"I figured you'd know better than me, but I'm beginning to regret it."

"Laevus has withdrawn for the time being but we need to be sure they won't come back. It's not like they will broadcast their abandonment of Amica. We need to pay attention and read between the lines. This step is very crucial."

"How much longer do we have to wait?" Napalm whines. "I want to fight!"

"In due time."

"How much time?" Nightshade asks.

Hunter sighs. "A week, at least."

"That's too long. By then Amica will mount some form of defense to wall us out."

"What fortress does Amica possess that is sufficient to withstand the might of us four?" Metis asks.

"They're desperate," Nightshade says. "A week would be enough time to establish a new deal with Laevus and get their protection. If that happens, then what?"

"Laevus won't come to their rescue, that much I assure you," Hunter says.

"Thanks to me," Nightshade snaps back.

Hunter freezes, a serious expression falling across his face. "What does that mean?"

"Because of me Laevus will be too scared to intervene again. I sent them a message and by the haste they left Amica in, they received it."

"What did you say?"

"What does it matter? They're—"

"What did you say!" Hunter yells, slamming his fist on the table.

Nightshade and Hunter glower at one another, their patience with the other running thin. "I don't need your ryken ability, Hunter, to inform you what Nightshade's message portrayed," Metis intervenes when it seems the two will come to blows. "He threatened them."

"I want to hear him say it," Hunter growls. "I want to hear him say how his obsession to be in control lost us our prey. I knew you were a fool, Shade, but this may be the dumbest thing you've ever done."

"I don't get it," Napalm says. "What's wrong with threatening them? It shows we aren't scared."

"It challenges them," Metis says.

Nightshade stands, turning his back to the others with a curse. "It's almost certain Laevus will return now to accept his foolish challenge," Hunter spits. "The only thing you had to do was keep surveillance with your shadows in the Amica Castle. No part of the plan involved you engaging directly."

"But I did." Nightshade turns around, defiantly. "Deal with it. Unless one of you wants to challenge me, I'm still in charge. If I don't make the best decisions, oh well. I'm calling the shots and you'll follow suit because if not," he smiles his sharp-toothed grin, "I'll kill you." Nightshade surveys his audience, taking note of Hunter's clenched fists. "No tough guys? Then shut up and listen. Here's our next move."

* * *

Akidiode is a chemical created for the sole purpose of neutralizing spirit energy. It can only be effective if the ryken consumes it or has it injected directly into their bloodstream. It's essentially a poison, mostly used to subdue ryken in prison. That is, of course, with the exception of the vigilante group known as ryken hunters. They use the chemical to wound or kill ryken, and unfortunately for Samané, he is their newest victim.

At least Samané escaped with his life. The same could not be said for the ryken hunter Rusco. Samané hadn't held back when he sent him into the mountainside. He'd hit a human with all his ryken strength. He knew better. Even if the scenario was unprecedented and Samané had to fight, going one hundred percent against humans spelled disaster for all parties involved. And now a man is dead because of it. No, Samané hadn't confirmed his death, but he has the sinking feeling in his gut that it's true. How could he condemn Metis for what he is doing, when Samané is doing the same? He's a killer. The Lutrio brothers both. *I wonder what Dad would say to us now.*

"Samané!" Serena calls out from the kitchen. "The food is ready!"

He swings his feet off the side of the bed. The akidiode is starting to wear off. Samané can move, slowly, but some progress is better than no progress. It's shocking how long the effects of the anti-energy fluid lasts, considering how little was used. Kato had given the Novice Pack a lesson on akidiode and because of that Samané has a rough timeline of what to expect out of the chemical. This time tomorrow he will probably be fully healed and back to normal, but the day drags. Pain does that to time.

This experience has opened Samané's eyes to pay more attention to Kato's lessons; they may save him one day. Still, it's one thing to hear about a particular subject and another thing entirely to experience that subject firsthand. In a way, he is thankful for being put through this ordeal.

Samané limps down the hall toward the dining room. He rounds the corner to see a buffet of food sprawled out on the table. He can only gape as Serena places the last dish down. "Well, eat up!"

"Who's all this food for?"

"Us, silly. You need your nutrients to be a big, strong ryken, right?"

"I can't eat all of this!"

"Hmm. I guess I did go a bit overboard." Her eyes start to water. "I just wanted to impress you, is all."

Samané holds his hands up. "It's okay. No big deal. What we don't eat, we'll have tomorrow. I don't mind leftovers."

She smiles. "You're so sweet. Sit down, husband. Let me get you something to drink."

Serena scurries back into the kitchen and Samané takes his seat. *She has got to stop calling me that. I'm only seventeen, I'm not ready to get married. How can Serena be so into me, anyway? I admit, it's flattering. She is cute. Really cute. But she doesn't even know me! Why is she doing all of this for someone she doesn't even know? I need to let her down easy. But how?*

Serena renters with tea, setting a cup on her side of the table then one on Samané's. When she sits Samané says, "Serena..."

She stiffens. "Oh no, there's somebody else, isn't there?"

That's it! "Yeah," Samané says, exaggerating his sadness. "I tried to tell you earlier, but I didn't know how."

Serena bites her lip. "What's her name?"

"Noctuama," Samané says reflexively.

"How long have you two been," she cringes, "a couple?"

Samané scratches his head. "Well, it's not official yet, but—"

Serena perks up. "So there's still hope?"

"Depends on what you mean by hope."

"I'll tell you what, you continue to chase her, and I'll chase you. First to catch their love is the winner. Deal? Great!"

"That's kind of a weird agreement, don't you think?"

Serena shrugs. "Things are only weird if you make it that way."

She begins humming to herself as she eats, dismissing the conversation. Samané picks up his fork and stabs the potatoes on his plate. *I'm not chasing Noctuama. Yeah, I went searching for her after the tournament, and asked her to join the Novice Pack even though I don't know anything about her, and I daydream about her occasionally. That doesn't mean I'm chasing her!*

Ugh. That's exactly what that means. But what Serena is doing is way different! She's being crazy. Saving my life, nursing me back to health, feeding me. She's insane! Samané puts a hand to his head, stressed. He raises his eyes to Serena and she looks up, offering a beautifully innocent smile. ...*Maybe I'm the crazy one.*

* * *

In the morgue, King Atrium views the body of Grade Culminary for the third time and still he's no closer to accepting his fate. This time around Atrium ordered the mortician and his staff away. Alone with the shell of his dearest friend, he allows his tears to reluctantly fall. Atrium vehemently hates this world, despite the fact he knows Grade wouldn't approve. He can't help it, and now he no longer has Grade here to advise him otherwise.

"These ungrateful citizens only curse that which I give them," Atrium says to Grade's corpse, "claiming the water provided is diseased and the wind wicked in nature. I've wasted years of my life giving this kingdom all of me and they've done nothing more than spit in my face. These citizens have killed the old king and appointed a bitter, selfish replacement on the throne. Now they have a right to rebel against what I've become. The king of this nation is doomed and tortured beyond measure. What man would desire this throne?"

Atrium pauses as if the corpse will reply and although it doesn't, Atrium knows what Grade's response would be. "Surely the kingdom is worth saving. Why else would I have died protecting it?"

"For Isabella," Atrium answers. "She singlehandedly keeps this country from devouring itself. I try to warn her, just as my father warned me, that these people aren't worth saving. Those who would take joy in seeing your blood spilled aren't worth sacrificing yourself for. But she's even more determined to restore this kingdom than I was. I don't want them to turn her into what I am today."

"I protected the kingdom for our future generations," Grade's corpse replies. "Not for the Amica today, but what the Amica of tomorrow could be. And I would sacrifice myself again, ten times over, so Isabella, Rhys, and many other kids may have the opportunity to succeed where we failed."

"Or fail themselves."

"But they deserve that chance."

Atrium grips the wooden handles of Grade's coffin so hard his knuckles turn white. After he releases it, he nods solemnly. "In your honor, I'll give them that chance."

* * *

"Are you really serious about coming back to Centrum City with me?" Samané asks over breakfast.

"Of course I am," Serena says.

"Where are you going to stay? My mom isn't going to be cool with you shacking up with us."

"I'll just have my parents send me some money for a hotel. It's simple."

"They'll just send you thousands for a hotel when you have a perfectly good house to live in here?"

Serena shrugs. "They'll be glad I finally found my husband and am getting out of the house."

Samané puts his fork down. "Listen, Serena. You've got to stop saying stuff like that. It makes you sound crazy."

She tilts her head. "But I'm not crazy."

"That's exactly what a crazy person would say."

"And a sane one."

Samané raises an eyebrow. "Valid point."

"I know I'm coming off a bit strong. I can't help it. I've never felt this way before. Most of the guys I run into are disgusting or weirdos. I'm not desperate, I just really like you."

Samané studies Serena's expression, her lips pursed in the cutest way as she awaits his response. How could he not respect her ambition, boldness and honesty? "Okay, okay. If you can promise to work on your presentation, I don't see any harm in being friends."

"And future lovers?"

"Stop saying stuff like that!"

Serena giggles, offering Samané the subtlest of winks.

Episode 19:

A Friend to the End

Kato scratches his head. "Let me get this straight. You went on a recruiting mission to bring back a human that provides the team with no foreseeable tactical advantage? Why?"

"This wasn't my original plan," Samané says. "I wanted to recruit a ryken, but things didn't exactly work out."

"You're being awfully secretive about your prospected Novice Pack candidate," Ventus says. "Can't you tell us their name?"

"Noctuama," Samané says, after a moment's hesitation.

"We don't need her," Serena snaps. "You'll all see I'm a much better girlfriend for Samané."

"Serena, could you not—"

"Oh, I see what's happening," Kato says with a giddy grin. "If one woman doesn't work, you snatch up another! It seems you've been paying attention to my lessons after all."

Samané sighs. "No, it's not like th—"

"Who knew Samané was so good with the ladies?" Gaudyme says in wonderment.

Lo folds her arms across her chest. "Jumping from one girl to the next isn't something to be proud of."

"If you guys would just listen—" Samané starts.

"I guess Lutrio does have *some* skills," Subnuba says, reluctantly.

"If I'm following correctly, you two are a couple?" Ventus asks after much consideration.

"Yes!" Serena exclaims, smiling.

"No!" Samané shouts. "No, we aren't a couple. We're just friends. You hear me? Just. Friends. Nothing more."

"He's just being modest. Taking things slow. He's so dreamy." Serena goes to lock arms with Samané, but he wiggles free of her grasp.

"I'm not being modest. I'm not taking things slow. I'm not into you!"

The room freezes, everyone's attention on Serena. Her smile remains obliviously unchanged. When Samané looks over, she winks and blows him a kiss. Ventus shakes his head, saying, "Relationships are confusing."

"Can we please move on?" Samané asks, sweat forming on his forehead.

"That's probably a good idea," Kato says. "I want to hear more about the ryken hunters you encountered, anyway."

Samané nods. "I thought my first run-in with them was by chance, but they had to have been keeping some type of surveillance to track me so far from Centrum City. These guys are targeting me."

"Which means you all may be on their radar as well." Kato strokes his stubbly beard thoughtfully. "They probably won't make a move on the rest of you because you aren't confirmed ryken, but be on guard just in case. From the sound of things, if any of you had taken a wound with that much akidiode, you probably wouldn't be here today. Samané was lucky to make it out."

"My husband is so strong," Serena purrs.

Samané ignores her. "There was something else too. It'll sound crazy, but it is what it is. The ryken hunters had spirit energy."

Kato raises a brow. "They had what?"

"That was my reaction too. Granted, it didn't feel exactly like ours, but they had spirit energy. And the physical abilities that come with it. Everything but a ryken ability, anyway."

Kato puts a hand to his forehead despairingly. "That Dr. Killinger just won't give up. Wait until Oki hears about this one."

"So what do you think?"

"To be honest, I'm not sure yet. I want to think on it before I start proposing random theories. Let me run this by Oki; in the meantime, you all can start your training session or whatever."

Kato heads for the exit, but before he makes it down the staircase Samané stops him, coming closer. His voice low, he says, "What do you know about the Books of Xenesis?"

Kato frowns. "They're books from a fantasy land. I've run into a handful of people who swear they exist, but I wouldn't take their word for it. They're a myth. Not real."

"This isn't real?" Samané reveals the Book of Xenesis in his possession. The dull appearing tome seems to have an inner glow once revealed. The inherent value of the book is unexplainable, yet undeniable.

Kato's awed expression reflects the grandeur of the book. His eyes move to Samané's, deadly serious. He points to the hidden chamber of his second floor. "Lock it away."

* * *

"Amicaaa!" Nightshade shouts from the roof of the second tallest building in the Amica Kingdom. The once-small crowd has grown quite substantially after having stood on the building's edge for nearly a half hour. Initially the spectators believed he was a jumper. When they find out his true intentions they won't be nearly as entertained.

Seven other shadowed silhouettes of various sizes and shapes rise on the rooftops of nearby buildings. Nightshade's voice booms from each one. "Behold today, the might of the Excessum! Amica has something the Excessum seeks and so we will take it! If you're smart, you will stand down and let us proceed as we see fit! If not, this kingdom will burn before the day's end!"

Amica begins to hum with apprehensive murmurs. In the distance Nightshade can see troops already filing out of the Amica Castle. "Why resist?" Nightshade hisses across Amica. "It doesn't make any sense to think you could oppose us. Have we not instilled enough respect in you, enough fear? Maybe it's because you don't believe us. Or maybe you don't recognize my face, although I can promise you after today you won't forget it. I am Nightshade, humble servant of Misery. It is through him, and by the power of our Lord Divineum, I declare the fall of Amica!"

Nightshade's shadows vanish and his attention is carried to the roof of the Amica Castle's center tower. He glares at the three men on the edge of the only building in the kingdom dwarfing the one he stands upon. Even at this distance Nightshade can confirm the identity of the stern, dignified man in the middle. "Jove the Legislator," he hisses.

Likewise, on the roof of the great Amica Castle, Jove glares at Nightshade. "He's the one. He is mine and mine alone." Jove turns away, heading back inside, Callisto and Prix following subserviently. "Disobey my order this time and he'll make sure you never live to talk about it." He stops before Princess Isabella. "The King?"

Isabella's face is flushed from a mixture of panic, frustration, anger and gratefulness. The last, solely belonging to Callisto. He kept his word. Because of it, Isabella too has a chance to keep hers to the kingdom. It's almost funny that her ability to achieve this is also up to Callisto. Callisto, Prix and General Jove—everything she loves is in their hands now. "Apparently he's locked himself in his chambers and refuses to come out. If you need him, I'll have someone break down the door and just deal with the consequences when we survive this."

"No need," Jove replies. "He's doing us a favor. He's staying out of the way, purposely. I'd even dare to say he's leaving things to you."

Isabella gapes. "T-to me?" She shakes her head after a second. It's now or never. Today, Amica either rises up or is devoured by the world. She can't have it fall. Not under her command. "You three handle the Excessum as you see fit. I'll move the citizens to a haven and manage the troops to put down the rabble rousers in the city. There's so much more to see to and not much time. Let's get moving. We have a kingdom to save!"

Jove bows. "As you command."

Prix and Jove head down the stairs but Callisto hesitates. "Be careful," he says.

Isabella nods, a determined gleam in her eye. "You too."

When Callisto departs, Isabella turns toward her frantic kingdom, a fire already roaring in the distance. "I will save you."

* * *

"You guys are still here?" Gaudyme asks Subnuba and Ventus after climbing the stairs to the Alair household second floor. Subnuba rests on a knee, breathing heavily, in a full sweat. To Gaudyme's surprise, Ventus appears out of breath as well, a feat he knows Subnuba couldn't accomplish a week ago.

"We are," Ventus says, simply.

"Last one," Subnuba says, standing.

"You said that last round," Ventus replies.

"That was before you busted my lip. Last one."

"Very well."

Gaudyme rolls his eyes and proceeds over to the stainless white wall. He places his hand against it, feeling carefully for the hidden button. When he finds it he impatiently presses three times in quick succession. A second passes before a square section of wall to the left begins to vibrate and move aside, revealing the small chamber beyond. Gaudyme immediately spots what brought him back after getting all the way home. On top of a ragged workout bench is the strawberry-filled pastry Gaudyme was saving for his post-workout snack. His mouth begins to water when he scoops it up. Before he knows it, the entire treat is sliding down his throat; he barely tastes it. Still, the little bit he does taste is enough to make his journey worthwhile.

The treat consumed, Gaudyme starts to leave, but something catches his attention. A book, surprisingly enough, considering how much he hates reading. A very old book by the looks of it. With a simple touch, however, Gaudyme can feel its immense value. It's as if with the simple connection his soul resonates with the tome.

Gaudyme marvels at the book, trying to recall where he'd glimpsed it prior. "This is Samané's," he remembers aloud. "He probably forgot it. Luckily he's got good ol' Gaudyme Admiratio as a friend to watch his back. He'll be so happy when I give this to him. He'll say, 'Forget Callisto! From this day forth, you're my best and most favorite friend for all eternity!'"

With a nod, Gaudyme stashes the thick book in his jacket and exits the room and floor, the grunts of Subnuba's and Ventus' sparring sounding off in the background. "Man, how much longer are those two going to go at it?" Gaudyme wonders aloud as he leaves the house. "I have to admit Subnuba is getting stronger, but it just seems like a weird friendship. It's not like I'm jealous that Ventus, super cool wind god, would rather spar with Subnuba than have tacos with me. It's okay, I've still got Lo. Even though she never wants to do anything fun and she always yells at me. That's better than nothing." He sighs. "I wish I was more like Samané. His new girlfriend seems really awesome. I can't believe I never noticed how smooth he is with the ladies! He constantly pushes Serena off him and she always comes back. Wait! Do girls actually respond to being unwanted?"

Crossing through a small park near Samané's house, Gaudyme suddenly feels very uncomfortable. He stops, hand on the hilt of his sword, listening to the night around him. A while passes before he discovers the reason for his uneasiness. An adolescent boy, around Gaudyme's age, emerges from the shade of night. He's Gaudyme's height but has a far more muscular build. Not too brawny, yet clearly the bruiser type. His hair is full, sitting atop his head like an auburn-colored lion's mane. His most fascinating feature, however, is his pupil-less eyes. Despite their absence, in his stare there is purpose.

"You have something of mine," the stranger says.

Gaudyme looks around, confused. "Me?"

"Don't play stupid," he snaps. "That book is mine and you stole it. Give it back. Or I'll take it back."

"Look man, I have no idea what you're talking about. This book belongs to a friend of mine and I know he didn't steal it from you. I don't know what else to tell you."

Gaudyme starts to walk when the stranger speaks out again. "Give back the book or face the wrath of Roye Amari. This is your final warning."

"I told you already, this isn't my book to give you. If you want it, you have to ask Samané."

"I think I'll just take it from you instead," Roye growls.

Almost before Gaudyme can draw the blade from his back, Roye's fist screams toward him. Flesh and metal meet and Gaudyme's arms buckle then give way under Roye's force. The flat of Gaudyme's blade slams across his chest, the impact sending him sprawling away, barely able to hold on to his sword. Blinking away the pain, he puts a hand to his chest, sure the blow would've crumpled his body had it connected directly. *This guy might be as strong as Samané. Still,* Gaudyme thinks as he rises again, *he's not getting this book.*

"You're weak," Roye says with a confused expression.

"You won't say that after this. Flashing Sunder!"

Gaudyme lunges and his sword is a blur. He whips the polished metal around with fluid dexterity, the tiny sonic booms of his blade cracking at every swipe. As wondrous as Gaudyme's movement is, Roye isn't impressed, and more disturbingly, isn't cut. He dodges every swing flawlessly and when Gaudyme's last stab misses, he realizes the gravity of his situation. *I'm outmatched...*

As hard as reality hits Gaudyme in that moment, Roye hits him harder. A punch, square to the sternum, sends Gaudyme sailing through the air. He tumbles into a fence on the edge of the park. He rests against it, trying to pull his mind away from the pain and toward a solution. *I can't win this, but I'm not giving Samané's book away either. That's not an option. If he wants it this bad, then it's probably just as important to Samané too. I won't be the one who loses Samané's most treasured possession. If that happened Samané would never prefer me to Callisto!* Gaudyme stands, the pain in his chest unbearable. *If I'm not giving up the book and I can't win this fight, there's only one thing left to do.*

Gaudyme makes a break for it, running as fast as his legs will carry him. Unfortunately, he only takes a dozen steps before his collar is grabbed and he is yanked back.

"Give me the book!" Roye demands.

"I can't," Gaudyme wheezes, the pain of his chest making it hard to speak. "It isn't mine!"

Roye grabs Gaudyme's arm, forcing him to the ground. "I'd rather not do this, but you're giving me no other option. Hand it over or I'll break your arm."

"I ca—"

There is a crack that stops Gaudyme's response in his throat. The scream that follows is sure to wake neighbors for miles around. The two stay frozen in their positions; the only sound in the wake of Gaudyme's earsplitting scream is his pained whimpering.

"What other choice did I have Dagon?" Roye whispers. A few more of Gaudyme's whimpers pass then Roye barks, "Fine! Don't answer me then."

Roye releases Gaudyme's left arm, cringing as it flops back by his side. He turns Gaudyme over onto his back, noticing his more infrequent whimpers as he slips into unconsciousness. Roye searches Gaudyme's jacket, finding the ancient text stashed away inside a large pocket along the side. Just as he removes it, Gaudyme weakly grabs his arm. "Please don't. It's Samané's book."

Roye wrestles free of Gaudyme's grip and stands. "No. It belongs to the Guardians of Xenesis."

Excessum Versus Ryken Squad

Jove, Prix and Callisto stand outside the gates of the Amica Castle, in the heart of the Amica Kingdom. Those on the roads scurry past with purpose, intent on finding a safe place for themselves or getting home to family. Shouting, pointing, pushing, running—*Chaos,* Callisto thinks. Pandemonium would be a better description if Callisto hadn't already used the word to characterize what was going on farther from the castle. Moving away from Amica's center, almost uniformly, the hysteria increases. In the distance Callisto can hear explosions, the work of a ryken's ability.

Jove starts forward, Callisto and Prix following, until Jove extends a hand. The two freeze instantly. A dozen or so steps then Jove stops too. A second later, a shadow slithers in front of him, crawling up the air into the silhouette of a man. The black blob solidifies, revealing the pale features of the lanky Excessum member.

Nightshade flashes his sharp-toothed smile. "Jove the Legislator."

Jove's expression is stone. "You're under arrest for terrorist acts against the Laevus government. Do not resist. It will only make the mercy of the High Council scarcer."

"You and I know both know that no one will show mercy to an Excessum member. If they did, we'd make sure it was the last mistake they'd ever make."

"If you refuse to come with me of your own volition, then you will be forced." Jove takes his stance.

Nightshade looks around. Not too far off a pair of men running in opposite directions collide, the smaller of the two falling down. Another man and woman yell at each other as if they aren't one foot apart. At their knees a two-year-old wails at the top of his lungs. Elsewhere, three children make way for a woman as she pushes an old man in a wheelchair. "Not here," Nightshade scowls. "Too much clutter and commotion. Let's go somewhere where there are no distractions."

Jove squints, studying Nightshade's coal eyes for a window into his motives. *What advantages are there for him should I choose to follow? A trap is possible, but improbable. Most likely, he only wants to draw me away from the castle, using himself as bait. Considering the situation, I'm willing to wager he is the strongest of the group sent here. That's the only bit of good news about our predicament. I don't know their numbers, but they can't be too great, otherwise they would have simply stormed the castle. So divide and conquer is their best strategy. Callisto and Prix aren't quite capable of handling Excessum members on their own, but I could be wrong. For their sake, I hope I am. If it means accomplishing this mission in the name of the Laevus Nation, I must take the chance. This is our best course of action. Our only course, really.* Jove turns slightly. "No tricks. We pick a location of my choosing."

"Lead the way," Nightshade says.

"Law 24: Beacon of Hope."

Suddenly, lights too bright to stare at glow high in the sky above both Jove and Nightshade. The two lights shine like miniature suns over Amica, increasing the brightness of the kingdom to an impossibly high degree. It's as if Heaven has opened its gates to witness Hell falling over the land. And under God's gaze, Amica continues to burn.

"Be sure to keep up," Jove orders.

"Just get moving," Nightshade hisses.

"Callisto, as my righthand, I delegate the remainder of Amica's defense to you. Do your best. Many are counting on you."

Callisto stiffens. "Yes, sir. Understood."

With that, Jove speeds off, the ball of light above turning into a vivid, luminescent streak above the world. If not noticed prior, the vibrant light demands the attention of the entire kingdom. All of Amica pauses, the commotion stalled by the awing spectacle above. Nightshade drops to the ground, a shadow once more, in pursuit of Jove. His movement causes the second beacon above to scream across the sky just as quickly. The grandeur of the lights imitates massive shooting stars. It's as if two small planets hurtle across space, shooting the gap between Earth and Moon. As the glowing orbs sail off they blend with the horizon, their light drowned by the undefeated might of the sun. Immediately afterward the Amican hysteria reignites. More explosions shake the ground, more smoke spews skyward and more panicked people stampede.

Prix regards Callisto. "Your orders, sir?"

Callisto frowns. The situation is dire, to put it simply. The Excessum bear down on Amica. The Amicans rebel against their government. And Prix stands beside Callisto in combat. What more could go wrong?

A lot, actually, Callisto thinks.

Yes, the Excessum are the strongest gang of delinquent ryken on the planet, but Laevus has the strongest regiment of ryken to counter. Justice will always trump evil. It will be difficult, but it's possible, inevitable even. Along the same logic, the rebel citizens of Amica could never win. Isabella is too determined, too righteous to be defeated by such a petty, mischievous evil. And Prix—well, there are much worse people to depend upon. Callisto would even go as far to choose him over any other recruit when it comes to combat. But before the punches fly and abilities flare, as his leader, there is something he must do. After all, this could be his last opportunity.

Callisto turns, squaring himself with Prix. "A few days ago, you apologized to me."

"I remember," Prix says, his voice hoarse.

"Is that apology still there to be accepted?"

Prix folds his arms across his chest. "I was wrong; I told you that once already. I don't know what more you want from me."

"Nothing. I accept your apology." Prix's expression softens, and he raises a brow. "I'm sorry it took so long, and I apologize for what I said to you then. You didn't deserve that. Just because you made a mistake didn't give me the right to disrespect you the way I did. So what do you say—do you accept my apology?"

Prix shakes his head, grinning slightly. "You don't have to be so uptight all the time. We're good. No need to do a song and dance."

"I'll try to remember that," Callisto says, a smile of his own forming.

Prix turns back toward the chaos. "We need to get moving. The only question now is where to start?"

Another detonation shakes the ground. "How about with that?" Callisto asks once the tremor ceases.

Just as Callisto and Prix set off, a child leaps out of a side road, nearly colliding with Callisto. Evading the child in stride, Callisto would continue forward if he didn't recognized the boy. "Rhys?" Callisto asks.

Rhys pants, his hands on his knees. "Your name is Callisto, right? Sutari told me to find you at the castle and bring you back. Please, I need your help. It's the only way to save my mom."

"Save your mom?" Callisto asks, trying to make sense of the situation. "Wait. He's the man that killed your father."

"I'll come too," Prix volunteers. "It's too dangerous. There's no reason for us to split up if we can help it."

"No," Callisto says. "I need you to stop these explosions. There's no telling how much damage they're causing if we can feel the tremors so far away." Callisto stretches, wrapping his right arm around Rhys twice. "I'll handle the murderer."

* * *

"Lo!" Samané yells out from Kato's guest room. "I think he's waking up!"

Not even three months ago, Samané lay unconscious in this same bed, the consequence of venturing to Ground Zero and challenging his older brother. But why Gaudyme is here is another matter. What could he have done to deserve being beaten so badly? Whatever the reason, Samané will get to the bottom of it.

Lo stumbles into the room. "Figures he'd wake up as soon as I walk out." Her tone is harsh despite her evident concern.

After a few more restless turns from Gaudyme, his eyes open slowly. Once his vision clears, he shifts his gaze between the anxious faces of Lo and Samané. "Hey guys," he croaks, his throat exceedingly dry.

"Here," Lo says, grabbing a lidded cup, placing the straw to Gaudyme's mouth. "Oki said you'd be thirsty when you woke."

Gaudyme drinks half of the large cup before stopping to breathe. Only a quarter remains when he stops to speak. He puts a hand to his forehead and says, "Oh my head. What happened yesterday?"

"It was two days ago," Lo says. "You were unconscious all of yesterday."

"Oki gave you some medicine and told us to let you rest," Samané follows up. "As for what happened, Lo and I were hoping you could tell us." Gaudyme grimaces as he sits up in the bed. "Careful. Your sternum was broken. It should be healed in about another day or so, but I'd take it easy until then."

"The same for your arm," Lo adds.

Gaudyme squints, his eyes sightlessly on his blankets as he sifts through his mind trying to uncover a relevant memory. Then it hits him. "Your book! Samané, I'm so sorry I lost your book."

"A book?" Lo asks.

"The Book of Xenesis?" Samané spits. "Someone nearly killed you over that?"

"I found it in Kato's secret room and figured you forgot it," Gaudyme explains. "I was on my way to give it back to you when some guy stopped me. He said it was his and you stole it. I didn't want to give it to him because I knew you didn't steal it. Then he attacked me. I didn't stand a chance." Gaudyme shakes his head despairingly. "So he took the book."

Samané's lip curls contemptuously. *Gaudyme nearly died trying to protect a book I know nothing about. He didn't deserve this. He was just in the wrong place at the wrong time.* "What was his name?"

Gaudyme sinks into the bed a bit, his recollections appearing to take their toll. "I think it might've started with an R. Other than that, I can't tell you. My head is still swimming."

"Get some rest, Gaudyme," Lo says. "You'll feel better tomorrow."

Gaudyme closes his eyes, lying back. "I hope you're right."

Almost immediately Gaudyme is sound asleep. Samané storms out but doesn't get far. "Where do you think you're going?" Lo snaps.

Samané stops at Kato's front door. "Anywhere but here."

Lo purses her lips. "How do you plan to find this guy?"

"Don't worry about it, just know I'll find him. I have to." Samané pauses to be sure that he doesn't yell. "Gaudyme didn't deserve that, Lo. He's too loyal for his own good. He should've just given the book away. Why would that idiot think a few pages were anywhere as close as important to me as he is?"

Lo shrugs. "Gaudyme is dumb; you know that. But you're just as dumb if you think I'm letting you do this alone. I'm coming too."

Samané shakes his head. "I can't. If we both leave Gaudyme all of a sudden, Kato would know what we're up to."

"Kato already knows what you're up to," he says, appearing in a doorway. "Seriously, how do you expect me not to with the two of you basically yelling? Do I have to teach you kids how to be stealthy too?" Kato leisurely cracks his neck. "So, let me get this straight. You plan to get revenge on someone when you have no clue what they look like or how strong they are? If anyone is dumb in this house, it's definitely you."

"I'll be okay," Samané growls.

"Not if they're more powerful than you. You've made progress, kid. But picking a fight with someone you literally know nothing about could be suicide. You're not strong enough to play big bank, little bank in terms of spirit energy or skill with a complete stranger."

"Fine, Kato. Then what do you think I should do?"

"Let it go. I'm all for you kids learning from your mistakes, but this isn't one of those times. You have a second Book of Xenesis don't you?" Samané nods slowly, reluctantly. "Bring it here. If anyone wants it, they can go through me."

* * *

Prix moves through the kingdom his attention honed, sharpened to every person, building, object around him. As he navigates, nothing can surprise him. Another explosion quakes the ground and a nearby building crumbles to the earth from the vibration. *I'm getting closer,* Prix thinks.

General Jove was always warning the team about the deadly might of the Excessum. He said the tall order of keeping the group subdued in Laevus belonged to the commander and colonels mostly, but sometimes fell to the generals too. Today Prix's duties will bring him in line with a task that even generals struggle to overcome. Today, Prix will prove himself.

Jove, Callisto, and Prix have been ordered to hold Amica against the Excessum attacks. General Jove follows orders. It's just that simple. Regardless of how petty, how mundane, how hopeless, if an order is given, General Jove gives his all toward accomplishing it, no questions asked. Luckily for Prix, this time it lands him in battle with one of the Excessum.

Prix places a hand on the stone wall of a building, peeking around the corner. His hand shakes; he is eager to see the infamously dangerous Excessum for the first time. The residents in this section of the kingdom have cleared out, leaving behind only the carnage of their homes and small businesses. Prix runs to the cover of a new building and not even a full second later another detonation sends wood, metal and other shrapnel through the air.

Laughter follows soon after. "Finally!" a voice exclaims. "Someone shows. As much as I love blowing things up, it gets boring after a while. Come on out so we can fight!"

Before he even finishes his statement, Prix rounds the corner, stepping over the shards of buildings, rearing to go. Prix approaches a child. A normal looking child. Brown, unbrushed, greasy hair falls over his eyes and ears. A button nose and rosy cheeks attempt to complete the facade of innocence, but Prix knows better than to judge a fighter solely on their looks. If there is one thing Prix learned under Jove in his three years in the ryken squad it is to never take chances. Child or not, the Excessum member will feel Prix's full strength before the day's end.

"The Excessum versus the ryken squad!" the child exclaims. "This has only happened a couple times in the history of everything! I wonder which of us will win."

"I can't afford to lose. Especially if Callisto wins his fight." Prix shakes his head. "It won't be a good look for me or the ryken squad. I have to win."

"Well, my dad is going to be really mad at me if I lose so I have to win too."

Prix takes his stance. "Sounds like one of us will be very disappointed soon."

For Glory

The calm before the storm. It's the weird moment of clarity preceding a fight where nothing else in the world matters. Everything that seemed important prior to this day, this hour, this instant, couldn't mean less. Glory, prestige, life—whether metaphorical or literal—lie on the other side of victory, and for the loser only the emptiness of defeat. Like a trained dog eager before his master, Prix struggles to remain patient, careful to not engage sloppily. It's been a long time coming, but finally opportunity rears its dangerous head. He just has to seize it.

Napalm's casual stance doesn't draw any similar reaction from Prix. His form remains vigilant, strong. Prix flexes his fingers, itching to move, but discipline won't allow it. Unlike his many sparring sessions endured under General Jove's tutelage, he only has one shot at this. Finally, Napalm attacks.

He makes a small circle in the air with his index finger. The circle glows, creating a box that, corner to corner, is the same as the diameter as the circle. Wheels form underneath the box as it is in free fall, landing at Napalm's feet. A flick of his other wrist sets both the box and the battle into motion. The tiny box moves quickly, but not too quickly for Prix as he evades its detonation.

Prix's hair dances in the wind of the explosion. *His power is impressive,* he observes, *but unrefined. He'll need to be more creative.*

Suddenly, a small explosion hits Prix, the pain of the blast evident by the deep anguish on his face. A ton of force slams into his chest, forcing him back and, without his knowing, another box slips under the heel of his foot.

"Gotcha!" Napalm exclaims.

The instant Prix's foot touches Napalm's contraption a tremendous surge of fire erupts. The explosion is so powerful that the felled buildings and debris surrounding the area are nearly obliterated. There is a heavy smokescreen that coats the flame-infested area afterwards, but only minutes pass before the rising wind carries it all away. In the wake of Napalm's ryken ability only a small crater remains, with Prix unmoving at its center.

Napalm dusts his hands off. "Welp! That settles that." A twitch from Prix causes Napalm to do a double-take. Another minute passes and Napalm turns away. "No way anyone could survive one of my bombs at point-blank range."

A glowing yellow disk whizzes by Napalm's left leg, taking a chunk of meat from his thigh with it. Burning pain follows immediately and Napalm covers the gash, trying to slow the bleeding. Wincing, he uses a tiny explosion to cauterize the wound. He turns back to see Prix on his feet, several burns running the length of his body. Anger from the nasty cut almost trumps Napalm's surprise. "How did you survive that?"

A grimace precedes Prix's response; still, he maintains his act of bravado. "You think a recruit of the Laevus Ryken Squad would be defeated so easily? You struck first blood, I'll strike the last."

Napalm's eyebrows rise, and an inexorable smile forces its way to his lips. "Oh wow! You're tough. Okay, second round. Let's see what you can do!"

Prix prepares himself, his burns screaming their extreme protest. Every movement, every gesture sparks a new sensation of agony for him. But it doesn't matter. Prix has no other choice but to continue fighting. This is still his long-awaited opportunity to prove his general-level strength. Something as trivial as pain isn't going to stop him. If nothing else, their first interaction only calms Prix further, his jittery nerves from facing the Excessum burned away in Napalm's explosion. Prix draws forth his spirit energy.

In a blink, two razor disks shoot toward Napalm. He turns, avoiding both in a fluid motion. Prix tries to close the gap between the two; however, before he gets into striking distance, he triggers Napalm's landmine. With every ounce of his ryken speed, Prix escapes the detonation, the sharp aching of his burns furiously returning when he dives to the charred ground.

Not offering Prix a moment's respite, Napalm sends another of his bombs wheeling over. Deftly, Prix conjures up a razor disk, firing it at the box. When the two spirit energy entities collide the detonation sets the area between the fighters ablaze. The flames of the explosion seem close enough to singe the hair on Prix's brows, but he hardly notices as he sends two more energy disks humming toward Napalm, using the haze of smoke as cover.

Not even a second later the child cries out and Prix very nearly smiles. *Stay at it,* he coaches himself.

Prix takes a hesitant step forward, wincing as his burns once again make their presence known. He concentrates to steady his breathing, needing all his senses at their keenest. Eventually, the smoke fades and the battered fighters glare at one another. Blood drips from the fresh cuts on Napalm's arm and chest.

The boy cracks another smile. "I might actually be able to try my hardest against you."

* * *

Callisto takes one last look back over his shoulder at Rhys and his mother Reyna. Their expressions are dubious, at best, a direct reflection of Callisto's chances against the Excessum member. Nevertheless, Callisto turns and forges ahead into the thick of the woods behind the Culminary household.

Initially, when Callisto approached the house with Rhys, he was hesitant because Reyna stood out in the open, alone. The situation had all the makings of a most primitive trap. Bait out in plain sight and the predator lying in wait, ready to pounce. Despite Rhys' most urgent objections, Callisto scouted the area for nearly an hour before approaching Reyna. Surprisingly, the trap never triggered; instead, Reyna informed Callisto that the Excessum member went into the woods and wanted him to follow. *Maybe I triggered the trap, after all,* Callisto thinks.

He proceeds slowly, carefully, unsure of where he's heading. Because of that, his journey takes another half hour before he reaches a clearing. It's there that Callisto sees him, the culprit responsible for Grade Culminary's death.

"Why must fate so cruelly gibe us?" Metis asks, his back to Callisto. Even though the question is rhetorical, Metis pauses a moment as if to ponder it.

Callisto approaches as if the man before him were a stranger, and in many ways, he is. Aside from this week, Callisto has not seen Metis in over three years. He hasn't had a meaningful conversation with him in over five. The two used to be close. In some ways, they shared bonds even stronger than Callisto and Samané had. But what does that mean when the world calls for justice? He can't turn a blind eye because they were friends. No, Callisto has a job to do.

"Why?" Callisto hears himself ask. It doesn't matter; the two will fight regardless. But for some reason, he must know. What makes people—ryken in particular, do such evil things?

Metis turns and stares at his old friend, stone-faced. The look of judgement is even more pervasive in Callisto's eyes than in Samané's back at Ground Zero. Callisto could never understand Metis' pain, his burden. It isn't so much that the two travel different paths, as is the case between himself and Samané; rather, Metis and Callisto journey the same road, only in opposite directions. If Metis could simply turn Callisto around, maybe... "For equality," Metis answers.

"How does murdering the Amican Protector move you any closer to equality?" Callisto asks, strangely calm.

"Don't be so short-sighted, Callisto. Look beyond the foreground. You should know that Grade was only a stepping stone, a piece in a much larger societal battle."

"Quit speaking in circles, Metis. All those words and you aren't saying a thing. Why did you kill Grade Culminary?"

"Open your ears, recruit. I hope you don't claim life is as absolute as right and wrong, yes or no. That's much of the reason for the impasse we now call the Laevus Nation. No ryken deliberates outside the box. Overwhelmingly, they either deny that which makes us truly distinct as ryken, knowingly or otherwise, or they twist their gifts in line with the will of humans, in essence being no more than a pet of bureaucracy. Not one tries to devise a system in which we can use our ryken prowess for the greater good. Will there be casualties? Indubitably. Let's not pretend we are holier than we are. Let us face it, own it, and use it to fashion a functional, fair society for those who will admit the same."

Callisto falls silent, trying to empathetically place himself in the mind of a once-dear friend. He puts a hand to his head, desperate to appreciate Metis' feelings. As children the two used to have talks of justice and truth frequently. They questioned philosophies of the kid-world plenty of times, Metis always instilling nuggets of truth in Callisto, despite the age difference being in his favor. In a subtle way, Callisto looked up to Metis' way of thinking. His thought processes were void of emotion, bias, and were as a result so objective.

"In truth," Metis continues, "I'm not sure what the Excessum has in store for the future. They're surreptitious for obvious reasons. I'd be duplicitous if I said I wasn't somewhat intrigued, but determining their intent is not my main objective. I simply require from them the means to change the world. To sharpen my mind enough to move the hearts of potential allies and acquire the power to bend the wills of my enemies." Emotion flickers across Metis' face for an instant. "I don't want to fight you. Instead, join me in my efforts to rebuild this world anew."

Callisto takes a slow breath. Hearing Metis voice his motives made Callisto nauseous, almost physically ill. Sweat forms on his forehead to cool him, but the body has no such protocol to extinguish his red-hot fury on the inside. "You are undoubtably the most egocentric person I've ever met," Callisto says, forcing his rage still. "You're going to sacrifice those unwilling, for your cause? That's called murder, you fool. No matter how you phrase it, it's nothing but mindless killing. Grade didn't deserve to die. He had a family, but you didn't care. You only want to create this Metis World of yours that doesn't exist. And it never will. Not as long as I have anything to say about it."

Metis doesn't budge, doesn't flinch from Callisto's rebuke. He only speaks, his voice completely flat, void of emotion, bias, and as a result, objective. "I am a fool. One day I will learn to cut the ties of my old life, swift and true. It will pain me far less."

Metis' eyes flash purple.

* * *

Prix scurries behind the cover of another building, barely avoiding the shrapnel of Napalm's latest explosion. Unsurprisingly, the juvenile Excessum member is strong—very strong. His spirit energy is his single most remarkable quality. Against logic, it seems limitless. One explosion after the other has had Prix running and ducking for cover with tiring repetition. And the child only laughs as if the entire fight were some deadly game.

And there is his biggest weakness, Prix thinks. Napalm has incredible power and a great ryken ability to boot, but his fundamentals are awful. It's obvious the child prodigy coasts off his talent, hardly having to critically think his way out of disadvantageous scenarios. Most likely, he simply imposes his will through force and not wit. *I'll show him the importance of strategy.*

Prix's left arm flexes and a second later a razor disk hovers above his fingertips. "I'm counting on you, little guy," Prix whispers.

"Come on out," Napalm yells. "This is going to get boring if you only run!"

There's no response until a razor disk sails off toward the sky, splitting the clouds on its way into the stratosphere. The maneuver betrays Prix's position and Napalm circles a box into existence. The cube, about the size of his fist, sprouts black wings like a bat and unsteadily flaps its way over to the building Prix hides behind. The instant it touches the concrete a ball of fire and air barrels outward with thousands of tons of force. A moment before the eruption, two razor disks curve around the building, heading directly for Napalm.

From his makeshift hole in the earth, Prix emerges once the explosion passes overhead. He lunges for Napalm, behind the cover of his razor disks. As expected, Napalm easily dodges the deadly saucers, setting his sights back on Prix, still too far away. Napalm pushes two more rectangular bombs, but Prix is faster, throwing ten razor disks in the allotted time. The first two razor disks slice through Napalm's bombs, detonating them immediately. The force of the explosion has Napalm stumbling back. Another razor disk nips past his cheek before he regains his footing. The rest of the razor disks are evaded, but Napalm's next move is anticipated, and Prix's fist connects clean to the child's jaw. Prix feels Napalm's body go slack at the moment of contact, as if he will fall, but immediately after, resilience flows back in him. Napalm takes the punch and the next three as well, each blow seeming to affect him less than the last. Prix summons a razor disk but just as he's about to throw it, Napalm deflects his hand, sending it into the ground. The disk splits the earth only a centimeter, but travels dozens of meters deep before its spirit energy dissipates.

Each fighter shares a thrown and blocked punch, but Prix is brought to a knee when Napalm's foot meets the side of his leg with stinging force. A shot to the chest hurls Prix through the devastated battlegrounds of scrap metal and half-standing buildings.

"You know," Napalm says, scratching his head, "I figured you ryken squad guys would be stronger. Sure, you got a few hits in, but you were barely able to draw blood. And, not counting the new guy, I'm the weakest person in the Excessum. Why does everyone compare the squad to us? Clearly we're stronger! Nightshade should've matched me up with the Legislator. He seems strong. Too bad Nightshade is going to kill him."

Prix tries to will himself to his feet, but his body is sluggish and defiant. Napalm leans forward, his voice dropping to almost a whisper across the distance. "Did you know Nightshade is even stronger than Hunter? I mean, I don't know for sure, but he has to be! Why else would Hunter let Nightshade boss him around? Oh, right, I almost forgot." Napalm steps to the side and just as he does Prix's razor disk rains from the sky, slicing into the earth. This time the ground divides as easily as flesh, creating a narrow chasm a meter wide and at least half a kilometer deep. The entire world seems to shake from the colossal rocky laceration. Napalm only smiles. "I can't believe you actually thought that would—"

His sentence is cut off when Prix's razor disk shoots from its cover, striking him from behind. Just as the disk touches flesh, there is an unprecedentedly big explosion. Prix, just barely standing, must dive behind the remnants of a building to avoid the wrath of Napalm's latest and most vibrant display of spirit energy.

Prix uses the seconds of inactivity to gauge the situation. Had the boy accidentally blown himself to bits? Maybe a typical ten-year-old ryken could commit such a blunder, but not one of the Excessum, regardless of how young. *So why did he suddenly explode? It doesn't make any sense.*

Prix sneaks a peak from his cover. With his plan taking an unexpected turn, it is best for him to proceed with exaggerated caution. Soon, the smoke in the area clears and the child comes into view. Pink, tender skin lies beneath the boy's tattered clothing. Napalm stands wearily, grimacing, wounded but alive. Burned but whole. It's then that Prix realizes the purpose of the explosion.

Defense. A last line of armor to protect him in a worst-case scenario. His clothing or maybe even his skin must have been lined with spirit energy set to ignite when in contact with a tremendous amount of another's spirit energy. Exploding being the trade-off to certain death. He used the detonation to not only move himself from the danger but obliterated the threat all together. Prix steps out into the open, his body futilely objecting once more. *It was a nice tactic to save him, but how much does he have left in the tank? After that, he must be worse off than I am. Now I just have to claim my prize.*

The two ryken glower at one another. Napalm sniffles, and with tears in his eyes, he cries, "You're dead!"

Episode 22:

Old Friends

It's better this way. Fighting with Samané at Ground Zero, and the same with Callisto now. It's better for Metis to sever the connections of his past life early in his journey to reshape the world. It's Fate's workings to create in Metis what he needs to complete his task. An early payment for the lives he will affect while traveling his path.

Back at Ground Zero Metis had only begun to truly wrap his mind around his course of work—his purpose, as the Wind god put it. As much as he hates to admit it, at the time, Ventus was right. Metis wasn't a killer. When Samané first showed at Ground Zero Metis' stomach turned and roiled at the implications of how it would end. Even if Metis didn't have to do the deed himself, how could he sit idly by and watch someone kill the one most dear to him? For every second Metis dreaded the outcome of Samané's presence there. Fortunately, miraculously even, both Lutrio brothers escaped with their lives. Since then, Metis has worked tirelessly on steeling his nerves to do what may need to be done one day. Only when he can set his emotions aside, honest and complete, will he deem himself the indiscriminate killer he must be to invoke change. Although he hasn't achieved that goal yet, Callisto isn't Samané.

This battle is more or less practice for Metis. A smaller scale representation of his love for Samané. If Metis can complete his objective in eliminating an old friend, it will show how far he's come since Ground Zero, mentally and emotionally; which was Metis' sole objective in joining the Excessum in the first place. Sure, physical strength is needed, but Metis could've obtained it other ways. The ability to detach himself from a situation emotionally is not so easily accomplished. The ruthless organization of legend seemed like the most efficient route to take. And so he did. Now he has no choice. It's either kill or be killed. And Metis doesn't particularly feel like dying today.

Callisto takes his stance when Metis' eyes begin to glow a deep purple. His sixth sense alerts him to the invisible walls Metis uses to box himself in. The energy summoned by Metis is tremendous and Callisto sweats at the mere thought of piercing through the defense, let alone doing so whilst trying to defend himself. Rather than work himself up wondering if he can conquer the barrier, Callisto charges.

He reaches the invisible wall without so much as a fidget from Metis. Though this is odd, Callisto doesn't hesitate. He rears his fist back, landing a solid blow. The wall transiently lights where Callisto's fist connects, rippling outward like a stone dropped in a purple pond. When the ripples cease, so too does the light of the wall. Callisto then kicks, shaking the wall, but only slightly.

"That's enough," Metis says, flatly. Just as Callisto moves his foot away, an aura punch connects to his side. He curls up but is still able to defend as he backpedals. Even when the aura strikes stop swirling around Callisto, his stance doesn't waver. Metis, on the other hand, stands relaxed, his forearms against the small of his back. "If you can't breech my fortress, you will be defeated. You must understand that."

"Shut up and fight," Callisto spits.

He lunges for the barrier again, but this time he doesn't get far before Metis' aura attacks are incoming. He must stop approaching to focus on his defense after a punch from Metis rocks his jaw. The exchange goes on for a minute straight, Callisto defending expertly. Each aura punch is stalled by Callisto's forearm, knee or met directly with a fist. When Metis relents, Callisto takes a step back, relaxing if just for a bit.

"This would be the time you reveal your ryken ability in the hopes that it may tip the scales in your favor," Metis says.

Callisto raises his chin. "Since you want to talk so badly, let's talk. Your father was killed. When we were kids, I didn't know the details; you and Samané never said much about it. You kept your feelings bottled up. But things are different today. We're older and more mature. Darn it, Metis, it must have been hard on you two."

"It was."

"Then why would you want to create that same feeling for another family? If anybody understands their pain it's you, and yet you're the culprit. You could transform Rhys into exactly what you are."

"If that came to fruition, I'd welcome it. To have more people broken to the point where they voraciously seek change would be a blessing to this world. It's the only way to eradicate the wheel we Laevinian ryken endlessly amble. Perhaps his pain will bring forth a plan for Amica to escape from beneath the thumb of Laevus."

"More of your egocentric talk. As if you're some sort of godsend people should want to copy. You're only adding to the hate this world is infested with. You're making the cycle worse."

"I'll admit that you've always been more logical than Samané, less prone to frivolous emotions. You've attained my respect because of it. But you're more stubborn and shortsighted than he could ever be once you resign yourself to a cause. If only you had more time to meditate on the matter, I don't doubt you'd comprehend my logic in its fullest. Unfortunately, we don't have the luxury of time. Let us continue. We are wasting our breath, and yours are precious and few."

* * *

Jove stops on a grassy plain a kilometer or so outside of the Amica kingdom. Nightshade appears after a moment in shadow-form. He retakes his human shape just as Jove repeals his Beacon of Hope Law. "The light was unnecessary," Nightshade says. "I wasn't going to run. If I need to go through you to please Master Misery, I'm going through you."

Jove barely hears the criminal. His attention is on his surroundings, surveying the area. But eventually Jove says, "That's what I don't understand about the Excessum. You all show signs of loyalty, in one way or another. That would mean you also understand right from wrong, even if in their most basic terms. Why hand yourselves over to injustice?"

"I'm loyal to only one thing and that's power," Nightshade says. "I go where there is strength, because the one who is strongest will always call the shots. Master Misery just so happens to be that person."

"Bowing to a man is foolish," Jove answers, his back still to Nightshade. "Man is imperfect and will always lead you astray. Give yourself over to a cause, something bigger than just one or two people. Order, truth, justice—these ideals will always win over any and everything else. The universe has shown this long before ryken and human roamed the earth and it will continue to show it long after we are gone."

"You're telling me to follow ideals? Can order overthrow a kingdom? Can justice wipe out an entire army?" Nightshade pauses, then says, "Will truth be able to save you?"

Jove tilts his head back, regarding the blue sky above. "It already has."

An eerie smile forms on Nightshade's lips. "Not from me."

* * *

His attacks are strong and fast, Callisto muses. *All from a distance. And what's worse, he remains behind that barrier. What can I do; what attacks do I have to counter? There's always a way, I just need to find it.*

Callisto's fist shoots out like a bullet, his arm stretching to Metis' defense, crashing into it with a booming thud. Metis tries to exploit the opening created on Callisto's extended side but his arm snaps back fast, faster than Metis can attack. In one fluid motion, Callisto blocks and fires another punch across the terrain, shaking Metis' wall again. This time Metis feigns an aura strike one way using a wisp of light, then fires a shot at Callisto's chin. He takes the bait and is jarred from the blow, ultimately taking a three-piece before falling to the ground.

There is silence as Callisto lies on the dry, pointed grass of the forest clearing. Eventually he stirs, rising to a knee. He wipes the blood from his lip, cursing to himself. Metis looks on, stoic. Callisto stands, his expression as determined as it was at the start of the fight.

"Hand Barricade," Callisto says, voice low.

On command, his hand grows and thickens to giant proportions. It stretches to three times Callisto's height and half that in width and thickness. Behind it, Callisto charges. Metis fires a dozen aura attacks in a blink, but Callisto only gains speed under its cover. Metis then tries to attack around the barricade, but his spirit energy diminishes to the point of near insignificance by the time contact is made and so Callisto takes every blow in stride.

When Callisto reaches Metis' defense, he drops his own, his hand shrinking back to normal size. Immediately Metis' aura swirls around Callisto, pelting him with several blows a second. He does well to defend the majority of Metis' onslaught, only a few attacks striking true. Each landed blow draws a grunt from Callisto, but nothing more. The young recruit's form and fundamentals are unyielding even as Metis' fatigue grows. Eventually, Metis begins to slow enough for

Callisto to strike the barrier and return to his defense without an exploitable opening.

Being so close to the Wall of Lutrio forces Metis to keep pressuring Callisto. Often Metis' opponents misunderstand his ability, thinking being farther away gives them more time to react to his aura attacks; however, nothing could be more untrue. Metis allows his opponents respite when they retreat as a kind of psychological reward for distancing themselves from his defense. Unfortunately, Callisto doesn't appear interested in Metis' petty compensation.

His fist slams into the barrier again. Metis' aura races toward Callisto's chest in response, but Callisto slaps the light from the air. The bout continues, but unlike Metis, Callisto somehow shows no signs of slowing. *Just one more punch,* he thinks. And no sooner another punch connects to Metis' defense. Still, Callisto doesn't back off. *Just one more punch,* he thinks, as if for the first time. What other options does he have besides digging deeper and giving this fight everything of him? Another punch to the wall is squeezed between Metis' aura strikes. *Just one more punch,* Callisto urges, teeth clenched in effort. His stamina seems limitless as he begins to trade every blocked attack of Metis' with one of his own to the transient defense. Several blows are exchanged a second, Metis' aura dissipating on Callisto's forearms, and Callisto's fists smashing against the unconquerable Wall of Lutrio.

Despite Metis' best attempt to not relent first, his hands cover his eyes almost involuntarily. The lack of blinking and overall stress of his ryken ability grow to be too much. Callisto, similarly, struggles with every strike to not topple over. "Just one more punch," he says to himself, swinging with every bit of spirit energy he can excavate from his body. "Just one more punch." Again, his fist collides. "One more punch!" Somehow, Callisto finds the energy to throw yet another punch.

But it's his last.

Finally, his fist rests against the transiently visible barrier, his body trembling from the effort. He slides down to his knees, too exhausted to even resist gravity.

For a while the world is quiet to Callisto, tranquil. The birds and other animals who initially called out in the background of the fight have all fled to safety by now. All is silent and, if Callisto allows his exhausted mind to reason, he'd dare say peaceful. The calming moment harshly concludes when Metis voice slides into existence.

"Memor Barrage."

Metis feels the spirit energy exit his body immediately, as draining as if he had just run for miles on end. But that's what is to be expected from the taxing technique. Metis' subconscious takes over, delivering a multitude of aura strikes every second. Callisto dances to the rhythm of Metis' subconscious mind, while his conscious mind focuses intently on another task. Metis closes his eyes as he concentrates, further releasing the restraints on his spirit energy, allowing all his strength to flow in a heavy torrent of controlled power. For nearly a minute Metis is motionless, a droplet of sweat curving past his brow. The time draws near, and so Metis braces himself, his heart hammering, his jaw locked. One thousand and ninety-six attacks of Metis' Memor Barrage all connect and just as the last follows suit his eyes snap open.

Callisto had began to think Metis' bombardment would never end. As the final crushing attack lands, he wishes he were still pelted by the lesser preceding blows. It's a wonder Callisto's chest doesn't cave in altogether from the sheer power of the aura strike, but for a few moments, his world does.

Everything goes black. There is nothing. No pain. No woods. No Metis.

Why am I even here in the first place? Callisto muses, his thoughts cloudy. *Not in this darkness. Not in Amica. Not in the ryken squad. Why am I here? For what reason do I exist? If I can't imprint justice on the world, for what other reason could I exist? How have things changed since I let Acura down? I have only taken on more responsibility with the same pitiful outcome. I boldly confronted General Jove about ideals and motives I'm not strong enough to instill. Maybe Metis is right. I can't deny that there is respect that comes with strength. Attention demanded when power supplements your words. But...*

Nothing could be more unjust.

I would rather die, right here, right now than to believe what Metis said was anything other than self-indulgent arrogance. I might not be strong, but I can still find solace that I'm not Metis and never will be. Even my burning desire for justice could never drive me to force it upon people. That would betray the very justice I attempt to instill. I tried my best and even though Metis emerged victorious, I gave it my all. What more can I demand from myself beyond my best effort? I left it all on the battlefield. I have no regrets.

His nerves hardened, his mind crafted to the task at hand, Metis Lutrio looks down on Callisto Socius. *Who would've thought it would come to this for us, Callisto?* The red-haired recruit opens his eyes. "Final words, perhaps?" Metis asks.

"Final words, huh?" Callisto says, introspectively. He takes a moment to think on the subject, but unsurprisingly only one thing comes to his mind. "If you see Lo, tell her I love and miss her so much."

Metis' expression doesn't so much as flicker. But he nods, almost imperceptibly. "I will do so. Rest easy, my friend."

A Veteran Battle

Laevus Ryken Squad General Jove Spinto and Excessum member Nightshade clash with booming force. Confidence, expertise, power—both men move with an evident display of each. It is a sight to behold and a lesson to be learned in every exchange, if anyone were around to witness.

The fighters separate, their unspoken warm-up completed. If this were a battle between less skilled ryken, perhaps they would collide several more times trying to bait out the other's ryken ability, then devise a plan to win the fight with said knowledge. For veterans, however, that strategy will leave you snuffed out by your opponent's ability before ever getting a chance to use your own. It's best to bring your best effort from the start.

"Law 19: Loan Shark."

Nightshade activates his own ability. He starts by delving into the recesses of his mind, tapping into the reserve power of his body. Immediately the energy flows forth, but even as it does the precious asset doesn't diminish, instead, it increases. It's as if the wealth of spirit energy within him is bottomless. Unexpected as it may be, Nightshade heedlessly mines the seemingly limitless reservoir.

Trembling with power, Nightshade extends a hand and Zacata and Declan spring into action. The two shadows crawl atop the grass as innocuously as a bird's shadow might, but at much greater speeds. In fact, Nightshade has never seen the manifestations of his ability move so quickly, a result of his newfound spirit energy.

Jove is barely able to react in the time it takes Nightshade's shadows to traverse the distance. The dark blobs shoot two spikes from the grass just as Jove hops back to evade. Unexpectedly, one of the shadows' darkness extends, reaching for Jove's ankle. Jove kicks his legs back, forcing his upper body toward the darkness and his legs away. The shadow changes its target, shooting for Jove's torso, but meets the general's fist instead. Unnatural as it looks, the punch lands and the shadow retreats.

Jove hits the grass on his hands and knees, then a shadow is on him. This time, however, it is the natural shadow of Nightshade standing over him. Jove barely sees the pale man's foot prior to the flash of pain to his midsection. He has little time to dwell on his anguish, turning his tumble into a combat roll. Jove rises to his feet just in time to dance around the spikes Nightshade's shadows shoot upward. It takes every bit of finesse in Jove's skillset to tip-toe around the shadows, until a third shadow seemingly spawns at his feet, latching around his ankles.

Jove rips one leg free just as Nightshade's fist meets his jaw, sending a pulse of pain screaming through his head, the sensation seeming to ricochet inside his skull, feeding back into itself in a miserable cycle of dizzying distress. Jove stops the wobbling of the world just in time to see the shadow spikes jutting for him below and another Nightshade punch aimed high. With his leg bound and Nightshade's power overwhelming, nothing can protect him.

Nothing, besides the Law.

Jove's ryken ability has always been difficult to explain despite how logical it seems to him. Twenty-five Laws govern Jove and whomever else he should choose. The Laws are absolute and are not to be broken, whatever those parameters, restrictions or costs may be. His ryken ability is unique in the sense that it gives no inherent advantage to Jove, as he too is subjected to the Law. Whether it is Law 14: Dangerous Ground that requires one to move constantly lest the ground give out beneath them, or Law 3: Passionate Sleep, that forces those with quickened heartbeats into a deep sleep, Jove is at the mercy of whatever Law he may initiate. In the end, he is judged equally.

From his depths, Jove once again confirms the maximum output of his own spirit energy. The essence of his strength at its limit, he reluctantly taps the bank of loaned energy granted from the Law. The power surges through him like an electric shock, his entire body jolting. Invigorating as it may be, Jove quickly clamps the lid of the bank, pulling out no more energy than absolutely necessary. The price he'll pay in spirit energy will be two-fold the withdrawal; best to not indulge. Had Nightshade known that he may have been more hesitant to accept the loan himself. Regardless, he will repay his debt.

Nightshade is inches away from the general when suddenly Jove rips his leg free of Etan. Surprisingly quick, considering his sluggish movements thus far, Jove dodges the spikes of Zacata and Declan then blocks Nightshade's fist. A parting shot to Nightshade's chest stuns him enough for the general to retreat. The shock of Jove's sudden burst of spirit energy causes Nightshade to pause. The man had seemed to move in slow motion until his situation was dire, then he'd maneuvered his way free with speed and strength Nightshade had seldom seen in his life. *He is up to something,* Nightshade thinks.

"I may have made the wrong choice," Jove confesses. "Although, in all fairness, I chose the best strategy, not the fastest."

"Enough of this," Nightshade hisses, "what is happening here?"

"You're causing me to repeal this Law sooner than I planned. You're strong, but that's to be expected with the Excessum. As for what's happening, well…"

With that, Jove stops his spirit energy from flowing to the Law, severing the tether and repealing its effect. Immediately after, Jove's payment is made and he feels more fatigued, though not unusually so. He feels only a bit worse than he would after an aggressive sparring session with Gwen, something his adrenaline will mask once the fighting begins again.

Nightshade, however, feels utterly exhausted. It's not unlike how he frequently felt in his first days with the Excessum, back when he thought he knew pain and Master Misery had proved otherwise. His legs wobble under his weight before he catches himself, refortifying his body with what remains of his spirit energy. He concentrates, removing all restraints in his mind, allowing his power to flow at one hundred percent. *It's too early for me to be at my maximum,* Nightshade thinks. *How could I go from fighting at the highest level I've ever achieved to showing my trump card?* "I don't like it," he hisses.

"You knew what you were doing," Jove says. "You knew as you reveled in the spirit energy and attacked me that it wasn't your own. Though you may not have known why or how, you chose to accept the foreign spirit energy with no regard to anything else. And now you have paid the price of the Law."

"That was your ryken ability? How was I supposed to know that it would do this to me?"

"Ignorance of the Law is no reason to not abide by it."

Nightshade scowls. "It doesn't matter. I'm still standing, and you'll see I'm just as difficult to defeat, with or without your mystical energy." Four more shadows pour out from Nightshade. They surround him in a large circle, moving like an intangible black rope on the grass. It's impossible to differentiate any one from the other six as they speed around.

Jove stands unimpressed. "Law 15: Punched Drunk."

Nightshade waits a moment, his senses keen to the slightest changes within himself or the environment, but there is nothing. The Law could mean anything and worrying about it will only cause hesitation, and hesitation invites defeat. No. If Nightshade is going to lose, it will be swinging wildly. And when he wins, it will be a result of the same. The pale man smiles.

The seven shadows disperse, all heading toward Jove. In response, Jove takes off in a full sprint at Nightshade. Two shadows shoot spikes from the ground; one is hurtled and the other Jove spins away from when he lands. Coming out of his spin, Jove slides on the dry grass beneath two shadow spikes that cross. Both his palms strike the earth to push himself back to his feet, never losing a step. A black tentacle rises from another shadow to ensnare Jove. He tries a side step that fails, leading to the tentacle almost snagging his arm. Instead, Jove's fist flashes, striking the tentacle and sinking it back to the earth. The last two shadows pass Jove and double back, joining the others that pursue him.

Jove engages Nightshade with a jab, wary of the shadows that begin circling both fighters. Nightshade deflects the blow then retaliates with two punches of his own that Jove stalls. Jove's foot is near to connecting to the side of Nightshade's knee when one of his shadows shoots out a tentacle to misguide the kick. Before Jove's leg returns to the ground, he leans away from another punch, but isn't so lucky to escape Nightshade's kick to his midsection. A grunt and a single step back are Jove's only reaction, but it is all the shadow needs to ensnare his ankle. Aware of the shadow's presence, Jove looks down, baiting his opponent closer. Nightshade throws a hook, but even as he does Jove lands a punch square to his nose.

Jove doesn't follow up as Nightshade's other six shadows are prepared to intervene should he overextend. As a result, there is a break until Nightshade re-gathers his wits. Without warning, the fight recommences in a blur of movement. Two spikes jut from the shadows and Jove, even with his leg captured, dodges. He then strikes one with a kick, dropping it back to the ground. When Jove sees Nightshade again, he is already mid-punch. Jove ducks the blow, coming back with an uppercut that lifts Nightshade from his feet, landing him on his backside.

Jove's deft maneuver doesn't go unpunished, as his left wrist is ensnared by a second shadow. A third shadow follows up, spiking behind Jove. With a loud cry of effort, he moves clear while pulling the shadow at his wrist into the line of fire. The movement happens so quickly neither shadow can adjust, and one pierces the other. The impaled shadow dissipates into nothingness with little more than a hiss. The five other shadows continue circling Jove, seemingly more hesitant, even while the sixth still renders his leg immobile.

Nightshade glares at Jove, his face twisted in rage. He lunges back into the fight. The two go back and forth with deflected punches, blocked kicks and evaded shadow spikes for quite some time, neither one able to land a clean blow. It is a testimony to the strength of both men, but Nightshade couldn't care less about that. To have the general still before him only shows his lack of control over the world. And nothing makes him angrier.

Nightshade's body burns with the effort of their exchange, but the same must hold true for Jove. No matter how quickly Nightshade seems to move, Jove's defense has no holes. Jove's attacks, however, are tempered by Nightshade's defensive tactic. One of his shadows, Brutus, lies in wait for the sole purpose of punishing Jove should he overextend with a predictable blow. The general seems mindful of that, until he finally missteps.

A solid punch lands to Nightshade's cheek and Brutus does exactly as he is supposed to, jutting up from the grass in a blink. Yet Jove doesn't back down. He goes back in to land a second strike. Brutus stabs Jove's thigh and although he is unable to pierce all the way through, considerable damage is done. Jove tomahawks the dark blo once, twice, three times before it sluggishly slithers back to the grass.

As stars dance before Nightshade's eyes, his shadows try to grab and poke Jove with endless repetition but despite his wound, the only thing they accomplish is eliminating one of their own with another stabbing miscue. After Declan strikes Hector down only he, Haan, Aldrick, and an injured Brutus circle the general, with Zacata at Jove's ankle. Nightshade's shadows await his command, but his eyes won't focus, the world still teetering after Jove's last strike. Nevertheless, Nightshade shakes his head and lunges once more.

Not long passes before a four-piece combo lands two punches on either side of Nightshade's nose. The combo ends when Nightshade throws a wild punch whilst his brain is still rattling inside his skull. He stumbles back, then falls, unable to catch his balance. As he lies, his eyes closed, the world reels around him in a nauseating rotation. No matter how hard Nightshade focuses to steady the world, his daze persists.

It's because of his ability, Nightshade concludes. *Every punch must have some lasting dizzying effect on me... But my shadows are a different matter.*

Ignoring his exhaustion, Nightshade scrapes the last bit of his spirit energy together. In his mind he sets the scraps of his once-elaborate feast of energy before his shadows, his team, the only friends he's ever known. And without hesitation, they eat.

Nightshade's punch hasn't affected Jove's mind and body too much, but still, because of the Law, Jove knows he isn't at his sharpest. Regardless, Nightshade lies motionless, his thoughts undoubtedly sluggish and dull. Jove tries again to pull his leg free from the annoyingly persistent shadow around his ankle, but to no avail. *The shadows aren't affected, of course,* Jove thinks. *But one more engagement should be all it takes now.*

Suddenly, the shadows around Jove speed up with not so much as a gesture from Nightshade. To the left of Jove, a shadow spikes and he evades. Unfortunately, he steps into another spike that moves into his blind spot. Scarlet blood is left behind when Jove twists away from the darkness. Another shadow shoots up from the grass as Jove's eyes are still wide with agony. Although the pain from the skewer is real, Jove's reaction is a bit exaggerated and he recovers when another shadow commits. He grabs the manifested darkness and smashes the heel of his hand against it two strong times. Before his eyes it dissipates, leaving no trace.

Once again Jove's arm is tethered to the grass by a shadow. The remaining two free shadows waste no time seizing the opportunity, jutting forth, one from behind, the other in front. Jove tries to force the shadow around his wrist in the path of the other as he had done prior, but this time it resists with more strength. The two shadows strike and Jove's entire body tenses in pain. A moment later the darknesses emerge from his stomach and back, coated in blood.

It's then that all four shadows vanish, and Jove is in free fall. His eyes begin to roll into the back of his head, but he wills them otherwise, catching himself with a hand and a weary knee. To lose consciousness now would mean forfeiting the fight with the finish line in sight. Jove places his other hand against his stomach feeling out the two holes in his flesh. As wounded and exhausted as Jove is, he is considerably more grateful.

He's run dry on spirit energy, Jove thinks. *And not a moment too soon.*

<u>Episode 24:</u>

A Losing Victory

In the most secret chamber of the Amica Kingdom comes whistling. Hunter rocks his head back and forth to the melody. The tune is of an old song his mother wrote when he was little more than an infant. She used to sing it to him often over the years before her untimely passing. That is, before he killed her with impeccable timing.

His first ryken prey, and what a nice prey she was. As a teenager, he had little appreciation for a quality specimen. She was a reasonable, resourceful woman and no one knew Hunter better. Unfortunately for her, the reverse held true. Not since has he found a prey as satisfying. Hopefully Samané Lutrio will blossom and change that soon.

Hunter whips his head, throwing the dreads from his face, over his shoulder. He surveys the Amican vault once more, noticing he almost overlooked a chest against the back wall. It's unlike him to miss details, even on the most minor scale, but odds are what he's searching for is not here anyway. Hunter crosses the cellar full of jewels and riches, documents and secrets, slotting a key in the fortified steel of the chest. He lifts the lid slowly, revealing its contents.

Akidiode. A tub of the viscous fluid. Millions of pines worth. Maybe even enough to neutralize the Laevus Ryken Squad if, by some divine intervention, one was granted the opportunity to inject it into them at once.

Garbage, Hunter thinks, slamming the lid shut. He rises, making for the exit. *The true treasure is nowhere in sight. I told Master Fulminate as much, but he loves these trinkets and toys. Too bad our boy Shade ruined his chances of obtaining them. At least for another ten years.*

Hunter makes his way to the staircase in the middle of the Amica Castle. He puts a foot on the first step and pauses. "I hate being watched," he growls.

Ryken Squad General Nicon Hornell leisurely sits atop one of the luxurious chandeliers hanging from the ceiling. "Man, these things are so uncomfortable. Am I right?" He takes the twenty-foot leap to the floor, landing lightly, then rubs his backside. "They don't really make lighting decor like they used to. Am I right? Anyway, it's about time you noticed me. I was a little worried I'd have to get on your shoulders before you did."

"You've been watching me for over a half hour," Hunter says. "My skin started crawling the moment you started. No one hunts the hunter. I only wanted to see how long it would take until you pounced."

"I'm more interested in the reason you're here than you yourself. I mean, am I right?"

"Ah, I see. You aren't as dumb as you look. That would explain why you didn't fall for the bait of the confined cellar. You knew that garbage masquerading as treasure wasn't what I sought, and only one escape for me held true for you too."

Nicon tilts his head. "Is this the part where I'm supposed to be afraid?"

Hunter squints. "You're awfully bold for a recruit."

Nicon's shoulders slouch. "Come on. You really don't recognize me? Here's a hint. Am I right? You have Clamous the Juggernaut, Gwen the Star Tamer... no? Jove the Legislator?"

"There's no way you're a general," Hunter balks.

"Yes! Nicon the Greatest!"

"I find it difficult to believe even your fans, as nonexistent as they might be, would call you that." Hunter puts a hand to his chin. "Nicon the Nameless would be much more fitting."

Nicon frowns. "Forget it. Let's just get to fighting. I mean, am I right?"

Hunter shrugs. "I'd rather not, with you being a general and all. Plus, I can tell you don't feel like fighting, just as much as I don't. Let's save us both some trouble and call it an early day. I didn't find what I wanted, and you just want to protect the kingdom. Am I right?" Hunter chuckles as he walks past Nicon. "Until next time, Nameless."

* * *

Power. It's what makes the world go round. Talks of racism, greed, hunger, love, life, happiness—what does it matter when power governs them all? Those in power make the laws, those with power bend the rules, and those who are powerful control the powerless. That's the way it works. It's the way things have always worked.

Nightshade lies in a daze, completely and utterly exhausted, at the mercy of Jove the Legislator. Why? Because Jove is stronger. Now he controls Nightshade's fate. As he should.

It has always seemed Master Misery could never understand that point. How could a man so immensely powerful not fully grasp the control he has because of it? Nightshade has never seen a ryken remotely close to equaling Master Misery in combat. When he first clashed with his soon-to-be master the battle lasted but seconds. Every challenge Nightshade issued as his subordinate henceforth ended even quicker, Master Misery's patience seeming to run thinner each time. He was repeatedly beaten to within an inch of his life, but Master Misery never snuffed him out. There is no telling as to why, but he has the power so who is Nightshade to question?

Master Misery says power won't make me happy, Nightshade broods. *How couldn't it? With power, true power, I would control all. With power even greater than Misery's or Divineum's I would control the very meaning of happiness. I'd control everything. If I could just get there, I'd show Master Misery happiness does exist... on the other side of power.*

Much to Jove's surprise, Nightshade begins to stir. As Jove limps over, a hand against the holes in his stomach, Nightshade stands to his feet. The Law still active, Nightshade's legs wobble and he staggers like a drunkard. The same cannot be said for Jove, but Nightshade's one landed punch does leave his thoughts a bit sluggish.

"Stand down," Jove orders. "This is your final warning."

"Don't tell me what to do!" Nightshade yells, words slurred, charging wildly.

A sidestep sends Nightshade stumbling past Jove, barely able to stay on his feet. When Nightshade turns to swing again, all he sees is Jove's fist before a curtain of black descends upon his world.

Jove falls to his knees, almost beating Nightshade to the ground. He looks at the scarlet red coating his hand, then returns it back to his wound. *Well, I won't bleed out. However, blacking out is a different matter.* He looks to Nightshade, unconscious, then regards the sky. *Hopefully the two of you were able to hold out thus far. If so, this is your reward.* Jove closes his eyes, retracting his spirit energy connection to the Law, repealing it. Nearing his limit, he once again allows a stream of spirit energy to tether him to a different Law. In his mind's eye there is only Callisto and Prix.

"Law 2: Void Essence."

* * *

If Prix had any question as to exactly what Napalm meant when he yelled, "you're dead," the dozen bombs hurled at him immediately after served as clarification. Tears stream down Napalm's flushed face as he pursues Prix in a fit of rage. With most of the buildings in the area obliterated by Napalm's ryken ability, Prix is forced to move farther away from the city to find more cover.

Just when Prix has begun to think he is wearing the Excessum member down, Napalm displays another surge of spirit energy. What more can Prix do but run, biding his time until some form of help arrives? Then again, can he even count on help? This is the Excessum, after all. If anyone can contest and defeat the Laevus Ryken Squad, it's them. And what will come of being rescued like some sniveling child, anyway? Prix worked hard for respect and this very opportunity to show his skill and growth. Now that he is here what will it mean should he choose to cry for help?

Simply, it will mean life.

There is nothing wrong with asking for help. Although Prix doesn't like it, he doesn't like dying more. At least surviving means he'll get another day to prove himself, one more chance to fight. If he can't defeat the Excessum today, he will just have to try again tomorrow.

If he can escape, of course.

Prix makes for a vacant house, diving behind it when an explosion goes off not too far away. He rests, his back against the brick, sweat coating his face and overwhelmingly tired. Suddenly, the building behind him explodes, blowing the recruit away along with an avalanche of bricks and other debris. When Prix comes to, he starts to squirm and wiggle his way out of the pile of wreckage, barely able to breathe under its smothering weight.

Emerging free, Prix sags against the debris, unable to move another muscle. Much to his dismay, however, Napalm is at the apex of the pile with a box twice his height beside him.

"This will show you to mess with the Excessum!" Napalm exclaims. He then slides down the wreckage onto solid ground and takes off at a trot. "Better luck in your next life, loser!"

Prix looks from the child to the explosive, the fight in him all but drained. In retrospect, he really did put up a good effort. Would he be remembered for it? Would Laevus commemorate him as the hero he always wanted to become? Probably not.

The detonation is massive, obliterating the entire section of the city where Napalm and Prix fought and more of the outermost area they were heading toward. The explosion might even be powerful enough to have eliminated Prix in one fell swoop when he was fresh and eager. *I stood no chance all along,* Prix thinks. Then, *Wait, why am I still thinking?*

Prix looks around and for a second longer he bathes in fire, but it doesn't faze him. The surreal occurrence is befuddling and it's not until the explosion is complete and Prix lays his head back upon the bare, scarred ground that he realizes what happened.

The sensation is subtle but unmistakable. It's the only thing Prix's body can feel besides the ground beneath him. A trace of energy, a tingling. Not General Jove's spirit energy, but certainly his doing.

"The general's second Law," Prix says, before passing out.

* * *

"Final words, perhaps?"

"Final words, huh? ...If you see Lo, tell her I love and miss her so much."

"I will do so. Rest easy, my friend." Metis pauses. "Valisious Slash."

From Metis comes a crescent shaped manifestation of his aura. It grows until it's a quarter of his height in an instant, moving toward Callisto just as fast. Callisto simply closes his eyes and waits for the inevitable. He hears a noise, but no pain.

He hesitantly opens an eye to Metis' confused expression, which devolves back to indifference. In that time Callisto recognizes the same subtle sensation he felt upon arriving in Amica. General Jove Spinto's second Law, Void Essence. The Law steals Callisto's ability to physically interact with other living creatures and, thankfully, their spirit energy.

Callisto puts a hand to the collar of his ryken squad uniform, or where it used to be, as it wasn't spared with Jove's Law. *Metis was going to kill me.*

"Why must it come to this?" Metis rhetorically ponders. "Misunderstandings, dissension, fighting, war; why must force always be the answer in the end...? I'm sincerely sorry to hear that you and Samané aren't on the best of terms. Although I'm bereft of details, you should consider rectifying the friendship as soon as you are able. True comrades are difficult to come across. And not many are truer than my little brother."

"I can agree with that," Callisto admits, slowly. "Maybe it is about time I forgive him. Life is too short to hold grudges, even when you feel genuinely wronged. What does that malice benefit me?"

"Objectively speaking, nothing. But sometimes we can't help but remain incensed, even against logic. Such is my curse."

"Against the humans?" Metis nods, once. "What's next for you, Metis? Where do you go after this?"

"Wherever the Excessum deem fit. Not even I know what that should mean for tomorrow. But it hardly matters. I've given myself to them, entirely. Even if just for the time being. It's not dissimilar to your commitment to the ryken squad."

"Don't compare us. I live for a cause and I fight justly. The result can never be more important than the method used to get there. That's what separates the Laevus Ryken Squad from the Excessum."

"But just how dissimilar are we, really? You and I specifically. We're two men on opposite sides of the same spectrum. Justice, you like to call it. That's what I seek. What's fair, right, and equitable for every person. We're slaves to it. You and I both. We can concur on the fact that our most distinct contrast lies in that I have resigned myself to do whatever is necessary, while you do what the world thinks is necessary.

"One day you'll see the ineffectiveness which accompanies that. When that time comes, I encourage you to trade your master from an inept variant of the Excessum to the authentic version. For your sake, and for what you can contribute with your strength and wit, I hope you realize the truth before our paths cross once more. I'd hate to be put in a position again where I'd have to snuff out such potential."

Metis recedes into the thick of the woods, but by that time Callisto has already receded into the thick of his unconscious mind.

* * *

It's Samané's third circuit around the city and he has yet to draw out the man who beat Gaudyme so badly. It may not have been the best strategy, but it's all Samané can think of to track down the culprit given his limited information and Kato's disapproval. However the man located Gaudyme initially could be repeated to find Samané. If only he would take the bait, this time he will find it much more difficult to wrestle the book away from its holder. That is, if Kato doesn't find Samané first.

A ryken's sixth sense works much like a hallway with two doors at either end. If both ryken have their doors open, either one can detect the other's location and gauge their strength with their ryken sense. Because of this, shutting the door has great value, but it's a tricky task for rookie ryken to maintain constantly. In fact, Samané has only just begun to do it involuntarily, excluding times when he fights in earnest. Only the deftest of ryken can maintain the seal on their spirit energy when going all out.

So even though it's unlikely that Kato will find him in the grand estate that is Centrum City, Samané is still uneasy about the situation. Anything that could stand in the way of Samané finding the culprit for Gaudyme's misfortune makes him uneasy. He must do this, for Gaudyme.

As the sun reaches its peak, Samané takes the Book of Xenesis beyond Centrum City's borders for one more lap. Not even a half hour later he stops on a dirt road. A dozen paces away stands a man. Samané scowls.

For Gaudyme

A calmness flows over Samané and his scowl lessens. As angry as he is on Gaudyme's behalf, there was truth in Kato's warnings about this fight. To swing first and ask questions later would be a foolish approach. Samané should handle this as he would any typical fight, with a relaxed, level head. Only then can he fight to his fullest for Gaudyme's sake, and that alone cools his boiling temper.

Samané stares at the man. He is a few inches taller and probably just a few years older than Samané. A strong, handsome man with regal features. A rigid jawline to contrast a soft, thoughtful countenance. Smooth, unblemished skin tells a subtle tale of a life of well-managed stress, even for a man of his youth. His dark blue hair would appear black under any other light aside from the harsh sun above. The man's eyes, however, are what truly catch Samané's attention. Even at their distance Samané can confirm his absent pupils.

An air of confidence surrounds the stranger as he places a hand on the pommel of the sword on his hip. His self-assurance is evident in his posture, expression, and tone. "My name is Eli."

"I don't care." Samané says flatly. He holds up the Book of Xenesis. "Are you the one who hurt my friend to get his hands on one of these?"

Eli shakes his head. "That was a hasty decision made by my friend. I sent him back home because of it. On his behalf, I apologize."

"I don't want your empty apology. What is that going to do for Gaudyme? What if your friend had killed him?"

"Roye is a bit too impulsive sometimes. A grave fault of his that he will work out, in time. But his actions weren't completely misled. The Book of Xenesis he recovered is very much needed and was very much ours in the first place."

"So that justifies beating my friend to near death? Even if I did steal this," Samané snaps, spiking the book to the ground in a giant plume of dust, "that wouldn't make what he did right."

Eli stares at the book embedded a foot deep into the ground with cool eyes, unmoved by Samané's flare of anger. "The way you imply that your actions had little to do with the consequence is foolish. You realized what you were getting yourself into when you stole the tome. I'm sorry for what happened to your friend, but perhaps he should have surrendered the book when asked."

Samané stretches his neck, then flexes his arms and legs. He takes a deep breath, Eli studying him quietly all the while. "Tell me," Samané says in a voice so calm it's soothing, "if Gaudyme had refused to surrender the book to you, would you have done the same?"

Eli nods. "I would have."

"Show me."

In a blink Samané is positioned in front of Eli, his right fist cocked back. Surprise wells in Eli's pupil-less eyes. Dust swirls around the fighters, displaced by Samané's speed. In an instant Samané's fist juts forward, but just as fast Eli composes himself and draws his sword. If Eli hadn't already had his hand on the pommel when Samané spoke his last words, there is no way he would've been able to position the steel between himself and the punch quick enough. Judging from the force that shakes the blade, and consequently Eli, from the blocked blow Samané might have ended it all in that one swing.

Eli takes the offensive, sure that Samané's momentum will leave him staggering and open, but somehow another punch follows, almost before Eli can reestablish his defense. A dozen punches meet steel before Eli finally accepts the fact that defense will be his only option until Samané decides otherwise. Thankfully for Eli's increasingly aching arms, not long passes prior to Samané relenting.

Samané retreats, feeling adequately warmed up. *More than warmed up, actually,* he thinks. *The way he's deflecting my punches instead of trying to block them straight on shows he's good. Very good. But it doesn't matter. I'm prepared for this.* He clenches his fists. "For Gaudyme," he whispers.

Samané sprints at Eli once more, but no sooner than his first step Eli touches the tip of his sword to the dusty ground. In anticipation of a counterattack Samané uses his speed to flank Eli before he can even lift his sword from the earth. Samané lunges but suddenly loses his footing. It feels as if the ground beneath him has completely given way.

Samané goes from throwing a punch on a dusty road to slapping frantically at swirling waters. He sinks into its depths for a full second, then the current pushes him back to the surface. Gasping for air, the first solid thing Samané sees is Eli standing atop the water, his feet glowing blue where his soles meet the surface.

"You're not a very strong swimmer, are you?" Eli asks, squatting down. "That's fine, wouldn't matter if you were. I'll be sure not to kill you. I've only come for the Book of Xenesis."

As Eli stands, Samané immediately begins to swirl around the whirlpool he summoned. Ten strides across, at least, the speed of the spinning waters is absurdly fast, pulling Samané under after two full rotations. Meanwhile, Eli patiently makes his way over to where the Book of Xenesis lies embedded in the ground.

Around and around Samané spins, becoming increasingly disoriented and increasingly suffocated. His mind races faster than the current, desperate to find a way free. Soon the light above, even the waters pressing all around, begin to fade, seeming more distant with every second. How does one stop a cyclonic whirlpool? The only weapons at Samané's disposal are his speed and strength. Little good speed does him, being suspended in water. Although one thing Samané discovered early on about his ryken ability is that if one aspect of it fails to be of use in any particular situation, the other is probably tailored to the task.

Samané balls up his fist, a grimace of effort on his face as he twists his body. He takes a long second to rally his spirit energy, pulling the ever-sacred stop off his most special ability. The energy flows forth furiously and Samané's body surges with its power. Against the force of the current Samané rotates twice. During the second rotation every muscle in his body bulges as if primed to explode. His leg extends, foot colliding with the swirling water with so much force a shockwave erupts from the point of impact.

"Corkscrew Kick!"

Eli turns back toward the sound of Samané's voice, an eyebrow raised. The whirlpool's waters slam against the once dusty road, muddying up the barren terrain with a sandy grime. A small wave pushes itself to where Eli stands, seeping into the hole where the Book of Xenesis rests at his feet. Samané crawls from his hole, coughing heartily.

"Impressive," Eli says, flatly.

"That won't happen again," Samané growls between labored breaths.

"Why should it?" Eli asks, bending down to retrieve the tome. "I've already got what I came here for."

Just as Eli touches the Book of Xenesis it vanishes. He waves his hand in the small puddle where the book once laid, utterly perplexed. He raises his eyes to Samané, who holds the treasure, hardly daring to believe anyone could move so fast. "And what is that?" Samané asks, forcing his heavy breathing steady.

Eli doesn't respond, or at least not to Samané. He murmurs something under his breath, waits a few seconds longer then murmurs something again. Finally, he raises his voice, "You're not half bad."

"Is flattery your next strategy?" Samané asks.

Eli scratches his head. "It doesn't make any sense."

"What doesn't make sense?"

Eli doesn't answer; instead, his attention is elsewhere. Another murmur.

"Okay, that's enough," Samané says. The next moment his fist screams through the air toward Eli. Despite Samané's speed, however, Eli evades with sublime agility. Samané tries another punch, but much to the same end. It isn't until after a dozen more swings miss that Samané recalls a similar frustration, back when he and Ventus Erubesco first encountered one another at Centrum City High School. Although familiar, the way Eli and Ventus move are distinctly different, yet achieve the same goal. If Ventus' movement is as elusive as the wind, then Eli flows with all the evasiveness of great waters.

Samané allows his thoughts to distract him and almost doesn't notice when Eli's sword touches the ground again. Just as before, the terrain transforms. Samané can retreat in time to escape, but doesn't. Instead he feigns his retreat, allowing Eli to relax just enough. When the water forms Samané can feel the touch of gravity dragging him down into the whirlpool. The weightless pit in his stomach ignored, Samané accesses the second of his most special abilities. His body responds accordingly, and he surges forward atop the water just as if it were solid ground.

Samané's ability, Hypersonic Dash, makes it appear as if the entire world moves in slow motion. Regardless of Samané's opponent, everything, strong or weak, living or dead, the air above or the water below, is sluggish in comparison to Samané. As a result, it seems he defies physics, running across the surface of the water.

From Eli's perspective, Samané goes from backpedaling on the transmuting ground to striking him in the next instant. Eli hurls through the air, landing on his feet after a flip. His hand immediately snaps to the corner of his mouth where he finds blood. He tries his best to suppress his surprise, but traces of it find its way into his expression.

"A fluke," Eli says as if talking to a third party.

Samané responds regardless, "You're cocky, you know that?"

Eli doesn't respond initially, then, "I don't want to, Ether. What's it matter? We have to retrieve the book, regardless." Samané is quiet when Eli pauses, evidently listening. "Fine. I'll try it your way." Eli focuses on Samané. "What can we do to settle this matter more peacefully?"

The question catches him off guard. Settling things peacefully isn't what Samané wants at all. He is far too angry to not repay the debt in violence. "Seeing you as hurt and broken as Gaudyme is right now is the only way I'll ever be satisfied," is what Samané would like to say. It's undoubtedly what he would say if he were fighting for himself, but he's not. This is all for Gaudyme.

"As much as I'd rather see you beaten, I'll settle for a peaceful end," Samané finally says. "I want you and your friend to apologize."

"Impossible. Roye has already gone back home. Besides, I have already given you an apology."

"You don't regret what was done!" Samané snaps. "Don't insult me by calling that an apology. Gaudyme deserves better. You agree to give Gaudyme an honest, remorseful apology and we can end this, right now. That's the only alternative I'll allow."

"You don't understand what we fight for," Eli says, shaking his head. "Your world, the people in it, the things you care about are all trivial. The Books of Xenesis are what's important. They have immeasurable value and, as their guardians, we are in charge of protecting them at all cost. We don't take the responsibility lightly and we won't fail. I am sorry your friend got hurt along the way, but it had to be done."

It takes every ounce of Samané's self-control to not sprint over and punch Eli in the mouth. Instead, he calmly says, "You're stubborn and prideful. If you truly are some guardian fighting for a higher order, Gaudyme would have believed you. It's the kind of guy he is. All you had to do was tell him. He's like a child. Too trusting, too naive, too loving. People take advantage of that. People are always taking advantage of him. I wasn't there to protect him then. But I'm here now." Samané looks at Eli. There is no malice or hate, but the glare is all the more unnerving for that very reason. "Keep telling yourself it was right to hurt him."

"Apâbici," is Eli's only reply.

Suddenly, two large rings mark the ground on either side of Eli. Each glows indigo before settling into the muddy earth. The outer circle of the ring is three leaping wolves, each mouth linking to the tail of the wolf in front. The interior of the circle contains hundreds of symbols and patterns of varied size in some ancient script.

Samané watches as Eli takes his stance and the runes beside him take effect. From the ground rise two massive whips made entirely of water. The tentacle-like pillars flail with impressive speed for their monumental size, creating sonic booms as they slice through the air.

Samané only nods at the challenge before him. "For Gaudyme."

He is a blur of movement as he hurtles the first water whip to slice toward him. The maneuver slows him down enough for Eli to dodge a punch and counterattack. Samané strikes the broad side of the sword, misguiding the swing. He then lands a blow to Eli's ribs, but a water whip closes in, preventing his follow-up.

From behind Eli the other whip approaches. Once it makes contact with him the whip passes through as harmless as any stream of water might. After, the whip solidifies again and Samané's speed is barely enough to avoid decapitation. Eli, however, anticipates his step, cutting him shallowly from shoulder to the opposite hip. Pain twists Samané's face as he backs away. Unfortunately for him, a water whip already covers that option. Well, tries to cover it.

Samané is there one moment and gone the next. Eli just begins to turn when Samané's fist hits him. With remarkable footwork and balance, Eli shifts his stumble into a spin, just missing a stab at Samané's side. Two missed punches from Samané lead to a kick landed to Eli's chest. It's then that the two water whips swarm around Samané relentlessly, licking him with fresh scarlet wounds in his growing fatigue.

Faster than Samané would expect, Eli is back at him, slicing and stabbing. Samané gets the better of him over the next exchange, breaking Eli's nose with a shot to the face and nearly rendering his off arm unusable after he blocks a kick. Samané takes minimal damage, only suffering a shallow puncture wound to his upper thigh.

Samané would swear Eli's next attack is lucky if his fighter's intuition didn't suggest otherwise. A masterful strategy of conditioning. It's not uncommon for any fighter to have a rhythm to the way they move; in fact, everyone does. Reading that rhythm, their pacing, their breathing, the chances they take and those they shun are what makes a battle. During the entirety of this battle Samané noticed a small pattern in the way Eli moved, a certain flow. Reading that flow is how he managed to break Eli's nose and send his eyes to dancing. This time, however, Samané is too eager, tipping Eli off to the blow that would finish him.

Samané overextends, connecting a punch that sends Eli tumbling, feeling the crack of his ribs on contact. A strong shot, but not worth the trade. When Samané looks down he sees the hole in his flesh created by Eli's sword, his own blood soaking through his clothes. He is almost too afraid to feel his back, checking if the sword made it through. He is thankful it didn't.

Nevertheless, Samané has trouble breathing. A ruptured diaphragm. Bad news. He tries to take a deep breath to stop his growing lightheadedness and immediately regrets it as mind-numbing pain seizes him. He forces his eyes to Eli, who has already begun to struggle to his feet. Samané takes note that Eli's water whips have faded, most likely a result of his injuries and fatigue, but that hardly matters, as Eli is still in a far better state than himself.

Eli staggers into his stance, and Samané falls from his.

He hits the ground with a thud and Eli can only stare. "There is nothing I can do for him at this point," Eli says solemnly. A pause. "I know it shouldn't have come to this, Ether. I know. Of course, I know."

Eli grits his teeth. "…It's my fault." A breeze rolls over the land. This time Eli's silence lasts for minutes, his expression increasingly distraught. "Why couldn't I admit it earlier? He only wanted to protect his friend. He meant me no ill intent otherwise." A tear falls, and Eli turns his back on Samané's unmoving body. "What does it matter now that I'm remorseful for my actions? But I am…

"I was wrong."

A noise behind Eli snaps him around. There stands Samané, unconscious.

Episode 26:

Consequences

If one word could be used to describe Eli, that word would be greatness. From as far back as he can remember he always showed promise at anything he truly gave effort toward. From the most trivial games of his childhood to the most difficult missions of today, he rarely failed and even more seldomly admitted defeat. This time, however, things are different.

As Eli stares at his motionless opponent he can't help but feel regret. What did he know about the person slain across the battlefield? The boy he cut down before his prime? Not much. Eli *knew* that the ryken stole two Books of Xenesis from him, but as the two clashed it became increasingly obvious he wasn't the culprit. Whoever pilfered the tome was stealthy, very stealthy. The thief used a type of trickery and finesse that Eli saw none of today. The person lying here is a straight shooter, both in combat and speech. *Well, he* was *a straight shooter,* Eli broods.

The ryken spoke with conviction, a heartfelt passion few could fake. Eli could detect a lie better than most, and Ether more than he. Both believed the ryken when he spoke of only wanting to avenge his friend. Yet Eli wouldn't budge. He couldn't. The Book of Xenesis was to be recovered at all cost. The price this world paid didn't matter. *I did the right thing.* But every time Eli thinks that it seems he believes it less and less.

He doesn't even know the ryken's name. Gaudyme? That's his friend's name. The one he died to avenge. It shouldn't have come to this point. Eli could have ended it. He should have ended it as Ether suggested... but pride. It's always pride.

"What does it matter now that I'm remorseful for my actions?" Eli says, turning his back. "But I am... I was wrong."

As if resurrected by Eli's confession, the ryken stands again, his eyes dulled in unconsciousness. He moves, a newfound speed upon him. His fist flashes and death looms over Eli in that instant.

If Eli could see the punch coming, he might have time to be afraid. Despite this, somehow he evades the blow, his body moving on its own. Another punch follows with the same blinding speed and yet again, Eli evades.

The ryken tries several more times at a speed and intensity twice that he was fighting at consciously, and astoundingly, miraculously even, Eli remains untouched. *But how?* Eli thinks. A moment ago he could hardly move and now he's dodging attacks he can't even see. He searches inward for Ether. He would know what is happening, though it's unusual he hasn't already voiced his thoughts on the matter. Eli poses the question to the part of his consciousness where Ether resides, the part of him that isn't him at all. There is no answer. Not only that, there is no presence of Ether at all.

That's what it feels like initially. Reason begins to find its way to Eli at once. His ability to continue fighting even after reaching his limit, Ether's apparent absence, and Eli's sudden calm mind and tranquil heart can all be attributed to one thing.

Resonance.

The consciousnesses of Eli and Ether are now one, linked and indistinguishable even unto themselves. The unfamiliar feeling is a wonder to both, but it feels right. *Perfect,* they think. It's then, and fleetingly, the two notice the change in their skin color. All over, where Eli's complexion had been so olive, is now translucent, as if a hazy light shines beneath their flesh.

As quickly as they are able to decipher their bond, it isn't quick enough. In the split second of their revelation the ryken's fist connects to their jaw and they are sent darting through the air. Eli and Ether hit the ground hard, their brain rattled from the blow. The two must shake off the daze quickly when the ryken looms over them, throwing another punch. They roll clear of the blow and his fist strikes the ground, the impact displacing the earth, forming a crater and blowing Eli and Ether away with the shockwave. A deft roll puts the two on their feet in time to evade the next onslaught of punches and kicks.

Although Eli and Ether have figured out the reason for their own sudden increase in strength, it doesn't begin to explain the source of their opponent's newfound power. From their judgement, this resonance increased their strength at least two-fold, and yet their opponent seems to hardly notice. It might be plausible that he has some ability that mirrors the power of his opponent, except he showed his power just before their resonance. *Something is at work here,* they conclude, but being attacked so relentlessly, now hardly seems the time to figure it out. Only one thing matters at this point. Surviving. *All of us surviving,* they think.

For a period longer than they'd like, Eli and Ether dodge the ryken's attacks with their water-like evasiveness. If defense were not their sole focus, there's no telling who would win the battle or how long that ending would take to come to pass. Even still, there are two close calls where, only by luck, Eli and Ether aren't dealt a lethal blow.

Eventually, the ryken begins to fizzle out. It's nearly imperceptible at first, but by the time Eli and Ether confirm it is indeed the case the remaining drop-off is almost immediate. He completely crashes, only wobbling a moment before collapsing to the earth. Eli and Ether approach slowly, cautiously. They squat, checking the ryken's vitals. Remarkably, the sword wound just below his chest that appeared fatal has already stopped bleeding. The two smile, breathing a sigh of relief.

Then, the earth comes up to meet them.

* * *

Callisto can feel the presence of the world around him, but stubbornly sinks back down into the comfort of the bed. There is always work to be done and Callisto is one to take that work seriously, but sometimes, just sometimes, he permits himself to indulge in the bliss that comes with intense relaxation. The all-consuming elation that is the dormancy of sleep. Eventually, his mind and body are satisfied, yet he clings further, only to recall the previous day's events in the twilight of consciousness.

Callisto snaps upright in his hospital bed, out of breath. The first thing he sees is the nurse by his bedside. He asks, almost desperately, "Did we do it? Did we save the Amica Kingdom?"

She gives him a small smile and turns to the window, pulling the blinds up. "Look for yourself." Sunlight drowns the room in a blinding light. After Callisto's eyes adjust he beholds the destruction left behind from the battle. From his bed in the medical wing of the Amica Castle, it looks as if a dozen tornados tore through the kingdom, leaving some lucky buildings untouched while completely obliterating other entire neighborhoods.

Callisto's heart sinks until the nurse continues. "Thank you." He looks to the woman, who now has tears streaming down both her cheeks. "Because of the efforts of you and your team my son is still alive. He was trapped after our house collapsed and..." She pauses, her voice catching in her throat.

Someone else calls out from across the room. "Really, Chyna? With the waterworks again? I told you not to mention it. We're only doing our jobs, simple as that."

Callisto turns to the person in the bed beside his. Prix flashes the biggest smile Callisto's ever seen from him. "I don't mean to be a bother," the nurse is saying, "I'm just so happy." She explodes into outright sobbing and runs out the door. "I'm sorry! I'm sorry!"

Prix turns the page of the newspaper he's reading. "You might think that was harsh, but you don't know Chyna. I've yet to go one conversation without her breaking down."

Callisto sits back, resting his head on the pillow, his disbelief obvious. "So we won?"

"If by *we* you mean General Jove, then yeah. And lucky for us that's all *we* needed. The two of us were beaten to the edge of our lives. Only saved by the general's second Law." It's then that Callisto takes note of the discolored pink splotches all over Prix's skin. "We were in pretty bad shape after the battle, by the sound of it. I had third degree burns and blisters all over. It wasn't until just before you woke up that they finally decided to remove my bandages. The good news is my skin should be completely healed by the time we get back to the Arena. But healing itches so bad, its driving me crazy!" Prix rubs his palm against his right pec furiously as his expression twists between the ecstasy that accompanies scratching an itch and the pain that is picking an open wound.

"You were worse off than me," Prix says, trying to distract himself from his discomfort. "The doctor said he'd never seen a ryken still alive with spirit energy levels so low. According to him, fighters like you are the reason the ryken's body evolved to have spirit energy reserves, otherwise you'd just keep pushing yourself until you collapsed and died."

Callisto doesn't doubt it. His entire body aches and he can't remember a time when he's felt so exhausted. He wouldn't be surprised if the effort from thinking alone left him short of breath. Nevertheless, here he sits, brooding, trying to digest everything that has happened. The past week's events, their implications and consequences. His attention is diverted when he hears the click of the door. It's Princess Isabella Vortane.

She falls to his bedside, throwing her ear against Callisto's chest and herself into his arms. Callisto squeezes her tight. "We won," he says, after a while.

"We won," she echoes back, voice steady. It's funny, Callisto had expected her to cry. She releases him and puts a soft hand to his face. To his own surprise, it comes away wet. "Cut that out or you'll make me cry."

Callisto smiles, it's then that he realizes how close the two of them are. "Ahh!" he shouts as he fakes a spasm of pain in his leg.

Isabella jumps up. "Are you okay? What's the matter?"

Her concern makes Callisto feel unexpectedly guilty. "Nothing. Don't worry, it's nothing."

A confused look from Isabella is interrupted by Prix's laughter. "Smooth, Elastoman. Real smooth."

The door swings open again, General Jove entering. Although his dignified demeanor is as present as ever, something is off about the general. "Good morning, General," Prix greets. "They decided to release you, after all?"

"Thankfully," he answers. "I should've never been admitted in the first place."

"I'm surprised you stayed," Prix says. "Although you might want to run a comb through your hair before leaving. You're looking a bit rough."

"I'm aware of that," Jove says, not unkindly. "I only stopped by because I was informed Callisto was awake."

"It's nice to see you alive, General," Callisto says.

"And you as well. I wanted to let you both know that I'm proud of you. To battle one on one with the Excessum and survive is not a feat to be taken lightly. We persevered and accomplished our mission, as a team. That's what matters most in the end. To be strong as an individual is easy. Selfishly pursuing power can be done by anyone. But to put your pride, ambition, fears, grudges and personal goals aside and unify with those around you to complete an assignment bigger than yourself—well, it's a Law of a task."

Callisto tries everything in his power to suppress the smile plastered on his face, but only ends up making the expression appear strenuous and painful. *We won,* he thinks, nodding to Prix. *This disorganized team actually rose against members of the Excessum and came out victorious.*

"Assuming the two of you are released tomorrow," Jove continues, "I want to head back to Centrum City immediately."

"What?" Isabella blurts out. "Did my father not talk to you? Our kingdom-wide festival and ceremony is being held tomorrow, in your honor."

"As appreciative as I am for your thanks and honor, as I told him, there will be no need. A mission completed needs no praise. The ceremony will not be necessary."

"But—"

Isabella is cut off and Jove is nearly knocked over when the door swings open, slamming against the wall. "What do you mean the ceremony won't be necessary?" Nicon shouts.

"I think the statement is self-explanatory," Jove answers calmly.

Nicon gags, covering his nose. "Whoa! Did you brush your teeth today, Jove? Your breath smells like you ate tortilla chips out of a pair of shoes, then ate the shoes. Am I right?"

"I've been kept prisoner in this medical wing and I refuse to remain here any longer than I must. I'll properly bathe and groom myself when I get back to the hotel. My presence now is a pitstop."

Nicon keeps his hand over his nose. "Let me make this quick then. Why do you have to be such a downer all the time? Relax and enjoy yourself once in a while. I mean, am I right?"

"We only completed our mission. Why thank us—"

"For doing our job, yeah yeah. The reason is because they want to. Am I right? Just enjoy it! At least ask your team what they would want."

Jove turns to Prix and Callisto. A rare sight of indecisiveness flashes in his eyes. He turns to exit. "Be ready to leave for the capital this time tomorrow morning."

The room is still for a moment, then Isabella storms out. "I'm going to go talk to him."

"Princess, no," Callisto calls out, but she doesn't so much as hesitate. He moves to pursue her, but pain seizes his body before he can even get the blanket off.

"Let her go. Am I right?" Nicon says. "She can't really make matters worse than they already are." He sighs. "I just don't get Jove sometimes. I mean, am I right? He pulls me aside yesterday and tells me how proud he is to be your team's general. How he wouldn't trade his position for anything in the world. Even gave you two his super-rare *Law of a task* compliment. All just to not listen to what you two want. Am I right? Now, I'm not your commanding general so I don't have the authority to give you permission to attend the ceremony, but you should."

"We can't," Callisto says. "You heard General Jove."

Nicon shakes his head. "Poor Callisto. Poor, naive Callisto. Just because a superior orders something doesn't mean you have to do it. Am I right?"

Callisto raises a brow. "That's exactly what it means."

Nicon shakes his head. "Poor Callisto. Poor, naive Callisto. You could simply disobey. Am I right?"

"As a general, should you really be advising me to be insubordinate?"

Nicon shrugs. "Probably not. Anyway, I'll talk to Jove, but after he brushes his teeth. I could hardly think with all that funk. Am I right?"

"You think he'll listen?" Callisto asks doubtfully.

Nicon smiles. "We're best friends. Of course he will."

Episode 27:

Aftermath

"You think he's dead?" Napalm asks.

Metis eyes the ten-year-old laid out atop the lengthy table, tossing a box of his own creation into the air and catching it. Two times already Napalm has misjudged, dropping the contraption, setting it to detonate, once on his face. Although, Metis must admit, for the couple of days they have waited in the cabin, only two drops is impressive.

"Who? Shade?" Hunter asks, sharpening a wooden arrowhead. "No chance. The ryken squad seldom kill their prey. They prefer to cage them. Feel it's more humane."

"How?" Napalm asks. "Nightshade is too strong to be kept in a cell. His shadows could get him out of there whenever he wants."

"I know I've told you about akidiode at least once," Hunter says. "They drug him up with it to suppress his ryken ability. With that stuff ryken become little more than humans."

"They just make him drink it?"

Hunter puts his fingertips to the bridge of his nose. "Why do I explain anything to you when you don't listen? You'll be asking me these exact same questions again, and again it'll go in one ear and out the other. Injections. You know, with a needle? They put akidiode right into his bloodstream. The only effective way to do it. Consuming it is basically poison. If you don't vomit it back up, it'll just kill you."

"Ohhh, that makes sense," Napalm says.

"That answer all your questions?"

"One more!" Napalm sits up. "Why are we still here?"

Hunter looks in Metis' direction. "Would you like to field this one, Sutari?"

To be honest, Metis isn't entirely sure. In fact, he feels more confident that he can surmise the reason for the other two still waiting around more than his own. Hunter loves the outdoors, the woods especially, so he's in no hurry to get back to his various businesses throughout Laevus. Since the attack on Amica he's spent sixteen hours a day destroying all the wildlife within a five-mile radius, each day trying to best his performance from the last. He even has a special (and intricate) scoring system based on prey. He once tried to break down the system to Metis; however, the monotony of his explanation left Metis inattentive and he was forced to excuse himself from the conversation.

Napalm's presence here is based off Hunter's. The boy follows the man. As for Metis, why has he yet to leave? His mission is complete. The team's goal as a whole may not have been accomplished, but he did as he was instructed. Master Misery told him to assist Nightshade in any way the pale man saw fit. Furthermore, Nightshade had given him straightforward commands, a few tasks to carry out, which he did. Without fail. There is no more to do, nothing left to be said. Yet for some reason Metis feels unfulfilled. Why?

A better query is: Why would I feel fulfilled? Metis thinks. *What have I done thus far? Not only in Amica, but since teaming with the Excessum. In short, nothing. My goal of equality is still far off, therefore I have no reason to feel contented. Those are notions that lead to complacency. Patience is an excuse for indolence. This emptiness within is a reminder of work to be done. It angers me.* Metis rises from the table. *And anger is my fuel.*

Hunter raises a brow. "Where are you going?"

"To Master Misery. My time here has expired."

* * *

"I'm sorry. Truly, I am," Eli says solemnly.

In the Alair household Samané, Eli and Gaudyme convene around a table, Kato Alair lurking on the darker outskirts of the room. The entire house is heavy with regret, mostly from Eli, but Samané plays his part too. A direct result of the decisions they made based on emotion, void of logic. And others made entirely with logic, void of emotion.

Gaudyme hardly seems to notice the somber mood. "Don't worry about it," he says, cheerfully.

Eli is hesitant. "You were hurt pretty badly from my understanding. Bruised, beaten and bloody. Maybe you'd like to think on the matter a while longer before you forgive my actions."

Gaudyme shrugs. "Nope. No need. Seriously, don't sweat it."

Samané lets out a small laugh. "That's Gaudyme for you."

"What?" Gaudyme says, looking around. "I don't get it. Am I supposed to stay mad? Doesn't really make sense if you ask me. Besides, Eli didn't actually do anything to hurt me."

"I did." Eli insists. "Under my instructions, my leadership, Roye did this. He did as I would have done."

Gaudyme waves his hand. "I get it. Still, I forgive the both of you."

Eli studies Gaudyme as if to discern the reason behind his apathetic mercy. Samané produces the Book of Xenesis. "Here. A deal's a deal. And you upheld your end of the bargain."

Eli shakes his head. "I want you to keep that for now. Until I return with Roye and he can apologize for himself, we don't deserve it."

"Are you sure?" Samané asks.

"I am."

Kato approaches the table. "We can't keep it. That book is known even in this world for the power it possesses. It took you days to track it here and look at the chaos it's already caused. What other trouble will it bring? Take it."

"As much as I would like to," says Eli, "I won't. Now, if you want to rid yourselves of it some other way I understand, but I won't take it until Roye has apologized."

"It's funny," Samané says. "Three of us almost died fighting over this and now no one wants to have it." Samané turns to Kato. "I want to keep it. Well, more specifically I want you to keep it."

"Oh, now you want to listen to my guidance?" Kato asks, his usual blithe tone painfully absent. He glares at Samané. "You shouldn't have gone in the first place."

Samané hangs his head. "I know—"

Kato cuts him off. "No. You don't know. Apparently not. I told you to bring the book here!" Kato pauses to regain control of his voice. "This is why I never wanted kids. They don't listen," he says, to himself. "If Eli had been a bit stronger, a bit more malicious, you'd be dead. You hear me? Dead."

A pause. This time Samané is smart enough to remain quiet.

"Being a ryken isn't all fun and games. This isn't a fairy tale or comic book where the hero always wins. This is life; you get one shot. That's it. You mess up and there are no second chances, no do-overs. You aren't as invincible as you feel. Trust me. I've seen far stronger men buried for thinking that way.

"One full day you were out there, unconscious. Anything could've happened to you. No one back here knew where you were. You did this for Gaudyme? It was selfish. You think Gaudyme wanted you risking your life for something that couldn't be undone to him?"

Kato takes a breath. His expression finally relaxes and his tone with it. "Shine trusts me to protect you, Samané. I promised Thralle that I would look after you. But if you continue to do reckless things on your own, how am I to do that?"

Samané is a statue of disappointment. His head hangs, shoulders slumped, eyes on the floor. The last of Kato's fury burns out and he turns to Eli, his expression now appearing weary. "We'll keep your book here. But under one condition."

"Name it," Eli says.

"Tell us about the world you come from. Tell us about Xenesis."

* * *

Idle time is not something Metis invites. Too much time for thinking, and that turns into mulling. So as Metis walks, he practices his energy control, performing figure eights with a wisp of his energy. At least, that's what he had been doing until he confirmed he was being followed. Since then he's speculated what the person could want from him. The reasons are infinite, but over-analyzing situations is Metis' least favorite pastime.

At last, the man shows himself, emerging on Metis' path. A lean, strong man with shadowy features. He has a menacing aura that is somehow simultaneously graceful, suggesting an underlying finesse about him. His long dark hair is pulled back into a ponytail, a few strands hanging loose by his face. "Metis Lutrio," says the stranger, his voice stern, grim.

"Introductions are so clichéd," Metis answers. "You ever consider skipping the tedium and progressing straight into the action?"

"I'm not here for a fight. Luckily for you, you're no use to me dead."

"I don't typically like being used," Metis says. "What's this request benefit me?"

"It concerns a person of mutual interest. I have reason to believe that a man of your organization serves two masters. A master of my world and one of yours."

"Your world?"

To Metis' surprise, the man's already intense expression grows even more penetrating. "The world of Xenesis."

The words mean nothing to Metis, and he doesn't pretend that they do. "Naturally that would pose a conflict of interest in the long term. What role do I play in this individual's two-faced endeavors?"

"Although your role is minor, it is important nonetheless," says the stranger. "I need your assistance in presenting the issue to your master, Misery."

Metis seems to think it over for a moment, then replies, "No. Are we done here? Or are you to threaten my life next?"

"Your life?" A mischievous smirk. "Why would I do that? Didn't I already state I needed you alive?"

Suddenly, a darkened presence comes about the area. An uneasiness creeps into Metis' expression, uncertainty devolving his poise. A shady mirror manifests beside the stranger. The reflection is initially blank, but slowly a face appears on the darkened glass.

Samané.

"He look familiar?" the stranger asks.

Metis stills for a moment, then forces his stoic countenance back to the forefront. "Samané can handle himself. I have my own life to lead."

"I see. You mean to say that he could die today, and it wouldn't faze you? Well, there's only one way to know that for sure."

Metis doesn't move. With little more than a shrug, the stranger begins to slip back into the shadows of the forest. But then... "Wait," Metis says, cursing himself inwardly. "Perhaps I can assist you."

The man expression doesn't change. "I thought as much."

* * *

Callisto can hardly believe how different Amica looks today compared to when he raced through the hectic roads a few dozen hours ago. Where there had previously been destruction and fire now instead has laughter and camaraderie. The nation that appeared hopelessly doomed now bustles with the promise of a new day during the kingdom-wide festival. Hundreds of thousands flood the streets, adults and children alike, weaving and winding around others, eager to reach their destinations. Each has their own agenda of how to make the most of the beautiful day.

Callisto—No, Division 1a of the ryken squad—did their job and this is the result, their reward. A second chance for Amica to get things right.

Callisto smiles at every person he passes, the expression almost as bright and warm as his heart. "You know, if you grinned any harder, you'd scare the children away," Prix says, cheeks already red from booze.

Callisto shrugs. "I have a reason to smile. We've done well. Shouldn't we enjoy it?"

"Of course we should!" Prix yells, a bit louder than necessary. "But you're different, Elastoman. I'm sure you've heard the phrase, wearing your heart on your sleeve. Well, you have a cardiac gown."

"Cardiac gown?"

"Yeah, you wear a dress of heart flesh. It's squishy and nasty. You should be more like me, or Jove. Yeah, the general! Be more like him. Ironclad with his feelings." Prix stumbles, spilling half his beer. "Aww. I was drinking that!"

"Maybe you've had enough. Am I right?" Nicon says, squeezing through a pack of people.

"Oh no!" Prix yells. "It's the squad! Run!" Laughter strikes him and he doubles over. For a long second Prix makes no noise; the only sign of his amusement is the frozen, open-mouthed smile on his face. Soon, a high-pitched whining sound escapes, preceding the crash of his laughter, the force causing a short, undignified fit of coughing. Prix puts a hand to his chest, talking through the episode. "Get it? Cause we're the squad!" Callisto's and Nicon's lack of response doesn't seem to affect him. Soon he begins to settle down and staggers away. "Welp, this bottle isn't going to refill itself."

"Shouldn't we stop him?" Callisto asks.

"Let him have his fun. Am I right?" Nicon says. He nudges Callisto with an elbow. "Well?"

The two start walking again. "Well...?"

"I told you I'd talk Jove into letting you stay, didn't I? Who's your favorite general?"

Callisto almost reflectively says Jove but hesitates. After all, Nicon did give Callisto an RS book when he desperately needed it.

Nicon continues, "I'm joking. Am I right? Man, you're way too serious, like a teenage version of Jove or something. You don't want to be like that, believe me. Don't get me wrong, Jove's a great guy, but he's way too tense all the time. He never stops to enjoy the fruits of life. Knowing when to rest is just as important as knowing when to push on. The three of you deserve to celebrate and enjoy this victory as much as Amica, and I'm not going to let you miss it."

Callisto is surprised to see the stern gleam in General Nicon's eyes. In fact, it's the first time he's seen him speak about something so passionately. *But what a thing to be passionate about.*

Nicon puts his easy smile back on. "We all know Prix is enjoying himself. Am I right? But what about you? Relax. Have some fun. Play some games."

"Nicon!" a familiar voice shouts in an unfamiliar tone.

He flinches at the yelling of his name. Storming over, soaking wet, is General Jove. "Nicon! You made an agreement to be the willing participant of the Amican dunk tank game at noon today. When you weren't around to honor *your* commitment," fire flashes in Jove's green eyes, "guess who they saw passing in the crowd to be your replacement?"

Nicon puts a hand to his chin, the lines on his forehead creasing in deep thought. Eventually, he sighs, "Can I at least have a hint?"

Jove sneers. "Law 24: Beacon of Hope."

Immediately, two radiant orbs of light shoot into the sky. Nicon smiles at Callisto. "You ever play a game of tag with someone as fast as Jove? It's a blast! I mean, am I right?"

With that Nicon and Jove weave through the crowd and out of Callisto's sight quicker than he would think possible. Above, the miniature suns glow over the generals. The spectacle allows Princess Isabella to sneak up on Callisto from behind. "Hi there!" she exclaims.

In a dazzling light blue dress stands Isabella. Callisto is a bit startled as he hadn't heard her approach, but he is far more taken aback when he sees her. Her beauty is undeniable.

"Uh..." is the best response Callisto can manage.

Passing the Torch

Samané can hear the chaos and commotion as he ascends the stairs. The second floor of the Alair household, the specially constructed training level, is triply reinforced with sound deadening material to keep all activity within, within. Despite this, his friends of the Novice Pack still manage to cause a ruckus.

Samané enters the stark white room and sees some variation of the commotion he anticipated. No sooner does he walk through the doorway than he must sidestep a fireball the size of a beach ball that screams toward him. The fire explodes when it collides with the wall behind him, small flames setting the back of his shirt ablaze. Samané arches his back, trying to pat the flames away, dancing across the floor.

By the time the fire is extinguished Samané has unintentionally traveled farther into the room. Gaudyme moves hurriedly in the opposite direction. Before Samané can react Gaudyme grabs him by the shoulders and moves him a single stride to the left. "Stand right there for me, buddy," he says, never slowing. Samané doesn't have the time to look confused. Sharp steel slices toward him and he ducks out of its path. He quickly lunges for the hilt of the sword, stopping it from swinging toward him again. The maneuver brings him hand to hand and eye to eye with the wielder.

"My love," Serena coos, fluttering her eyelashes, "this is so sudden."

No time to respond as Samané pushes Serena backward and out of the way of another raining fireball. He snaps his neck toward the source.

"Quit running, you coward!" Lo screams.

"I'm not running, I'm evading," Subnuba responds. "There's a difference."

Lo balls her fist as ice trails in Subnuba's wake. "That's exactly what a coward would say!"

Two fireballs rain on Subnuba's path, but he slides beneath them, the heat close enough to singe his eyelashes. "I could keep this up all day," he taunts. "You're nowhere as fast as Ventus. How could you ca—"

Subnuba, allowing himself to be distracted, moves to the center of the floor where Ventus had been peacefully meditating, in direct contrast to the rest of the room. Subnuba trips over the silver-haired ryken, forcing both to the floor. Lo seizes the opportunity and creates an ice block above both in an instant, accepting Ventus as a casualty of war. The glacier drops but immediately stops, midair. Subnuba and Ventus look up.

"I really can't leave any of you alone for more than five seconds," Samané says, the massive ice block resting in his palm.

"Because Cheesehead here doesn't know how to talk to women!" Lo shouts.

Samané tosses the block of ice up and it falls onto his fist, shattering into an infinite number of crystal specks. "I don't find that hard to believe."

Suddenly, Serena is latched around Samané's other arm, the sword still in her opposite hand. "But you sure know how to, sugar dumpling."

He squirms from her grasp. "What are you even doing here, Serena? How many times do I have to tell you to not interfere with our training? You're not even a ryken."

"Aww," she adorably pouts, "that's discrimination."

"I don't believe that's how it works," Ventus says, standing.

Subnuba frowns at Ventus. "Remember what I told you about taking things too literally?"

Gaudyme walks up, snatching the sword from Serena's hand. Then, eyes wide, he points the tip at Samané's throat. "Your girlfriend is crazy."

Samané's glance flickers toward her as she smiles expectantly, then back to Gaudyme. "She's not my girlfriend."

"Just keep an eye on her when she's around anything sharp," he responds.

Samané waves his hand. "Can we focus for just one second, please?" Surprisingly, the room falls silent. "The Novice Pack has our first mission."

* * *

All of Amica lies stretched out before their gaze. The mountainside view that the old Amican Protector, Grade Culminary, discovered is simply breathtaking. The people below move like ants raiding the picnic that is Amica. The tightly packed crowd flows, shouts, laughs, lives, breathes, because of Callisto's efforts. *He really is amazing,* Isabella thinks.

"It's funny, isn't it?" Callisto asks, taking in the dazzling sight. "How fragile life is? Ryken or human, it doesn't matter. We always focus so much on what separates us we never pay attention to what draws us together. The same spark of life that makes us people, that's what I want to protect. So we may all have the opportunity to live. From the most powerful ryken to the weakest human and everything in between, I'll fight to protect their right to life. Because in the end," Callisto turns, finally meeting Isabella's stare, "we all die the same."

Isabella resists the urge to look away. On Callisto's mind is life, justice, honor, duty, and all the other virtues that make him perfect. *Not perfect,* Isabella thinks. *No one is perfect, but if Callisto has a flaw, I haven't seen it. How many people are willing to stand up to their superior and question their motives for a stranger's sake? When I'm around Callisto I feel like we can reshape this dark world. Surely, side by side, we could change anything we put our hearts and minds toward. I know there's still a lot of work to do here in Amica but look at the impact he's had. For the sake of Amica, for the sake of the world... for the sake of myself, I can't let him leave.* "Callisto," she says, her voice tiny.

But Callisto is already shaking his head. "I can't." He pauses, as if working up his courage. "My journey doesn't stop here. I've done all I can for Amica. Tomorrow I must head back to Centrum City and continue improving myself until I can have the same impact in Laevus that I've had here. There's so much more to be done. But I will change Laevus, and I'll do it justly."

Hearing Callisto speak so passionately about his goals always seems to put a smile on Isabella's face.

But not this time.

Maybe I could... she thinks.

"And your place is here, Princess," Callisto continues as if in Isabella's head. "You've already done so much for this kingdom, but you're far from finished. There are so many people down there counting on you. Don't let them down. They're trusting you with their lives. People like us have a gift, a power we can't take for granted. We can't afford to be selfish and allow the world to fall deeper into injustice. It's up to us, it's up to you to make a difference. To be the difference." Callisto turns back to the kingdom, his voice dropping to a whisper. "They need you, Isabella."

The Princess of Amica tries to respond but her voice catches in her throat. A moment passes before light footsteps betray her retreat. She can only make it halfway down the mountainside before she must stop. She leans against a large stone, her heart leaden.

And Isabella Vortane cries.

* * *

As great as Callisto felt this morning, somehow, he feels that much worse now. After waiting an hour on Mount Virran it became apparent Isabella wasn't going to return. Callisto could pretend that the princess' mood didn't affect him, or that her feelings were a mystery to him, but he'd rather face the reality of the situation. To face the pain and accept things for what they are is something Callisto is learning to do more and more every day.

So, with his dampened mood, Callisto decides to seek the only person he believes could make him feel worse. *When it rains, it pours. But if I'm already soaked, what more is there to avoid?*

Callisto enters the throne room, looking for King Atrium Vortane. When the room is vacant, he locates a guard who directs him to the King's personal chambers. Callisto knocks on the door.

"Come in," Atrium's gruff voice calls out.

"Your Majesty," Callisto says, entering, shutting the door behind him. King Atrium sits at his desk, his glasses on, a pen scribbling furiously around his large belly against the page of a thick book.

"I almost forgot how tedious this paperwork could be," he says. "Good thing I won't be in charge of it after today."

Minutes pass as Callisto stands silently, watching Atrium. Finally, his pen stops moving. He stashes his glasses away, regarding Callisto. "Do you have any idea how it feels to lead a country that hates you?" Callisto just stares, his expression grim. "Of course not. You're nothing more than a toddler. Your bold claims to restructure the world prove as much. Experience will show you, just as it showed me. A lesson decades long."

Atrium stands, pressing his knuckles down onto the papers scattered atop his desk. "I've wasted too much of my life giving this kingdom all of me and they've done nothing more than spit in my face. These citizens have killed the man I used to be and appointed a bitter, selfish replacement on the throne. Now they have a right to rebel against what I've become. The king of this nation is cursed and tortured beyond measure. What man would desire this throne?"

Atrium's demeanor shrinks under the weight of the unspoken answer. However, Callisto isn't satisfied with the implications of the unsaid. "I know a woman who does," he replies.

Atrium sighs, his expression desperate. "My little Isabella is a lot like me. In more ways than I'd like to admit. For the past year she's been the one keeping this country from devouring itself. I try to warn her, just as my father warned me, that these people aren't worth saving. Those who would take joy in seeing your blood spilled surely aren't worth sacrificing yourself for. But she's just as determined to restore this kingdom as I was in my youth, maybe even more so." He pauses. "I don't want them to turn her into what I am today."

"Isabella is strong," Callisto says, his voice low, but intense. "If you support her, she will succeed. I know it."

"Ah. What I would give to be young and innocent again." A smile cracks through Atrium's thick, white beard. Then it fades away, his disdain coming forth in full. "I don't like you Laevinians. I dislike you especially. Your self-righteous ideals and your illogical determination. It borders on stupidity. It makes me sick that I even know your name. *Callisto Socius.* I hate everything about you." Atrium's lips peel back from his teeth in a nasty scowl. "But most of all, I hate that I respect you."

* * *

"How do we get to this world?" Lo asks, all attitude. "A spaceship?"

Samané squints. "Haven't you been listening to anything I've said? We get there by magic."

"I'm confused," Ventus says, tersely.

"It's my second time hearing this and it only makes less sense," Gaudyme adds.

"Look," Samané says, "it's not really all that complicated. I'll break it down again. We're traveling to Xenesis. It's a parallel world that's only reachable through the effects of magic. We don't have magic here, so there's nothing we can do to journey there on our own. Still with me?"

The Novice Pack all nod.

"Now, we're traveling there to help someone named Eli. He's a guardian of something in their world referred to as the Books of Xenesis. Apparently, these books are incredibly powerful when all sixty-six are gathered together. Eli and a team of three others are responsible for overseeing these books. Since one has fallen into our possession, I feel liable for making sure it isn't misused, even if it's not necessarily our world that's affected. That's pretty much the gist of the situation."

Subnuba crosses his arms. "It sounds like we're sticking our noses into business that isn't ours."

"I agree," Ventus chimes.

"Be that as it may, I still want us to take on this mission," Samané says. "According to Eli, this isn't the first time a book has traveled between worlds. He even believes the Excessum may have their hands in the affairs of their world. If that's the case, I feel it's necessary that we aren't left in the dark about something this important."

"I have a question," Gaudyme says. "Where is Eli now?"

"He left yesterday. He said that even in Xenesis, magic used to cross worlds is very rare and very taxing. He has to make arrangements for us."

Suddenly, Subnuba flexes his right arm and slaps his bicep. "You know what, count me in. This sounds like the perfect opportunity to show the lot of you what I've been up to these last few weeks."

"Me too!" Gaudyme exclaims. "Going to a new world? Magic and spells? Sounds like a lot of fun!"

Lo shrugs. "Can't let you idiots hog all the action. And who knows, maybe I'll meet a cute boy."

Serena laughs. "Talk about a long-distance relationship. Glad my man is always right by my side. Because of that, I don't really have a choice but to tag along."

"I will make the journey as well," Ventus says.

Samané surveys his team, pride welling up inside him. Then he turns to the door.

"Now to convince Kato…"

* * *

The festival and ceremony all went well. Much better than King Atrium Vortane could have ever imagined. To see the kingdom come together like this was something he had worked his youth away to achieve and now that it's here he couldn't care less.

More than likely the sensation is psychological, but Atrium can swear the crown atop his head is the cause for his terrible headache. The useless piece of gold never ceases to affect him this way. It's the first time in years he's even touched the thing because of it. And hopefully it will be the last time.

The crowd goes crazy after Atrium's last words. He barely even remembers what they were. *It doesn't matter,* he thinks. *Leadership is more smoke and mirrors than actual effort. It's not what you do for the people, but what they think you do for them. The perceived results are infinitely more important than the results themselves... But what if you could satisfy both?*

Atrium half-turns to Isabella, his voice still carrying to the microphone. "And now to close today's ceremony!"

The hundreds of thousands in the crowd fall silent, curious of what's to come. Atrium traverses the stage to where his honored guests stand, Callisto Socius and his team. The king does his best to block the Laevinian group out of his mind, his focus utterly on his daughter standing beside them.

"When I was a young king, I was so self-sacrificing," Atrium says. "I would've laid down my life for this kingdom, and, in a sense, I did. Time and time again. Over these three decades this country has taken all that I am, leaving this bitter, broken man you see now. I loved this country with everything I had, I promise you that. But how many times can one be betrayed before it becomes okay to hate? I am only a man. I have seen fields of deceit and acres of corruption. Today, I can say, without a hint of doubt, that I hate this kingdom with all my being. A kingdom that I once loved with the same intensity as my only daughter."

Isabella's eyes start to water, but Atrium continues regardless. "What kind of father would say that to his daughter? What kind of king would do this to his country? Don't cry, Bella. There's still a bit of the younger Atrium deep within me somewhere. I've been fighting inside myself to decide if I would go through with this charade of a ceremony and hand over the Excessum criminal to the Laevus nation. The result would be beneficial to both parties and that sickens me.

"But then I look at you. I could never destroy something you care for so deeply. Somewhere along the line I've transformed into the catalyst that will turn the future generations of our nation into the exact monster I am today.

"I've said all of this to say that I won't be able to lead a country I hate into a more promising era while working alongside a country I hate even more in the process. So it's your turn. I'm asking—No, Young King Atrium, the man I used to be, is asking you, Princess Isabella, not as my child, but as a ruler: Will you take the throne from an unworthy man's hands?"

Just as it appears that Isabella's tears will spill over, she bites her lip. Then she nods. "Of course I will. And I promise I won't let you down."

The two stare at one another, the same determined gleam in their eyes. Isabella throws her arms around her father and Atrium hesitantly embraces her. In this moment his great love for Amica flashes, fading away just as quickly as it sparked. He squeezes his daughter tighter. "I pray that this land doesn't scar you the same way it has scarred me... but just as much, I pray you do not wound Amica either."

<u>Episode 29:</u>

Fall Upon the World

Callisto steps off the road, eyeing the house he'd been searching to find for the past hour. He woke up early this morning to retrace his steps from the other day, the journey just before he fought his second most dear childhood friend, Metis Lutrio.

Callisto couldn't help but feel during the celebration yesterday that Amica as a whole, and maybe even himself included, was a bit too happy. Amica had taken a crucial blow in losing Grade Culminary, their kingdom's Protector. Although there was a segment during the ceremony to commemorate his sacrificial effort and lifetime of service, Callisto still felt his honor was short-lived. And so he decided he would pay his respects to the family in person.

Callisto knocks and after the third try Grade's widow, Reyna Culminary, answers the door. Her sunken eyes and messy hair make her look much older than Callisto knows her to be. Her clothes hang over her as though meant for a woman of a size or two larger.

"Can I help you?" Reyna asks. A flicker of recognition. "Wait, you're the ryken squad officer."

Callisto offers a sorrowful smile. "I just wanted to come by and personally give my condolences for the loss of your husband. Although I didn't know Grade personally, any man who would lay down his life for a cause bigger than himself is a man I strive to imitate every day."

"Thank you," Reyna says softly. "You have no idea how much I appreciate your kind words." She takes a deep breath. "It's still so surreal, like something from a nightmare. One day he's here lying with me and the next he's gone. My Grade. They took my Grade from me... took him right from my arms. What—how do I go on without him?"

Reyna sags against the door, crying. Callisto reflexively reaches out to ensure she doesn't fall, her emotion tugging at his heart. Despite his best efforts a tear escapes. *Look at what you've done, Metis,* Callisto thinks. *This woman has lost her way because of your selfish actions. Why would you do this? No, that doesn't matter. I can't allow you to hurt another person like this without consequence. I won't let you hurt others like you've been hurt.*

Callisto is dragged out of his thoughts by Reyna's shaky voice. "How can I forgive him for taking my husband? Grade wouldn't want me to live bitterly. He wouldn't want me hating anyone, but I don't know if I can do this. I don't think I can forgive him."

Callisto wipes his cheek aggressively. "I'm not sure if I can forgive him either, but I know we have to. If we don't that same hatred will consume us. Eventually we'll be just as he is, bitterly hurting others because he hurt us."

Reyna bites her lip. "Will you promise me something? Promise me you'll stop him before he makes another wife feel as empty as I feel right now."

Acura's innocent smile flashes in Callisto's mind and for the first time he doesn't suppress the memory. Instead, he embraces it, the image fortifying his will. "No. I won't make a promise I'm not sure I can keep. I learned that lesson the hardest way there is. What I will do is promise to stop him at any cost to myself. I'll pour my life into ensuring that one day he is made to answer for his crimes."

Reyna's reaction surprises Callisto. Through her tears, she smiles. "As long as you give it your all, the absolute best you can manage, I'll learn to rest easy again. Something tells me you won't fail."

* * *

Since his unexpected meeting with the ominous stranger, Metis' mulling has evolved into brooding. The stranger, who went on to identify himself as Danté Erebis, hit Metis right where it hurt. He attacked the weakest part of Metis, the part Metis has been recently working so hard to eliminate within himself. Now, as he walks, heading toward a destination unknown even unto him, he is disappointed. Very disappointed.

If Metis had thought his time thus far with the Excessum had been wasted before, he *knows* it to be the case now. How is it that Metis could destroy what someone else holds most dear for his end goal, but isn't willing to sacrifice the same?

Metis dwells on the topic for an extended period, not even noticing when the terrain changes from forest to fields of crops on either side of him. He tries to resume his figure eight exercise of energy control but quits when his mind won't focus. It's then the cloudy sky darkens. Metis stops, a deep-rooted, primal fear coming over him. This fear always precedes *his* presence. Knowing that, however, doesn't make it any more bearable.

"The mission didn't go as planned," Misery says. If Terror itself had a voice, it would have received its vocal cords from Misery's throat.

It takes every ounce of Metis' courage to stand firm in Misery's presence. Every fiber of his being screams for him to flee but somehow, he wills his body still. Or perhaps, more likely even, his fear has him petrified. "Indeed," is all Metis can chirp.

Misery is quiet for a moment, then says, "No matter. The ordeal was nothing more than a shot in the dark."

Metis starts to respond, but fear causes his voice to catch in his throat. He nods once instead.

"You've grown," Misery says matter-of-factly. Metis is confused. He had just been thinking the exact opposite. "Your heart has hardened more. But I'm far from satisfied. To think I've sacrificed my bishop for the growth of a pawn may look foolish. But you will be great." An order. "You will ascend to levels even I have not achieved." A command. "You have no choice." A threat.

"You will be crushed and built anew as I see appropriate," Misery continues. "Those phantom notions of love and loyalty you have won't only be erased, but decimated. Into the flames of Hell you will plummet and when you are nothing but ashes, I will reform you into the greatest version of yourself. Only after misery can there come understanding."

Metis swallows.

"I heard everything Danté Erebis had to say," Misery says. "I've known for a while what Cupid has been up to. I'll allow you to accept the invitation to Xenesis on my behalf. Intuition tells me this journey will be your breaking point. When you return, we will get started on what you joined the Excessum to do."

He turns, walking away.

"You've dabbled in darkness. Honed it's power when it was convenient for you. I'll teach you to embrace it, let it flow through you. You will become darkness itself. Your wrath for humans will be your fuel. And then, because of Sutari, under Lord Divineum's reign, misery will fall upon the world."

* * *

Since fending off the Excessum attack, Callisto has suffered through a wide range of various emotions. Guilt, joy, hope, sadness, pride—Callisto has experienced each one to a crippling degree. Now, he isn't sure what to call the mood he's feeling. Whatever it is leads him to General Jove's door.

"I suppose we might as well settle this before we step back on Laevinian soil," Jove says, leading Callisto into his provisional chamber. Jove takes a seat but Callisto remains standing just inside the doorway of the room.

"I have so much respect for you, General Jove," Callisto starts, each word coming slowly, carefully. "The way you operate, your unyielding sense of justice. I admire you. If one day I can be half the man you are, I'll consider my life meaningful."

"And that's why you continue to challenge me the way you do," Jove says, not unkindly. "To refine my character where you see flaws. It's to ensure that you not only understand why I do what I do, but so I can understand myself on a deeper level as well. You force me to further evaluate *why*. The most important aspect of what we do. We must always have just purpose behind our just actions."

Callisto nods. "To make a difference. That's my just purpose. To leave whatever I come across better than I found it. My efforts left Amica better and for that I regret nothing."

"What about Laevus?" Jove asks. "Is Laevus any better off because of our efforts here? I would say no. What have we gained? I can understand your drive to make the world a better place, but we must focus on putting Laevus in the best position to achieve that. Home needs to always be our first priority."

"I can't say you're wrong," Callisto replies. "I wish I could, but I don't know for sure. That might be the best way to bring about change. But I can't guarantee that I'll sit idly by while others suffer in an attempt to *focus* on Laevus. Maybe I'll learn how to prioritize my efforts, or maybe I'll rid myself of the entire notion. I don't know. What I do know is that I still have a lot to figure out before I move forward. Actually," Callisto lets the word hang in the air a moment, "I should probably take a step back first."

Callisto makes his way to Jove while detaching the badge that indicates his righthand status from his uniform. "It was a great honor to be the righthand of Jove Spinto." *What am I doing?* Callisto thinks even as he proceeds. *Am I really about to give up everything I've achieved so far? Stop, Callisto. Reattach the badge and leave.* But he only continues speaking. "Hopefully the next time I wear this I will do it the justice it deserves."

Callisto sets the badge gently on the stand next to Jove. Then he heads for the door. "You have been a great honor as my righthand, Callisto," Jove says. "Your resignation from the position doesn't change much beyond a label. You'll be the same pillar of righteousness to our ryken squad as you are growing to be. And regardless of your title I know one day your justice will fall upon the world."

* * *

Samané finds Kato leaning against the rail of his porch, his head tilted back, studying the moon. Samané takes a seat on the steps leading up to the house. Nothing is said for a while, until Kato speaks. "You're really planning to do this, huh?"

"I am."

Kato shakes his head. "I don't get why. There're so many other battles to fight here on your own soil. We haven't even begun to address things in Centrum City, let alone Laevus as a whole, and you want to go off and fight someone else's war. I get that these Books of Xenesis may be important in the long run, but we have more prominent issues to tackle today."

Samané shrugs, the gesture more helpless than nonchalant. "I don't know why, but I feel drawn to help Eli. It's hard to explain, but I know I can make a needed change in their world. So why shouldn't I? If it's because it doesn't benefit me, I think that's pretty self-centered."

"Naivety at its finest," Kato says. "Your father was the same way. I didn't understand it then, either. Always going out of his way to help others, no matter the cost to himself. Honorable, but foolish. He was too giving.

"Me, I'm wired differently. Self-centered maybe, but practical. Low risk efficiency... but that has its flaws too." Kato's voice is laced with regret. "You need to find balance. Don't be too sacrificing, because you'll run yourself into the dirt long before your time. But don't be a coward, either. You'll live longer than you should, always kicking yourself for the friend you didn't save...

"Balance is key. Everything in moderation. Equal parts emotion and logic. This is who you are, Samané. You have a good heart and a strong mind. Trust your instincts. I have no doubt the same equity that is within you will one day fall upon the world.

"In saying that, for the future I need you to listen to my advice. I can't have you running off getting yourself killed. But even if instinct leads you to do something against my judgment, don't hesitate. You have a group of fighters, a team of friends, counting on you as their leader. You hear me? I'm not their leader. You are. I don't call the shots. Just because I feel a certain way about venturing to Xenesis doesn't make it right. Only what you say goes."

Samané stands. He makes his way to Kato with a patient gait. The two regard one another as coolly as enemies might. Samané extends his arm and Kato mirrors him. Each grasps the other's forearm and pulls themselves in, embracing.

"I say you're coming with us, Kato."

* * *

At the west gate of the Amica Kingdom, Queen Isabella stands with the ryken squad soldiers.

"I truly wish the kingdom of Amica the very best in the future. Take care, Your Highness," Jove says, bowing his head.

"Thank you, and you as well," Isabella says.

Nicon hands Nightshade—cuffed, gagged and disarmed with akidiode—off to Jove. "Queen, it was short but fun," he says, cheerily. "You all sure know how to party. Am I right?"

Isabella laughs. "If that's true, be sure to come and visit. You're always welcome."

Prix comes next. "Congratulations and good luck on being queen. I expect to hear great things."

"I won't disappoint. Do me a favor and keep him out of trouble for me, will you?" Isabella gestures toward Callisto.

"I'll try, but he just has a knack for finding it."

With that, the group falls back out of earshot and Callisto steps forward. "So I guess this is it," Isabella says, her voice soft.

"For this chapter at least," Callisto says.

Isabella bites her lip. "Do you think our paths will cross again in the future?"

"Of course they will. I plan to have an impact in Laevus for a long time to come, and with you as Queen of Amica our paths must be intertwined."

"I look forward to it! As the next generation it's our duty to overcome the hatred and corruption of those that came before us."

"You're right. I thank you for showing me that. You helped me to see that all combat isn't done on the battlefield. It starts with the prestigious leaders. As a ryken in a human-dominated nation my voice can only be heard by few, but I won't use that as an excuse. I'm determined to change Laevus.

"But I must change myself first. I have to reshape my own convictions and constantly test my own resolve. Forgiveness is the first task for me to tackle. I have a good friend back home whose apology has gone ignored for too long. In the future, I'll try to be more merciful. I hope to be as forgiving as you one day. Even with all the wrong this kingdom has done to you, you still find a way to forgive. I don't know if I could ever be that merciful, but it won't stop me from trying."

Isabella finds herself smiling. "Why do you have to be so perfect, Callisto? Someone like you is impossible to come by. How am I supposed to let you go?"

Suddenly Isabella lunges forward, embracing Callisto. He wraps his arms around her, squeezing her tightly. After a few seconds he moves to release her, but she just squeezes tighter. For a minute longer he cooperates but eventually lets go, despite her best attempts to persuade him otherwise. He is careful to avoid eye contact, being so close to her. As a result, he turns and walks away quickly, joining the others. Isabella has to resist the urge within her to pursue.

"Goodbye Callisto," she whispers.

As he shrinks into the horizon, Isabella doesn't think she can feel worse. That is, until Callisto disappears from her sight. Not once looking back.

The End